KU-415-474

Odalisque

'Darling Gerry,' said Auralie, 'I want to make love to a woman.'

Gerry drew in a sharp breath. Auralie knew the calculated shamelessness of her statement would excite him. She slid a hand under cover of the tablecloth, surreptitiously undid a couple of buttons on his trousers, and wormed a finger into the opening so she could stroke him. They were in a public place and she knew it would arouse him. Through half-closed eyes she took a long look at Gerry, then whispered into his ear.

'You know I've never done it. We could have her together.'

'No,' said Gerry, resisting her. He gazed at his chic, petite French wife. You lying bitch, he thought.

WITHDRAWN

By the same author:

Conquered
Hand Maiden of Palmyra
Bonded
The House in New Orleans

Odalisque
Fleur Reynolds

BL

This book is a work of fiction.
In real life, make sure you practice safe, sane and
consensual sex.

Published by Black Lace 2008

2 4 6 8 10 9 7 5 3 1

Copyright © Fleur Reynolds 2008

Fleur Reynolds has asserted her right under the Copyright, Deisngs and Patents Act
1998 to be identified as the author of this work.

*All characters in this publication are fictitious and any resemblance to real persons,
living or dead, is purely coincidental.*

This book is sold subject to the condition that it shall not, by way of trade or
otherwise, be lent, resold, hired out or otherwise circulated without the publisher's
prior written consent in any form of binding or cover other than that in which it is
published and without a similar condition including this condition being imposed
on the subsequent purchaser.

First published in Great Britian in 2008 by
Black Lace
Virgin Books
Thames Wharf Studios
Rainville Road
London W6 9HA

www.rbooks.co.uk

Addresses for companies within The Random House Group Limited can be found at:
www.randomhouse.co.uk/offices.htm

The Random House Group Limited Reg. No. 954009

A CIP catalogue record for this book
is available from the British Library

ISBN 9780352341938

The Random House Group Limited supports The Forest Stewardship Council (FSC),
the leading international forest certification organisation. All our titles that are
printed on Greenpeace approved FSC certified paper carry the FSC logo.
Our paper procurement policy can be found at www.rbooks.co.uk/environment

Printed in the UK by CPI Bookmarque, Croydon, CR0 4TD

1

'How wicked I am,' thought Jeanine, as she removed the severe black band that held her thick blonde hair securely in place.

'So very wicked,' she thought as she picked up the brush and applied rhythmic strokes. Jeanine knew she would have to confess her sins. What would she say? How much should she tell? Thank God her eyes would be lowered and her blushes hidden.

She unzipped her soft, deep, cream cashmere skirt and let it drop to the floor. Slowly she undid the front buttons of her pale, patterned silk blouse, enjoying the feel of its languid sensuousness. That, too, she let fall on the thick pile corn-coloured carpet. She sat down on the high, brocade-covered chair opposite the cheval mirror and leisurely removed her dark brown, fine kid shoes. At last she was free. This was the first evening of her new life. She was her own mistress.

Jeanine felt pleased with the way she had managed to organise the conversion of her home into a hotel. On Monday she would be open for business, but for now she had the weekend to herself. On Monday she would be putting the last-minute touches to the rooms, buying fresh flowers and interviewing chambermaids. She must also choose a cook and a handyman-cum-porter. Perhaps, she thought, it would be nice if they were a husband and wife team. A nicely rounded roly-poly woman as the cook, and a sensible man who would understand how the electrics worked as well as being strong enough to carry guests' luggage up the Georgian staircase.

It was cause for regret that there was no space for an elevator. Jeanine stretched lazily. On Monday she would be busy sorting, choosing, organising people and distributing leaflets. Tonight and the next couple of days were hers alone, to do with as she wanted.

But what should she say to her Confessor? She stood up and unhooked her pale-pink Chantilly lace bra, unhurriedly stroking her breasts. Lingering over the nipples, she allowed her fingertips to coax them into a pleasant stiffness. She smiled to herself as she picked out a lipstick from her dressing-table and painted her lips a deep, fiery red.

Those people in her old office had no idea who she was, or what she really thought. She had deliberately played down any vestiges of her sexuality. It was there for all to see if they had only looked beneath the prim exterior and beyond her no-eye-make-up face. She'd worn only a soft pink lipstick and had coiled her hair into in a bun that never betrayed her flaxen glory, now so evident.

Her clothes, sensual to touch and easy to shed, were an invitation, but her manner was wholly contained. Throughout her meteoric four-year career her attitude had remained as cool and aloof as her brain had been fast and incisive. She knew she had been nicknamed The Ice Maiden, and that the more unkind and outspoken had called her, bluntly, The Frigid Bitch. But now all that was behind her.

Jeanine sighed with relief. Never again would she have to push through rush-hour traffic, climb the marble and glass stairs into her office or sit at her desk with its computer and stupid rubber plant, avoiding the gossip of the women and the men. She had earned enough both in salary and in respect to go her own way. Now, with her late husband Laurence's money finally through and her employment contract terminated as planned, everything had come together very nicely. Jeanine took a long, deep and contented breath; the decorators had finished in the house and all was fresh and sweet smelling.

Jeanine removed her slip and stood in front of the mirror, naked except for her Directoire knickers. What would her Confessor say if he could see her now? She had avoided him for the past few weeks on the false grounds of pressure of work. But soon, very soon, she would have to face him, report to him, tell him. Her Confessor, who had taken her under his wing when his nephew, Jeanine's husband, had died so tragically three days after their marriage. Her Confessor who had given her the extra money she needed for her hotel. Her Confessor who, when she initially refused to take his money, told her it was no more, no less, than a business arrangement; a good investment for him. He had many friends and acquaintances constantly coming and going, all needing somewhere where they could stay, away from the public gaze, in perfect peace, safety and security. Her hotel would suit them very well. She conjured up a vision of her Confessor. She shivered slightly. Petrov always had an uncomfortable effect upon her.

Somehow she knew he spelled danger to her inner being. She could never quite put her finger on what it was. He was charming. He was polite, with old-fashioned good manners. He was caring and considerate of her feelings. What Jeanine failed to recognise was the potency of Petrov as a supremely sexual man.

She thought of him as she saw him on her last visit, made before the reawakening of her sexuality: a great bull of a man in a black cassock, with grey-blue eyes that bored into her and a magnetic presence that overwhelmed her. His iron-grey hair was, as always, perfectly cut but curled slightly at the temples. This gave him a somewhat raffish air, an air almost unbecoming in an abbot. Jeanine trembled slightly at the memory.

Alerted by the porter at the main gate, Petrov had stood at the massive open door of his large, rambling Tudor mansion, which he had had modernised at great expense. It was his pride and joy, and also the headquarters of his religious order. It was a mixed order, one which both men and women could enter. Jeanine rarely met anyone on the inside of the building, but whenever she visited she noticed a plethora of male and female novices in their dark-green robes tending the gardens.

Petrov, his arms outstretched in welcome, had greeted her with a platonic peck on her cheek before leading her across the great hall to the confessional box hidden slightly behind a raised dais. Petrov had entered on one side and sat down. Jeanine entered on the other side, closed the door and knelt in the darkness in front of the grille. There had been very little to confess; small jealousies, little lies, but never anything that had warranted much penance. Not then. But now, now she had rediscovered physical desire. That was why she had spent the last month avoiding him. She was frightened of confessing this to him. Something inside her told her that this discovery and telling him about it would change their relationship: for all Petrov had ever asked of her was that she remained pure and faithful to her husband's memory.

He had promised that within the year she could have her wish, join his order and withdraw from the world. But for the moment she must be of this world, subject to its temptations and resist them. She must continue with her life of purity. He had also told her he would know if she ever deviated, if she failed to tell him the truth or infringed any of the rules he had laid down for her. And she believed him.

Sitting down at her dressing-table she painted her nails with bright-red lacquer. The colour reminded her of the tropics. South America. Brazil. Brazil was the one place in the world she had wanted to visit. She had been overjoyed when Laurence suggested they go there for their honeymoon.

Hazily, she pictured him: his lithe muscular body, his deep-brown eyes and sun-bleached hair. His face permanently suntanned from the hours spent in the open air searching for, collecting and naming plants.

They had arrived in São Paulo quite exhausted after their long flight from Paris via Lisbon. They had been met by Laurence's Aunt Rosario and her new husband, Edson, who had driven the long miles to his large estate whilst Rosario and Laurence chatted happily of old times in Paris and of mutual friends. Jeanine had been happy not to talk; content to hold Laurence's hand and watch the changing landscape. After a five-hour drive they eventually arrived at an enormous house. There, in the soft hours of a Brazilian morning, Laurence had taken her virginity. He had introduced her to the delights of lovemaking.

She remembered the soft touch of his hands as he stroked her body. He made sure she was not afraid. His fingers gently loosening the ties of her negligée and lifting her night-dress, revealing her secret place suddenly wet with desire. She relived his lips touching hers before kissing her neck, her eyes, her hair, her breasts. Then he showed her how to hold him, how to stroke his penis so that it became stiff as a rod, fully extended and ready to plunge into her. Parting her legs he moved between her thighs and then slowly, with great patience, his erect penis gliding on her moistness, he entered her. Sensations she had never known before flooded through her, took her by surprise, engulfed her. For hours they lay moving and moaning, shaking and taking until, sapped of all desire, they had curled up in each other's arms and fallen asleep.

During that night she had been attacked by mosquitoes. They had gorged themselves on her fresh English blood and debilitated her. If they hadn't she would have died with him. Laurence was a keen polo player. Rosario and Edson had placed a private jet at the honeymooners' disposal, suggesting they both fly the five-hundred-mile journey to where a game was to be played. But Jeanine had been too ill to go. The mosquito bites had caused an allergy that set a fever raging through her body, so Laurence went alone. Then came the news. Her husband had not arrived at the match. It took them two days to find the tangled wreckage of his aircraft in the depths of the Brazilian rainforest, but his body was never found.

That was four years ago. Four years in which to recover from the shock and learn to stand on her own two feet. Jeanine had found that difficult, suddenly deprived of status, support and love. She had always been protected by family, especially her mother, Penelope Vladelsky, who only a few months later was herself plunged into mourning for Jeanine's step-father, Stefan. Penelope's grief had left her incapable of sustained thought and action for herself, let alone anyone else, even her only child, Jeanine. Because Laurence's body had never been found, the trustees were loath to pay out on the will. The insurance company was loath to pay out, too. With some money of her own, but not enough to keep her going for a protracted period, Jeanine decided that work, for which she had no real or sensible training, was the answer, not only financially but also to ease the pain of Laurence's death.

Petrov had helped her find employment with a young public relations company. Jeanine had not enjoyed it. She had not looked forward to the daily grind, the drudgery of being with people she did not like, of being at their command, but she had done it and done it well. Recently, Laurence had been declared officially dead and all monies due to her had come through. She was able to stop working like a drone and have her own business. Jeanine was utterly determined it was going to be a great success.

She looked at the beautiful drapes, carpets and upholstery so wonderfully designed by her clever cousin, Auralie. Dear Auralie, so very different from her. Dark, where Jeanine was blonde; petite, where Jeanine was voluptuous. Creative, where Jeanine was practical; sexy, where she was . . .

Jeanine stopped herself in mid-thought. She was pleased her cousin was now happily married, but knew that her own marriage to Laurence had been a blow to Auralie. The two had been very close, although Laurence had gone to great lengths to tell Jeanine he and Auralie had never been lovers. They couldn't be, he had explained: they were first cousins. Jeanine had said she didn't think that mattered, but Laurence had insisted it did. Jeanine had expected Auralie to be jealous but she had been sweetness itself. She had even helped Jeanine choose her wedding dress. She could not understand why her mother detested Auralie so much.

Auralie had proved her worth and friendship again, providing Jeanine with the refurbishment of her hotel at cost price. When her mother returned from her cruise, Jeanine would tell her how kind Auralie had been. Jeanine could not bear dissension or undercurrents, nor rows or violence in any form. She wanted everybody to be happy. She would bring the two of them together. It would be like it was when they were young, before her step-father Stefan had died.

Jeanine's thoughts switched from Stefan to his youngest brother, Petrov, the cadences of his hypnotic booming voice piercing her thoughts. Soon she must see him. She must, but not yet. What would she say? How explicit should she be when her thoughts were less and less of Laurence and now more sexual, deeply sexual? Should she tell him she lay on the bed with her legs and arms apart, bound by leather straps holding her down while a strong muscular body came up between her legs, a mouth licking her thighs, and fingers slowly opening her secret entrance? As she thought about this, Jeanine's hand moved slowly over her body and under the waistband of her knicker elastic. Her forefinger, as if of its own volition, began exciting her most tender parts. Jeanine began to feel the sensations of want and need. She could feel the blood rushing through her body, suffusing her face, filling up, opening up, and expanding her hidden places. She could feel her cheeks tingle. Her tongue peeped through her half-opened mouth and she licked her own lips. She could feel her inner self ripening, unfurling. She could feel herself blossoming.

Jeanine removed her knickers and sat down on the cane chair in front of her dressing-table. The mirror on the opposite wall was so positioned that with the aid of the cheval mirror she had a perfect view of herself from every angle. She gazed at her breasts and touched her nipples, making sure they stood firm and erect. She bent slowly with the unconscious grace of a natural dancer and stroked her inner thighs. Then she stood to admire the plump, rounded softness of her pale-skinned bottom, now slightly reddened and criss-crossed from the cane chair. This sight unexpectedly aroused her and she trailed her red-nailed fingers along the fresh marks. Jeanine walked over to her beautiful walnut inlay tallboy and opened a drawer. Excited by a sense of guilt, she took out her secret purchases: a black lace and leather basque, a pair of black satin, split-crotch panties and black silk-seamed stockings.

Standing in front of the mirror Jeanine laced herself into the basque and stepped into the crotchless knickers. She liked the feel of the cool satin against her buttocks and how the elastic held her in at the top of her legs so that her hidden softness was gently edged forward and constantly rubbed together in a spiral of enticement. It opened her, encouraging the moistness to flow. She opened further, becoming more than moist, becoming wet. She opened still further, her juices oozing out and dampening her thighs.

Jeanine turned her stockings inside out then pulled them on and up her shapely legs. She checked that the back suspenders were hitched at the point where the seam began and that they were perfectly straight. From her ornate walnut wardrobe she took a pair of high-heeled, laced-to-the-ankle boots and thrust her feet into them. She smiled at her reflection. Her transformation was complete.

Would her Confessor understand when she told him her need to feel that man's penis in her mouth? To close her lips over his masculinity and suck him? Would he understand her need to turn over, raise her buttocks and feel that masculinity within her? Or would her Confessor punish her for her wickedness? And how would he punish her?

Jeanine, facing herself in the mirror, noticed her secret self was no longer secret. Now her fingers were not enough. She wanted something more. She opened another drawer of her tallboy and removed a pink leather dildo. She caressed it. She put its tip into her mouth, sucked on it and remembered how she had come to buy it.

Until recently she had lain night after night alone in her bed and sobbing. But one restless night desire had begun to form within her. It started when she was suddenly cold. She put her hands between her legs to keep warm. Enjoying the unaccustomed feeling of being held and the twin satisfaction of warmth flooding through her cold fingers and the sense of security provided by her hands, she moved slightly in the bed. Her fingers shifted and accidentally touched her closed opening which immediately responded to the pressure. It tingled and waited expectantly for those fingers to move again. There was a tightening in her throat and a flutter in her belly. Jeanine touched again. Tingle. She touched again and again. She uncurled from her foetal position, spread her legs apart and, in the darkness beneath her bedcovers, searched out her hidden self. Without a conscious thought, just the excitement of flesh touching flesh, she luxuriated in the thrill of discovery. Her sensitive fingertips caressed her equally sensitive secret parts – her sex. After a while nebulous fantasies began to take shape. Jeanine started to look forward to her nights instead of dreading them. She also felt the need for something thicker, bigger, longer, throbbing inside her. She decided to buy a dildo, but that would mean going into a sex shop. She had felt an acute sense of shame and had blushed at the thought. However, the overriding desire, the wantonness of her desire, overcame her shame. She had put on an old Burberry raincoat, thick pebble-lens spectacles, covered her head with a Hermes scarf and had walked unabashed into the shop.

Amongst the blow-up dolls and whips and canes and jellies and creams and garments she thought existed only in her imagination, Jeanine saw an array of plastic and leather penises in a variety of sizes. Almost immediately her eyes had fallen on one in shell-pink leather. It was beautifully shaped and formed, its leather balls supple and malleable and yielding to her touch. She felt her legs begin to tremble and her knickers cling with a sudden dampness. In a daze, Jeanine began fondling its hard erectness. A hardness that in her mind had taken on a dangerous quality. She had bought it, together with a small vibrator.

The memory now made her want to see herself brazen and swollen. She took off her panties, then opened a drawer in her dressing-table and removed a bottle of sweet-smelling oils. Carefully, so none dropped on the carpet, she coated the dildo with solicitous strokes. Standing in front of the mirror, keeping her legs apart, her pelvis thrust forward, she rolled the dildo up and down her thighs. She held it behind her back and let its hardness peep through the space at the top of her legs. Quivering with anticipation and aching to welcome something thick and stiff she let the dildo caress her soft, dark-pink inner lips, normally completely hidden from view but now showing, open, tactile and wanton.

Jeanine imagined the hard, taut body that would possess a member like the one now teasing her oiled thighs. She imagined the hands that would pull down the lace and leather that covered her breasts. She envisaged those hands holding her breasts, massaging her nipples. And she thought of the mouth that would kiss and suck them. She imagined those hands moving down from her breasts, over her belly, to stroke and play with the fair down covering the mound at the top of her legs. As she fantasised, so the muscles inside her begged to be enclosing, manipulating, the beloved object. Jeanine envisaged the face and trembled. A very real man. A forbidden man. She knew she would have to tell her Confessor about him; have to relate to him her wickedness, her sin. Confess your thoughts, he always told her, for they are father to the deed. But Jeanine knew she would never ever let those thoughts become reality. The idea was preposterous. Nevertheless, her mind continued to visualise him – Auralie's husband, Gerry. Gerry bending over her whilst she was tied and powerless. Powerless to stop him twisting her hair in his hands, jerking her head backwards so that her mouth opened involuntarily as he inserted his penis, commanding her to suck him whether she wanted to or not.

Jeanine held the dildo at its base. She sat on the cane chair, spreading her legs apart over its arms. With her vulva exposed and one hand resting on her enlarged and engorged clitoris, she let the dildo glide into her shameless opening. She shoved hard. Harder. Imagining and feeling. Tingling and trembling. Taking and tightening, working herself up to the pitch of ecstasy. Every pore of her body was alive. She gripped the dildo, pushing it in and out, in and out, her mind conjuring fantasy upon fantasy. Men were sucking her. Men were taking her. Taking her from the front, taking her from the back. Men were holding her down, making her suck them one after the other. She was panting and squirming, bringing herself to the point of no return.

Then, on a whim, with her back arched, the pattern of the cane chair digging into her buttocks, she stopped thrusting. She decided not to come. She would tease herself. How stupid to use up hours of pleasure in a few short moments. She would do something she would be unlikely ever to do again. She would roam through the house playing with herself. She would play with herself in front of every mirror in every room. Then in future, when that room was occupied, she would have the memory of what she had done. How she had stamped her sexuality on the fabric of the house. *Her* sexuality. *Her* fantasy. She would pretend she was a hooker visiting clients.

She was no longer Jeanine, ex-director of a PR company, now the owner of a small private hotel. She was Jeanine, the high-class hooker visiting clients and having to dodge the owner. She set the dildo to one side and began to paint her face, first the foundation, then the silky powder. She put blue on her eyelids, then black mascara on her eyelashes. She brushed mascara on her eyebrows, enhancing their curve, then put rouge on her cheeks and more bright red on her lips. She brushed her hair again. She checked that her stocking seams were straight and touched herself at the top of her legs. She was still wet. Glistening wet.

What to wear over her basque? She moved across to the wardrobe. She saw herself in the mirror. She caught a glimpse of her reddened, marked bare bottom, her black silk-stockinged legs, her ankle-high leather boots, her breasts with their erect nipples jutting forth, and she smiled. What a shock her old colleagues would have if they could see her now. The Ice Maiden, The Frigid Bitch, enjoying her fantasies. Rifling through her wardrobe Jeanine chose a floor-length, black leather cape. She draped it over her satin-smooth shoulders, bowing its thongs around her neck. She decided she would go into the kitchen and take a bottle of champagne from the refrigerator. She would christen each room in every possible way. And no one would know. This added to her sense of wickedness and gave her a sharp stab of pleasure. Next week she would tell her Confessor. She would have to because she could not continue to avoid him; he might become suspicious. Next week she would allow herself to be covered in shame and mortification, but tonight, and for the weekend, she would wallow in her fantasies. She picked up the dildo and left the quiet, golden charm of her bedroom.

Jeanine had no way of knowing that soon her secret would be discovered. That it would be the man she most desired who would find her dressed in her secret, exotic and erotic clothes, and he would find her sexually hungry and wantonly aroused.

2

Gerry de Bouys surveyed his new office with enormous satisfaction. It was elegant and businesslike; exactly what he had
wanted. Auralie had done an excellent job.

Auralie was his wife, and the designer. He gave her a
mental, though grudging nod of respect. Grudging, because
today he was displeased with her. More than displeased: he
was angry with her. But his anger did not extend to the design
of his office. He was very happy with the deep silver-grey
carpet, the pale-grey walls with white ceiling, the white
skirting board, the white doors and the ebony desk. This was
cleared of almost everything except fresh paper, a pen, a
telephone and fax and a chrome table lamp. Gerry's father
had drummed into his son from an early age that an untidy
desk represented an untidy mind: that an untidy mind is an
inefficient mind, and inefficiency has no place within a
successful company.

Gerry sat in one of the chrome-and-black leather chairs,
momentarily staring at the restful sight of the variety of plants
set in pebbles round a small pond in a corner close to the main
window. This window, running the length of the room, gave
Gerry a panoramic view of London and the River Thames. He
glanced out, noticing how the day's dying sun lit up and
enhanced the city's famous landmarks.

He walked into his private bathroom where, for want of
anything better to do, he washed his hands and combed his
hair. Everyone else in the building had gone home, but Gerry

had stayed on. He was anxiously waiting for a coded fax from his father, the industrialist, Sir Henry de Bouys.

Sir Henry had decided to go into the airline business. He was going to gatecrash the monopoly held by the world's major airlines and planned to beat them at their own game. Gerry's office, adjoining his father's, would be at the heart of the new empire. Nobody knew of their plans, not even Auralie. There had been times when Gerry was tempted to tell her. Now, reviewing the events of the last thirty-six hours, he was glad he had not. Total secrecy was all important. It left the advantage with them.

Gerry was waiting to hear if his father's deal for the aircraft had gone through. If it had, then he could activate the next phase of the operation – the corporate identity, the designing of the logo, the carpets, the furnishings, the uniforms and the VIP suites at the airports where the aircraft would touch down. Everything they had planned rested on a fax in the affirmative. It depended on Sir Henry's ability to get the right aircraft at the right price.

Gerry looked at himself in the mirror. He was as neat as his office. His well-cut, navy-blue chalk-stripe Savile Row suit fitted his athletic figure perfectly. His pale-pink Egyptian cotton shirt showed off his tightly knotted old school tie. His deep-blue eyes twinkled in his lightly suntanned face. His dark-brown hair, always cut by his hairdresser in Curzon Street, fell easily into place with a quick flick of the comb. As he washed his hands some water splashed onto his classic English black brogues. He opened the door beneath the wash basin, took out a shoe-cleaning pack and gave his shoes a slight polish.

He wondered if his father might appear at the office in person instead of faxing. It was a little unlikely, but there was an element of the mischievous in Sir Henry's character. Gerry was convinced that it was his father's ability to surprise that frequently gave him the edge on his business rivals. Gerry hoped it was a characteristic he had inherited.

He walked back into his office, sat down and started doodling. He was so busy thinking about the business it took him some time to realise he had absentmindedly drawn two women: one slim, one voluptuous. The voluptuous one was standing tied to the pillar of a four-poster bed. The slim woman had one hand over the curvaceous woman's pubis, the other on her breasts. He realised that the slim one bore a likeness to his wife, Auralie.

Gerry had often dreamed of watching two women make love, but at the slightest mention of his fantasy his wife had rolled away to the far side of their bed, expressing her disgust. The previous afternoon he'd returned home to collect some important notes and had been completely taken by surprise to find his wife making love to a nubile and plump young woman.

Gerry stared at the drawing. It made him horny. He could feel his cock straining against the cloth of his pants. He would have his wife tonight. But he needed relief immediately. Gerry stood up and locked his office door. He knew the building was empty but Gerry was a careful man; he always took precautions. Vividly recalling the scene he had silently witnessed, he returned to his seat, unzipped his trousers, let his erect prick leap out of its imprisonment and began caressing himself.

He thought about the previous afternoon. He remembered how he had let himself in through the white stucco and porti-coed doors of his South Kensington house and checked the bureau in the hall for the missing notes. Unable to find them he decided he might have left them on his bedside table. He started up the stairs to the bedroom. The thick carpets disguised his tread and he was about to push open the bedroom door when he heard a deep sigh; an intensely sexual sigh. Something inside him told him to stay where he was. Jealousy suddenly raged through his body at the thought of Auralie having an affair with another man. He peered into his bedroom and was completely astounded by the sight that met his eyes.

A vaguely familiar plump young woman with short brown hair and dressed in a nun's habit had her arms above her head and was tied to the bed post. Gerry's wife, stark naked, was standing beside her, one hand inside the long slit-front opening of her habit, playing with the young woman's breasts.

'Have you had many women?' the plump girl asked his wife.

'Oh yes,' replied Auralie. 'That, Margaret, is why Petrov sent you to me.'

Gerry's mind raced. So this Margaret had something to do with Auralie's uncle, Petrov. Well, he had never liked the man. Never. True he could be very charming – very old-world Russian. But on the few occasions that Gerry had met him he had always felt the deepest scepticism towards Petrov's professed sanctity.

Gerry's thoughts were interrupted as he watched Auralie push the girl's habit to one side, uncovering the full opulence of her large breasts. The licentiousness of their massive white round-ness made Gerry's mouth go dry with instant lust. He watched Auralie knead their lusciousness while licking the girl's neck and kissing her lips. Gerry, surprised by Auralie's admission of female lovers, was even more surprised by her evident expertise. She quite obviously knew and enjoyed knowing a woman's body.

Margaret let out a long moan of pleasure. Auralie's other hand began lifting the long skirt of her habit.

'Open your legs,' ordered Auralie. The young woman did as she was told. 'Wider.'

On the command she opened them wider. With a vicarious

thrill Gerry watched Auralie reveal more and more of the girl's plump white thighs, then finally expose the neat black triangle at the top of her legs.

Shocked, yet titillated and mirroring the girl's attitude, Gerry leant against the door post. He gently rubbed his balls and penis through his trousers.

Auralie put her hand over the girl's black mound, pressed her breasts to the other woman's, then slowly began to move one finger backwards and forwards along the visual reaches of Margaret's sex.

'I want you very wet,' Auralie said.

Her words galvanised the girl into making sensuous, undulating hip movements. Auralie stopped playing with her, put both hands on her breasts, then allowed her tongue to trace the outline of Margaret's mouth.

'What am I going to do to you now?' Auralie asked the girl.

'I think you are going to suck me,' said the other woman breathlessly.

'Yes,' said Auralie, squeezing her breasts, 'I am going to put my head between your legs and I'm going to lick your stiff little clitoris until you don't know whether you are in heaven or in hell. After that we'll have today's lesson.'

Gerry watched Margaret as she arched her pelvis, offering her sex to Auralie who knelt down and buried her tongue in the depths beyond the black triangle.

Gerry thought he had seen few things more erotic than the tied girl swaying and jerking to the rhythm of his wife's tongue.

Still leaning against the door, Gerry felt an intense desire to punish Auralie. He wanted to bend her to his will and spank her bare bottom. He also had a strong desire to burst into the room and take Auralie, then take the woman tied to the bed post.

He recalled the first occasion that he had proposed bringing another woman into their bed. It was within a week of their marriage. They had been making love when he had mentioned another woman. 'I would love to have another woman in our bed,' he had said. 'I would love to see you touch a woman and then watch as I fucked her.'

Why, he had later asked himself, had he said such a thing when they were perfectly happy enjoying each other's bodies? But he had, and Auralie had frozen. Though disappointed at the time, he had thought it was possibly a normal reaction. But now, as he watched the neatness of his wife's body, her rosebud breasts, her taut belly, the shape and swelling of her arse as she licked and kissed the woman tied to their bed, he wondered what the real cause was.

This thought stopped abruptly as Auralie stood up and unhooked the ties that bound Margaret's hands. Gerry undid his flies and squeezed the base of his cock. He mustn't come. He wanted to know what else Auralie was going to do. He wanted to know what the next lesson was.

Auralie made the girl lie down flat on her back putting her hands in place over her little black mound.

'Play with yourself,' she commanded, then placed her own knees either side of the girl's head, her juicy open sex hovering over Margaret's mouth. 'Exactly as I showed you last time. Put out your tongue and lick me.'

Gerry thought he would explode as he saw the chubby girl's small fat tongue come out and enter his wife's sex. Auralie's hands came down and played with Margaret's creamy breasts as she rode her mouth.

'You've learnt well,' Auralie said. 'Now go deeper, deeper. And keep playing with yourself.'

The girl, spreading her legs wider and wider, began to raise her hips and shake and tremble.

'You mustn't come. Not yet,' said Auralie, suddenly standing up. 'Turn over and put your arse in the air.'

The rounded plumpness of the girl's bottom was utterly inviting and Gerry's member was thick, erect and at bursting point as he saw his wife's expert fingers slide into Margaret's arse. The girl gave a sharp cry.

'All of you has to be open for Petrov. And you are too tight here,' said Auralie, adding, 'My husband likes to take me like this.'

'You enjoy sex with him?' asked Margaret.

'Oh yes. Gerry has a wonderful prick and he knows how to use it,' replied Auralie. 'Now stay like that whilst I give you your next lesson.'

Gerry felt a flush of pleasure at this unexpected overheard praise, but wondered why, if she liked him so much, she didn't allow him to have sex with her more often. Perhaps this girl was the reason. Perhaps his wife had sex here on a regular basis. Whilst he was at the office maybe she was here screwing. Screwing women. But could she also be screwing men? Jealousy whipped through Gerry, searing his ego.

Auralie disappeared from Gerry's view for a moment, then came back and bent over the girl. She had a cane in her hand. He and Auralie seemed to be more in tune than he would have guessed. He wanted to grab that cane from her, bend her over and sting her bare bottom with it.

'Now, Margaret, I am going to spank you,' said Auralie.

Her words made Gerry hold the base of his penis and squeeze very hard to stop himself coming.

'Why?'

'For keeping me waiting.'

'But . . .' protested Margaret. 'But I didn't know . . . didn't think . . . didn't realise.'

'You didn't realise! When I kissed you goodbye on your first visit and let my hands pass across your breasts, you didn't realise?'

Now Gerry remembered why the girl's face was familiar. Some weeks ago he had arrived home from work to find a nun sitting in his drawing-room. It was the same girl. Auralie had said she was interviewing for a book-keeper. He had thought it odd at the time. Why interview at home and not at her office? And why a nun? However, he was busy with his father's new project and dismissed it from his mind with the thought that nuns, too, had to earn a living, and possibly Auralie did not want her current book-keeper to know she was getting rid of her. Gerry never interfered in Auralie's business.

'I didn't realise. I thought it was an accident,' said Margaret, responding to Auralie.

'No. That was no accident. Didn't Petrov tell you?'

'He told me nothing except I had to come with the accounts and learn from you.'

'Yes, and you are learning very quickly. Petrov will be delighted. I shall give you a good report for all your figure work. Stay there. Stay exactly as you are. Don't move, close your eyes and raise your arse up.'

Margaret did as she was commanded, but it wasn't high enough for Auralie, who readjusted the girl's position.

'Higher, higher,' Auralie urged. 'Your shoulders on the floor. I want your tits, your lovely big fat tits, flat on the floor.' Auralie gave them a quick squeeze as she said this. 'Flat on the floor, so you can feel the roughness of the carpet against your nipples. And after each stroke you will thank me, is that understood?'

'Yes.'

'Yes *madam*,' corrected Auralie. 'And you will never keep me waiting again, will you? Answer me.'

'No, madam.'

Auralie brought the cane down across the girl's bare bottom. The girl cried out. The cane left a bright red mark.

'You say "thank you",' hissed Auralie.

'Thank you, madam,' whispered Margaret.

'Louder!' instructed Auralie.

'Thank you, madam.' The cane came down again, leaving another red mark.

'Next time you come here you will be ready for me. Do you understand?'

'Yes, madam.' The cane hit the girl's bare flesh once again and she flinched. But Gerry couldn't help noticing that her face was flushed with pleasure.

'Keep still. You will not be wearing anything underneath your skirt, and when you arrive you will kneel down and beg to suck me.'

'Yes, madam.'

'What are you going to do?'

'Kneel down and beg to suck you, madam.'

At these words Gerry loosened his grip slightly and rubbed his prick faster.

'You are going to suck me exactly as I showed you, aren't you?'

'Yes.'

'Yes, *madam*,' said Auralie, the cane descending once more. The girl yelled out, then offered her buttocks for another stripe. 'Now repeat what I told you.'

'Next time I come I will not be wearing any panties and I will kneel down and beg to suck you.'

'That is correct. Your arse is looking very pretty, *ma petite*. Very red. Two more.'

'Oh no,' she cried.

'No?' queried Auralie. 'But, *ma petite*, you don't understand. You take what I give you.'

Gerry watched as his wife caressed the reddened bottom, then slid two fingers into the girl's open wet sex and thrust hard. Then she administered two further stripes.

'And where did this disobedient girl learn to take her punishment?' Auralie inquired, lasciviously.

'At my convent.'

'On your bare bottom at your convent?'

'Yes. Reverend Mother used to spank me.'

Auralie began to caress and stroke Margaret's breasts. 'You have exceptionally nice tits. Now tell me what you had to do for the Reverend Mother.'

'I had to bend over her desk, pull down my panties and pull up my skirt. Then she would feel my bottom, tell me it had to be soft and wobbly and when it was to her liking she'd bring down the cane.'

Auralie caressed the girl's reddened, delectable, rounded soft arse, then quickly took up the cane and gave her yet another two stripes. Margaret screamed with a combination of pain and pleasure.

Gerry had always wanted to spank Auralie. He had always wanted to see her reddened bottom and feel her blind obedience, but she had never allowed it. Now he understood why. She had to be in control. But he was the man, the husband, and his wife must do what he wanted. He would have her tied and he would spank her. The very thought of this increased Gerry's desire and his penis throbbed and ached. He rubbed it, feeling the exquisite sensation of near orgasm.

Auralie stroked the weals she had left on the girl's backside, then licked them. The girl relaxed onto the floor in an attitude of total supplication and Auralie untied her hands.

'Stand up and play with my pussy whilst I play with yours.' In Auralie's lilting French accent those words added to Gerry's arousal and excitement. Eyeing the tableau in his bedroom, watching the two women kiss and probe each other to orgasm, Gerry held his balls and moved his hand faster and faster as he imagined thrusting into Auralie. Uncontrollably he came, silently spurting into his own hands.

He left the house as noiselessly as he had arrived and went to the pub for a drink. When he returned sometime later Auralie and Margaret had gone. There was no sign that they had ever been there. He found his notes and went back to his office. His concentration was not as high as it should have been. All the while he was thinking of what he had seen and then imagining what he would do to Auralie. In the end he had given up and gone home.

He had not mentioned what he had seen to Auralie. He had been tempted to imagine that his wife had done it to act out his fantasy so that she could tease him with it afterwards. But then he decided that was not the case. He had felt certain Auralie would tell him about her escapade. He had waited and waited. Throughout supper and the entire evening, he had waited. He had waited patiently, but he had waited in vain. He had anticipated her whispering into his ear as they settled down in their enormous four-poster bed, but had experienced an acute sense of anti-climax and disappointment when she said nothing. He had hinted at sex. Started to talk dirty. He had tried to kiss her neck and breasts and had mumbled about his various fantasies. He had told her how he longed to watch her being taken by another man and how much he would like to see her making love to a woman. Her response had been the same as always. She had told him not to be so disgusting. He had made overtures to her body, touched her breasts and let his hands wind down between her legs; she had feigned tiredness. Clenching his mouth in anger he had rolled away from her.

Gerry wondered why he didn't face her with what he had seen that afternoon. Why was he keeping silent? He started to think that perhaps he had not witnessed anything at all, that the whole incident was some bizarre invention of his own imagination. But, remembering the tide of conflicting emotions that had engulfed him, he knew it was not. He had been hit by sexual excitement, extreme sexual excitement, but he had also been assailed by anger. He decided it was the anger that kept him silent. He knew something about his wife that she did not know he knew. This, he mused, was control, and something that could be traded.

This was why, since then, he had been thinking up various scenarios for his revenge. He was determined she would pay. He would think of something. She could not take a woman and then reject *him*, her own husband. He had lain in the darkness, seething with anger. It had been her unobtainability that made her worth conquering. She had never had sex with any of his friends, although he knew they wanted to. She had kept her legs closed until after the wedding ceremony. Now she was his wife and he could take her whenever he wanted. He thought that was the deal, but it had proved otherwise. It would, he thought ruefully, have been better if he had not put such a store on her purity, her untouchedness. They might now be enjoying a better sex life. He might have discovered more about her.

Was she so pure because she preferred women to men? This horrific thought suddenly hit him. But if so why had she chosen to marry him? There had been plenty of other, and richer, men on her horizon. There must be a reason. If she was trading her sexuality it had to be for a reason. He had thought it was for love but now he wasn't so sure. He would wait and watch.

But he still wanted her. He had put out his hand and stroked her back. She had flinched. He withdrew his hand, feeling a sudden rush of jealousy and a desire to take her whether she wanted him or not. He thought about it, then had a vision of her cousin, Jeanine.

Jeanine, the blonde, voluptuous, virginal Jeanine. Maybe he could have *her*. Maybe he could hold *her*, take her large breasts between his hands, roll his tongue around her nipples, let his hands drift between her legs. He thought of the difference between the two women. Auralie, tiny, slim and dark, her fiery green eyes flashing, her sleek black hair severely cut. Jeanine, big and blonde, her blue eyes almost doelike and her thick blonde hair kept in a bun that had the promise of tumbling sexily over her shoulders. Gerry thought of his wife's neat, pert breasts and her flat, almost boyish, stomach. He surprised himself by making an unfavourable comparison with Jeanine's larger, fuller, more rounded figure. The harsh compactness of the one against the soft lusciousness of the other. Jeanine seemed so cool and self-assured but it was Auralie who, for all her exotic looks, had an icy coldness about her. No, he decided rather than screw his wife when she did not want to know he would leave her completely alone. He would occupy his mind with thoughts of having Jeanine. But how could he manage that? Gerry had gone to sleep thinking about it.

When he woke up next morning he began to plot revenge. He looked at his wife lying beside him, her dark nipples showing through the pale thin cambric of her night-dress which was wound around her waist, revealing her slim bottom.

She was going to discover what anger, jealousy and dominance meant. He put out a hand and brought the palm of his hand down hard on her small rounded cheeks. Auralie jumped with surprise. Gerry got out of bed without saying a word. He bathed, shaved and dressed, and left for the office without acknowledging her existence.

Auralie had called her husband's office a number of times during the day but he had not allowed her calls to be put through. She was worried, just as he wanted her to be. That was the opening move in the plan, his plan, for getting what he wanted.

He was still playing with himself when there was a knock on the door. Gerry pressed the intercom on his desk. 'Yes?' he said, sharply.

'It's Caroline,' came a voice.

Gerry half-covered his prick before pressing another button that would allow his father's secretary to enter his office.

'Sorry,' she said, standing framed in the doorway, 'I left something behind.'

'In here?' he asked.

'Yes, for safe keeping,' she replied, smiling. There was a hint of naughtiness in her smile.

Gerry stared at her lasciviously. Caroline Turner had been his father's secretary for two years ever since she graduated from the Knightsbridge School for Young Ladies. But they had known each other for longer than that. Caroline's parents had bought a house close to Sir Henry's London mansion in an ultra-smart part of Chelsea. Caroline's brothers had attended the same school as Gerry and they all went to the same balls and other seasonal functions.

There were times, Gerry thought, when he had forgotten how good-looking she was. Her short, blonde feathery hair, cut to shape, accentuated her deep-brown eyes, her clear skin and her high cheekbones; her mouth, heavily coated with a deep shade of pink lip-gloss, picked out its full sensuousness. She was wearing a well-fitting, dark-pink linen suit which showed her trim figure to advantage. With a clutch bag held under her arm Caroline swept elegantly into the room, her fine long legs very much in evidence beneath her short skirt.

'Kit's picking me up here,' she said.

'Really!' said Gerry from behind his desk, his fingers inside his flies and gently running over the tip of his prick.

Kit was his oldest friend. They'd been at prep school together. He thought they had no secrets from one another, but his friend had not mentioned that he had been seeing Caroline. Kit, otherwise known as Viscount Brimpton, was heir to large estates in north-west England. He was wealthy and had no need to earn a living, but as a four-goal player he hired himself out during the polo-playing season and made what he considered useful pocket money.

Gerry knew that Kit and Caroline had had a fling some years ago but he had no idea they were still an item. He wanted to ask her but decided that prying into his father's secretary's private life was bad form. There had been a time when he had known everything about her. Before she was Kit's lover she had been Gerry's. Gerry's cock stiffened more at the thought of the hours spent screwing Caroline.

'What did you leave behind?' he asked.

'Some toys,' she replied, walking across the deep silver-grey carpet and pressing a switch on the wall. Immediately a part of the pale-grey wall slid sideways revealing a row of black-lacquered filing cabinets. Caroline strained on tip-toe to open the high top drawer. As she did so her short skirt rose up and Gerry saw that she did not appear to be wearing any panties. Caroline fished around in the open drawer. Although she was tall, she was not quite tall enough but Gerry did not offer to help. He was enjoying the sight of her bare, slightly suntanned thighs and the curve of her bottom. He put his other hand down between his legs and gripped his balls.

'I can't find where I've put them,' said Caroline. 'I think I need a chair.'

'Are you sure you've got the right cabinet?' asked Gerry.

'Oh, I think so,' she replied, collecting one of the chrome-and-black leather chairs from beside the window and placing it in front of the filing cabinet. She kicked off her high-heeled shoes, lifted first one leg and then the other onto the seat of the chair and bent over in her search. Gerry heard the rustle of paper. His eyes were transfixed on the soft, light-brown, downy mound at the top of her thighs.

He had a great desire to run his hands along Caroline's legs and bury his fingers, his mouth and then his prick deep into the sweet juiciness of the lips almost revealed. Then he remembered Kit, and decided that Caroline was taboo.

Quickly, he covered himself up but did not have time to do up the buttons. He decided he would be more in command of the situation if he moved away from his desk, away from the immediate sight of her. He stood up, walked over to the window and gazed once more at the panoramic view of London.

'Found them,' said Caroline triumphantly, waving a shiny black carrier bag.

'Good,' said Gerry, staring purposefully, but to little effect, out of the window.

Caroline closed the drawer and stepped down. She looked inside the bag.

'Bugger,' she said. 'They're not all here.'

She stood still for a moment. Gerry could see her, soft, sexy and pink, reflected in the window.

'Oh, I've remembered, I put the others in your desk drawer.'

When Gerry turned round he saw that Caroline was bent over his desk removing something from the top drawer. He couldn't see what it was. All Gerry noticed was that Caroline's legs were straight out and apart, her toes gripping the carpet, steadying herself, her skirt high, and the inner lips of her swollen vulva clearly visible. Gerry's prick shot to its full length and he swallowed hard. He put his hands inside his flies and held his thick throbbing erect penis. He had an absolutely violent desire to possess Caroline.

'Caroline,' he said. 'You're asking to be screwed.'

'That's right,' she said, turning her head to look at him.

Gerry needed no further invitation. His trousers, socks and shoes were removed in a trice. He came up behind her, gripped the back of her neck with one hand and his shaft with the other, then shoved his cock into her in one hard, almost vicious, thrust. She opened and yielded to him instantly. With every sharp thrust she opened more and more, jerking beneath his touch. She clutched at the edge of the desk. She didn't sway or heave, or moan or groan, but silently accepted the forcefulness of his movements.

As he took her Gerry felt an enormous sense of release. She was a body known to him. He knew its capabilities and its erogenous zones. He held onto Caroline's slim hips and pressed deeper and deeper inside her. He was panting, gasping, wanting to cry out. She remained silent. Why didn't she yell, he wondered. Why didn't she scream as other women screamed? It had always been a mystery to him. In the months they had been together she had never made a sound either during sex or when she came. He knew she was very excited. Her labia were blooming, flowing, beneath his constant ramming. Gerry made a decision. This time he was going to break down her inhibition, her control. He would make her voice her ecstasy.

There was a strange passivity in Caroline that increased his masculinity, his potency. He had not thought of her in sexual terms since he had married Auralie, although he had had sex with her the night before his wedding. His goodbye present to her, he had called it. And she had enjoyed it. She had even said that she would be available if his marriage didn't work out, but he had told her not to think about it, not to consider it. And he had meant it. As far as he was concerned, faithfulness was to be the order from that moment on.

Caroline moved slightly backwards, edging her feet closer together so she could take him even deeper. He continued to swoop into her, his hands on her buttocks and his nails digging into her flesh.

Why today? he asked himself. Why had she appeared wanton and sexy today? What essence had he emitted for her to pick up on? Was his deprived sex life so obvious? He thought he had kept it remarkably well hidden.

Gerry was riding Caroline with a familiar rhythm, but she was no nearer crying out than when he first entered her. He decided to slow down, work her differently, be more gentle. Then the intercom buzzer sounded on his desk, making them both jump.

'Kit!' Caroline exclaimed.

'Jeez!' said Gerry, standing quite still. He picked up the receiver. 'Hello?'

'Gerry?' It was Kit's voice. Caroline suddenly gave a sharp cough as if she was clearing her throat. 'Are you screwing my woman?'

'Yes,' said Gerry. It was the last question he was expecting and the reply left his mouth before he could think.

'Is your cock rammed up inside her right this minute?'

'Yes.'

'Well, let me in and we'll both have her.'

Gerry pressed the buzzer.

'Was it Kit?' asked Caroline.

'Yes.'

'Oh! What did he say?'

'He asked me if I was screwing you. When I said I was he suggested we could both do it,' Gerry replied, thrusting violently into Caroline's open, wanton, juicy sex. 'Does that appeal to you?'

'It might,' she answered, licking her lips and wiggling her hips.

Without allowing Gerry to remove his prick from inside her Caroline eased herself up and began unbuttoning her suit top, and then her slinky blouse. Casually jerking his shaft into her, Gerry removed his own shirt and threw it with abandon across the room. Then he brought one hand round and, lifting Caroline's breasts clear of her pink lace and satin brassiere, began playing with her nipples. Gerry found he was intensely excited at the idea of them screwing Caroline together.

Neither of them heard the door open or noticed Kit standing in the office doorway. Watching Gerry's arse tense in and out as his cock slid backwards and forwards on Caroline's wetness, Kit removed his charcoal-grey pin-striped suit, his pale-blue silk shirt and old school tie. He slipped off his black handmade shoes and grey fine silk and cotton socks.

Kit was a taller, blonder and a more muscular build than Gerry; his cock was slimmer but longer. He stood for a moment watching the two of them, then began to rub his penis so that it stood proud and erect.

Kit walked to the far side of the desk, lifted Caroline's head up by her hair and shoved his cock into her mouth.

'One inside your pussy, one inside your mouth, bitch,' he said. 'Now suck. Do it exactly as I like it. As I've trained you to do.'

Caroline formed her mouth into an 'O' shape and then placed her lips over the hood of his penis, letting her tongue wander down its length. Gerry's hands slipped along her body and gripped her hips whilst Kit took hold of her breasts.

'Did she come in and show you her pussy?' Kit asked Gerry, as his prick continued to ride Caroline's mouth.

'Yes,' replied Gerry.

'What exactly did she do?'

'She stood on a chair whilst looking for something in a filing cabinet and her skirt rose up.'

'And you saw her pussy?'

'Yes.'

'Got you going, did it?'

'Yes.'

'I thought it might. She's a dirty little cow, aren't you?' said Kit, tweaking Caroline's nipples, whilst enjoying the sensation of her tongue sliding up and down his penis, her luscious lips enveloping and squeezing it. Kit loved talking dirty to Caroline. He knew it excited her.

Caroline smiled inwardly. She was remembering the conversation she'd had with Kit when he had telephoned her earlier that day.

'Honestly Kit, Gerry looks as if he needs a good screw,' she'd said to him. 'I don't think that bloody wife of his is delivering the goods.'

Caroline didn't like Auralie. Instinctively she had taken against her. There was something hard and dispassionate about the French woman that made Caroline feel distinctly uncomfortable. One day she had caught Auralie staring at her breasts, staring at them as a man does to a woman he fancies. Could Gerry's wife be bisexual? A lesbian even? If she was, her not wanting to be touched by a man might account for Gerry's constant hang-dog expression. But if that were the case, surely he would have divorced her by now. There was no reason these days for a man or woman to put up with a bad marriage.

'Caro,' Kit had warned her, 'don't you go screwing Gerry. You're my woman, and your secretarial duties do not extend to giving his cock the once-over.'

'The thought never crossed my mind,' Caroline had commented.

But Kit had not been fooled by Caroline's assurance. He had

frequently felt threatened by Gerry. Kit was in love with Caroline but thought that she retained remnants of her affection for Gerry, who had unceremoniously dumped her after meeting Auralie. Kit was never able to figure out why Gerry had married Auralie but he did understand the attraction. Auralie was French. She was different. An enigma. Perhaps that was her allure. Kit thought that men always went for the same physical type. *He* certainly did. He liked long-legged blondes. All his girlfriends had been the same and Caroline was part of that pattern. Auralie was not part of Gerry's pattern; she was petite and dark. But then, he reminded himself, so was Sally. Sally was the new woman in Kit's life that Caroline knew nothing about. Kit was busy checking them both out. He couldn't work out which one he preferred. Caroline was a friend of long standing as well as a lover. Sally was new and something of a challenge. Kit was being faithful to both of them in his fashion. He wasn't letting either of them know the other existed. Although he hadn't yet got into Sally's panties, he was trying to work out whether Sally was an over-heated sexpot keeping it under control, or as frigid as hell. Screwing Caroline was still his safety valve.

'No, screwing Gerry was not on my agenda. Not until you just put it there,' said Caroline, adding, 'He used to be a very good fuck.'

'So am I,' replied Kit. 'And just you remember that.'

'Kit, have you heard anything about Auralie. I mean she isn't screwing anybody else and Gerry doesn't know about it?'

'Not to my knowledge,' said Kit. 'Nothing's come through on the grapevine. All I know is she's a very hard worker.'

'Well, she's obviously not working too hard on Gerry. Of course there was a time when she did,' said Caroline, ruefully.

'When was that?'

'When she got him to marry her. Then butter wouldn't have melted in her bloody mouth.'

'Was she always running after him?' asked Gerry.

'No, quite the reverse,' replied Caroline. 'She played hard to get, and now I really begin to wonder why. Do you think she really loves him?'

'I don't know,' said Kit honestly.

'Well, you see the two of them together,' said Caroline, challengingly.

'Well, yes and no. I go to their house, but they're not often together. She's working and . . .'

'Something is wrong,' said Caroline. 'Know what? I bet I could seduce him.'

'No.'

'Listen Kit, he told me that his marriage was for ever, no unfaithfulness. Now if I was to lift my skirt a little bit, just to give him an idea of rumpy-pumpy and he was to fall for it then I would know my intuition's right. If he doesn't fall for it then I'm wrong.'

There was a silence from Kit.

Caroline was worried. Had she gone too far? The idea of having Gerry again did appeal to her. Her legs opened slightly. She could feel a tightening in her stomach and a loosening in her womb.

'Kit?' she said.

Kit was thinking. He was wondering how he would feel, knowing Gerry was screwing Caroline. Then a thought crossed his mind. If he was actually there he would know how he felt.

'Very well, but on one condition,' he said. 'That you have it with both of us.'

'Both of you? You mean together?' Caroline was astonished by Kit's suggestion.

'Yes.'

A frisson of licentiousness rushed through Caroline. To be screwed by two men at the same time had been one of her fantasies but she never thought she would contemplate doing it. She never imagined that she would trust two men enough to allow that particular fantasy to come to fruition. She was suddenly aware that her juices were flowing and her panties were damp.

'Caro?' Kit said, to break the silence. 'You've gone quiet.'

'Yes, I was thinking.'

'It wasn't thinking that stopped you talking,' said Kit. 'I'd bet a pound to a penny you came and now you've got wet drawers.'

'Actually, you're right,' she admitted.

'So you fancy having two cocks, do you?'

'Yes, but how are we going to manage it?'

'I suggest you wear that pretty pink suit with the short skirt and no knickers. Pretend to have left something behind in his office. The rest is up to you.'

'And if he doesn't react?'

'I'll take you out for dinner.'

'And if he does?'

'I'll still take you out for dinner, but later.'

'But how will you know how things are going?' Caroline asked.

'Tell him I'm on my way to pick you up. Then, when I ring through, give a cough to let me know he's screwing you.'

'And?'

'Then I'll join you.'

'But how will you do that?'

'Leave that to me,' said Kit with assurance.

Caroline was brought sharply back to the present as Kit began to remove her clothes. She continued to suck his cock whilst Gerry filled her sex. Kit carefully removed her jacket and threw it across the room to join Gerry's abandoned shirt. Then he took off her blouse and her brassière.

'I want you naked,' he said, then spoke to Gerry. 'Undo the zip on her skirt and take it off.'

Gerry did as he was asked. There was a certain protocol to this affair and, as Caroline was ostensibly Kit's girl, Gerry felt he had to obey. But this meant removing his cock from Caroline's pussy, something he was loath to do.

'Have you ever been up her arse?' Kit asked Gerry as he stepped back from the bending girl.

'No,' replied Gerry.

'She likes it, don't you, bitch? You like having my cock stuck up your tiny arsehole.'

Caroline, still with Kit's member in her mouth, nodded.

'Change places, Gerry, and I'll show you.'

Kit came round the desk and stood beside Caroline, proprietorially running his hands over her body. His hands tingled as he touched her naked flesh. He kissed her mouth, letting his cock rub against her thighs and his hands trail down from her neck, lingering over her breasts.

'But she also likes to be sucked,' said Kit. He pulled her back against him so that his cock was thick and throbbing against her neat buttocks. Jealously, he sucked her ear lobes and played with her breasts whilst staring at Gerry, admiring his penis. 'So, whilst I'm getting my cock ready to take her arse why don't you suck her pussy.'

Gerry was suddenly aware of Kit's rush of jealousy. But he was deeply aroused and, desperately wanting to feel the softness of Caroline's sex on his tongue, knelt down in front of her. She pushed her hips out to meet his tongue as Kit held her slightly backwards.

Gerry guided his tongue past the light-brown fur and quickly found the swollen pink folds. She gasped out loud as his flesh hit her clitoris. She gasped again and almost came as he slurped at that hard little point growing under his tutelage. Gerry was amazed. These were the first sounds he had ever heard from Caroline. This prompted him to become more adventurous.

He brought up his hands and began to caress the unfurling inner folds, the soft lining of her labia, with a touch so gentle, but firm, that an exquisite sensation rent her belly. It travelled up to her nipples, hardening them, then quickly burst downwards in sharp explosions of delicious near-pain.

Whilst Gerry was busy at the front of her body Kit brought one of his hands down and began to caress her buttocks, gradually easing a finger inside her anus.

'Did you bring your toys?' Kit whispered to her.

'Yes,' she answered.

'Where are they?'

'In that carrier bag, but one's still in the top drawer, left-hand side of the desk.'

Placing Caroline's hands on Gerry's shoulders, Kit moved away from her. He found the bag and removed a tube of lubricant. He coated his prick then covered his fingers in the same goo. Kneeling behind her, his greasy penis running along her calves and ankles, Kit began to massage her buttocks, gradually moving inwards towards her bottom-mouth. He spread her hindquarters apart then let his forefingers roam in tinier and tinier circles until it touched the point of her orifice. Then he eased inwards, slowly opening her. Caroline gasped. Again and again she gasped as first one finger then another travelled upwards, widening her, making her long for the moment his member would penetrate her forbidden hole.

Caroline moaned wantonly. The sweetest, most delirious sensations were engulfing her as the two men played with different parts of her aroused body. Her sex was open, and tingling and swollen, and wanting more, much more. She was at a point where she would take anything that anyone wanted to give her. She was basking in the sensual delights that were flooding through every pore and nerve-ending in her body.

'If you lie on the desk,' said Kit to Gerry, 'this dirty bitch can suck your cock whilst I'm screwing her arse.'

Gerry duly positioned himself so that his trunk lay on the desk, his legs over the sides. Kit took hold of Caroline's hands and held them firmly behind her back. He guided her between Gerry's legs then jerked her forward so that her mouth hovered over his thick erect prick.

'Suck it, bitch,' said Kit. He was caught by the twin emotion of wanting to see her take his friend's prick into her mouth, watching her lips envelop it, and a desire to screw the living daylights out of her for doing it.

Caroline's lips opened and her mouth slid down Gerry's tool. Kit let go her hands. She immediately put them over Gerry's balls and began to gently roll them between her fingers as her mouth did its work on his shaft.

Kit positioned her legs, stretched her buttocks apart, stood firmly between her thighs, made a couple of short forays on to her well-greased arse, then plunged with all his might deep into her. She was jerked violently forward, taking Gerry's prick far into her throat. Gerry began to play with her breasts and her hard, dark-brown nipples. Kit, noticing the other man's hands massaging her hanging, swaying tits and seeing her head bob up and down on his friend's cock, gripped Caroline's hips tighter and thrust into her like a man possessed.

Caroline couldn't take any more. She lifted her head from Gerry's cock and collapsed her body over Gerry's. But the two men had other ideas. Gerry put his hands down and started to play with her clit.

'Open that carrier bag beside you,' Kit said to Gerry. Gerry swerved slightly, picking up the bag and looking into it. 'Take out the smallest of those objects.'

Gerry removed a small vibrator.

'Turn it on, then put it on her clit,' said Kit.

Instantly, with the touch of the tiny machine on her most sensitive point, Caroline was once more galvanised into motion. Kit's prick was still pounding at her behind and the vibrator was shuddering on her clitoris as she began to roll and move.

'Put some of that lube on your hands,' Kit instructed Gerry.

Caroline, unwilling to forgo any pleasure whilst this was happening, took the vibrator and held it against her sex whilst Gerry coated first his hands and then her body with the jelly. She was aware that he was making a conscious effort to avoid her pussy and her arse. She wondered why, and then realised it was an inhibition. He might accidentally touch Kit's prick. That, she thought, was a great pity as she found the idea of two men having her and touching each other at the same time incredibly exciting. Caroline decided that she would have to take the initiative.

Kit's rhythm slowed down. Caroline grabbed one of Gerry's hands and stuck it between her legs.

'Feel his balls banging against me,' she said.

Gerry opened his hand to encase Kit's scrotum. It was the first time in his life he had felt another man's sac. It was quite a hurdle, but he enjoyed it. So did Kit. There was a major difference in the feel of a large hand, like his own, expertly and instinctively knowing how to touch his balls. Knowing exactly what to do with them, how to roll them.

'Ring his cock with your hand, feel it entering me,' she said.

Gerry did as she asked. His own cock was stiff against her belly. He could feel her juicy wet opening slithering and sliding against his hand. Kit pounded into her harder as Gerry's hand held him. Caroline moaned and swayed and lifted higher as she enjoyed the feel of their hard masculine bodies.

Gerry took his hands away from Kit and picked up the vibrator. Running it gently over her clitoris it sent shudders of pleasure through him whilst she jerked to the rhythm of Kit's cock in her arse. He lay back, revelling in the feel of Caroline's body leaning against his, her soft breasts flattened against his hard chest. Gerry suddenly had a desire to kiss Caroline's lips, to feel his tongue push through and explore her mouth. Gerry turned Caroline's face to his, closed his eyes and brought his lips down to hers. Then Gerry's eyes shot open at the harsh sound of a hand slapping flesh. Kit was spanking Caroline.

'You're a horny bitch,' said Kit. 'A horny bitch who deserves to have her bottom spanked.'

Far from putting Gerry off, this made him more horny. Many times he had lain in the darkness beside his sleeping wife, wanting to beat her neatly rounded buttocks. Wanting to feel her writhe in pain under him. Gerry's cock stiffened. He dearly wanted to have Caroline. He decided that Kit had had his way with her for long enough. It was his turn. He pushed her to one side and rolled away from the table.

'What are you doing?' asked Kit.

'I want to screw Caroline,' Gerry replied.

'Where, back or front?'

'Front,' said Gerry.

'How do you feel about that, bitch?' Kit asked her, jabbing at her arse and striking her bare bottom once more with his hand. 'Gerry wants to stick his dick in you.'

'I want her flat on the floor,' said Gerry. 'Missionary position. I want to feel her under me. I want to feel her legs wrapped around my waist.'

'Does that appeal to you, bitch?' asked Kit, pulling Caroline's head backwards and kissing her lips.

Caroline was aware that there seemed to be a battle of wills going on between the two friends. She didn't want either of them to lose face, or his hard-on.

'Kit,' she whispered, running her hands along his body, 'why don't you lie on the floor with me on top of you?'

Kit was about to withdraw, but Caroline stopped him. 'No, keep your cock up my arse while we lie down.'

Kit lay on the floor with Caroline on top of him, her back on his chest and his cock still rammed deep inside her anus.

'Now, Gerry, if you put your knees between Kit's legs and mine I think you could get inside me.'

'The two of us together?' exclaimed Gerry.

'Exactly,' she said.

Caroline put her hands down between her thighs and began stroking herself. She was very wet. She was very excited and the feel of Kit's cock still moving inside her back passage was making her muscles contract and expand.

'First, give me the vibrator again.'

Gerry handed her the little machine. She ran it along her sex-lips then along Kit's thighs, finally ending between the crack of his buttocks. As she did that he jerked again harder and deeper into her.

Gerry knelt in front of them, watching Kit's hard-working penis glide in and out of Caroline as she lay on Kit's chest, glistening with sweat and desire in an attitude of total abandonment. Kit's hands were massaging her breasts. Caroline let the vibrator fall beside her and put both her hands down between her legs and held her thighs apart, silently inviting Gerry to enter her swollen, pink, unoccupied opening.

Gerry positioned himself between the two sets of legs, bent his head and began to lick Caroline furiously. He licked her thighs, he licked her belly, then he licked her clitoris. He felt her muscles tense, stiffen, then relax beneath his touch. She gasped. Gerry positioned his penis at her juicy, wet entrance.

'I want it,' she said, gasping between Kit's thrusts into her arse. 'Gerry, I want your cock. I want you to take me. I want it up there, inside me, and I want it hard.'

Her anal muscles tightened around Kit's shaft. She wasn't going to let one go in favour of the other. She was going to take them both. Have both men at the same time. One cock stuck hard in her pussy, the other jammed in her arse and the vibrator playing on her clit.

Every dream Caroline had ever had, every sexual fantasy she had ever possessed, was about to be played out in Gerry's office and she intended to savour each moment. Each delicious minute was going to be relished. Her entire body was trembling, tiny tremors shook each particle of her body as she waited for the final onslaught – Gerry's entry into her ripe, swollen, tingling, wanton sex.

Slowly he began to enter her. Caroline let out a long gasp as she felt the tip of his prick push through her tremulous juicy folds. He had never known her so vocal. Perhaps this was what she had always wanted – two men. Slowly he eased his way up inside her, her sex opening further and further to take the thickness of his highly charged and engorged penis.

Gerry, like a gentleman should, took his weight on his hands, and held his arms straight beside their waists as he lowered himself into Caroline's creamy wetness. Kit's hands had manipulated Caroline's nipples until they were stiff. He offered them to his friend's mouth and Gerry fastened his lips over them as his penis pushed deeper inside her. Gerry's cock was able to feel Kit's prick inside Caroline's arse. This sensation excited them both. Then Kit released his hands from Caroline's breasts, allowing Gerry's mouth full rein on her nipples, whilst he gripped her hips, sliding her along his sweat-lubricated and aroused body and pumping her up and down onto his ever-thrusting cock.

The two men gathered momentum. Kit began to bite Caroline's neck. Gerry kissed her lips and both of them pounded into her, filling up every crevice she possessed. In a sea of undulating motion their bodies were moving with total accord and none of them knew where the other began; each felt the grip and tightening of the stomach and the downward flow of that exquisite magic that everyone yearns for and remembers long after it has happened, but finds its essence difficult to record. It was then, in a wave of ecstasy, they came.

Exhausted, the three of them lay on the carpet for some time. Caroline was the first to move. She kissed them both then sashayed into the bathroom to take a shower.

Both men lay still, taking sideways glances at the other's body.

'A hell of a pecker you've got on you,' said Kit.

'I could say the same about yours,' replied Gerry.

They laughed awkwardly, propping themselves up on their elbows. They watched silently as Caroline came back into the room, towelling herself dry.

'That was a great screw,' she said, combing her short wet hair. 'I never thought I'd be able to take two cocks.'

'Neither did we,' said Kit.

'Let's do it again sometime,' she said, much to their surprise.

'You really want to?' one of the men exclaimed.

'Why not? It's fun. Really good fun,' she said. 'We could come to your place, Gerry. You never know, perhaps your wife would like to join in.'

'No,' said Gerry, a touch of irritation in his voice. He didn't want to be reminded of Auralie.

'Why not? Doesn't she like sex?' asked Caroline.

'Don't push it,' said Gerry.

It was obvious to Kit that Caroline had hit a sore point. Her intuition had been correct. There *was* trouble with Gerry's marriage.

'My turn in the bathroom,' said Kit, jumping up and making a quick exit.

It didn't take Kit and Caroline long to dress and for the room to be restored to order. Nobody would have known what major screwing session had just taken place.

Caroline and Kit said goodbye to Gerry and left for the restaurant. Gerry mused on what had happened and wondered when he would hear from his father. He relaxed, gazing out on the twinkling lights of night-time London. He was in a state of duality, tired but refreshed. Refreshed, almost cleansed, from screwing Caroline, but tired from physical exertion and suppressed anger. The anger that engulfed his body as he thought that he should have been, could have been, having sex with his own wife. Where had he gone wrong? He knew he wasn't a bad lover, so was it her?

Suddenly the fax machine sprang to life. He stopped instantly and read the coded message the machine was printing out. Sir Henry had clinched the deal. The aircraft was his. Now they could start the next phase. His father added a rider. He was not coming to England immediately. He had changed his plans. He was stopping off in Rome.

Gerry looked out through the window. He also had a plan. He washed, zipped up his trousers then picked up the telephone and dialled his wife.

'Oh, 'ello *cherie*,' greeted Auralie. Gerry detected a hint of relief in her voice.

'Darling,' he purred. 'I want to take you out to dinner to-night.'

'Oh, lovely,' said Auralie. 'Where?'

Gerry named her favourite Italian restaurant in Knightsbridge. Auralie cooed her delight and agreement. Gerry, feeling a rush of adrenalin, replaced the telephone and adjusted himself. With the air of a man about to take many more of life's opportunities he walked out of his office, out of the building and hailed a passing taxi.

3

'Wearing this uniform, it will be very easy for you to fuck standing up,' Auralie said briskly to the two pretty long-legged girls and the beautiful man sitting in front of her.

It was lunchtime at Petolg Holdings – Auralie's office in the heart of Mayfair. On her desk there were various bags and boxes and a couple of samples of chambermaids' outfits and a waiter's uniform. Auralie was holding a private meeting behind locked doors. It had nothing to do with her design business but everything to do with her cousin Jeanine's new hotel.

'I designed them.' Auralie held up a pair of trousers. 'Look, no flies. More like sailors' flaps. And these – sweet little skirts, aren't they?'

The two girls nodded in agreement.

'And the blouses button down the front. The little apron hides nothing but is very decorative. You can let your tits hang out.' Auralie held out the short bias-cut skirts, the Peter Pan-collared and pin-tucked blouses and the tiny white lace-edged, bib-fronted aprons. 'Put them on and you'll see.'

The two girls removed their jeans and sweat shirts, revealing their complete nakedness down to their shaven pubis. The beautiful man got an instant hard-on.

'Looks like he can't wait to screw you,' said Auralie. She went over and felt the young man's bulge. 'Perhaps I should see what the three of you can do before I send you on your mission. Terry, put those trousers on and remember to button them up.'

The young man removed his jeans and put on the waiter's trousers.

'You have to wear stockings,' Auralie instructed the girls, 'and no knickers. Here . . .' She threw them a couple of black, lace suspender belts wrapped in cellophane wrappers, 'and these shoes.'

From some boxes she took out a couple of pairs of high-heeled, lace-up shoes. In a moment all three were regaled in their outfits.

'Now, Jill,' said Auralie to the taller of the two girls, 'undo Terry's buttons, take out his prick and play with it.'

Auralie watched Terry's large cock stiffen to its full length under Jill's expert handling.

'And Mary,' Auralie said to the other one, 'lean against the wall.' The girl did as she was told, placing her legs apart and bracing her shoulders against the wall. Auralie continued, 'OK, let's put this to the test. Jill stand back and let Terry screw Mary. Do it standing up, Terry. Mary, hold that skirt up so everything you've got is on show.'

Mary held her skirt high. Terry bent his knees slightly, positioned his cock against Mary's shaven mound, then, with a great lunge, went straight up her wet pussy.

'Excellent,' said Auralie, enjoying the sight of his large prick entering and re-entering Mary quickly and smoothly. 'Jill, undo your buttons, let's see your breasts, then start playing with yourself. Yes, yes, that's good. Lift that skirt higher; let's see your pussy. That's better. I like it shaved. It looks good. Very inviting. You enjoying that, Mary?' Between her sighs and groans Mary nodded. 'OK, Jill, do you think you could get a hand down there between Terry and play with Mary's clitoris?'

'I'll try.' Mary tried, but found it awkward.

'All right,' said Auralie, 'don't bother, just carry on playing with yourself. That's sexy, really sexy. Lean against the wall next to Mary. Terry, if you can suck on one of Jill's tits, do that, OK.'

Auralie was immensely pleased with her orchestration. All three were young and firm and very beautiful and what she was seeing made her extremely turned on. She was wet and aching between her legs. She wanted to feel a hand running up her thighs, and fingers entering her sex. She rather liked the idea of sex with Terry, having his cock ram up into her, but she resisted any desire to interfere. She would keep herself on a knife edge. Keep herself horny. Auralie sat back in her chair and watched Terry's virile cock glide in and out of Mary. They were writhing and moaning in unison. She watched Jill's fingers playing with herself, her hips jutting forward and her legs shaking.

'This, *mes amis*, is what I want you to do at Jeanine's,' said Auralie. 'Make sure you're on an upstairs landing and, just as a guest is about to come up the stairs, start screwing.'

'The best assignment I've ever had,' said Terry enthusiastically.

'But you must make sure Jeanine never catches you,' Auralie added. 'She must not know what's going on. Is that understood?'

'Sure,' said Terry, adding, 'Can I come now?'

'Jill,' said Auralie, turning to the girl still playing with herself, 'are you bringing yourself off or do you want Terry to screw you as well?'

'Why should I miss out?' said Jill.

Terry put his hand down and played with Mary, then screwed her until she came. Then he pulled out and thrust his prick straight up into Jill and took her too. Auralie was delighted with their performances. She knew they would devastate Jeanine's trade. Guests would flee in droves from her respectable hotel and the silly bitch would never know the reason why. Auralie was thrilled. Jeanine and her mother, Penelope, would get their come-uppance. And that, thought Auralie, would teach the doe-eyed bitch to marry Laurence.

Auralie had been in love with Laurence. She and Laurence were first cousins on her father's side. They had been lovers. Laurence had said they could never marry. She had accepted that, but when Jeanine had arrived and taken her place in his affections Auralie had been furious. She was far too canny to allow anyone to see her fury, but had vowed revenge. The opportunity had taken years to present itself but now, with the opening of the hotel, Auralie knew she could achieve her ambition: Jeanine's downfall. The prissy madam would fail. And that would reflect on her obstinate mother.

Jeanine's mother and Auralie had a running battle. This had not always been the case. For most of her early years Penelope had looked after Auralie; brought her up as her own. But everything had changed on her eighteenth birthday. When Auralie was a baby, both her mother and father, Amelia and Boris Vladelsky, had been killed in a car accident in the Alps. The young Auralie had been in the back of the car but had been thrown clear. Penelope, Amelia's twin sister, had immediately rushed to the scene and taken Auralie back to England. Years later Penelope met Boris's brother, Stefan, had married him and gone to live in Paris. Stefan was the cause of the rift between Auralie and Penelope.

Penelope had given a huge party for Auralie in their elegant Parisian apartment. Jeanine, being a few years younger than Auralie, was still at boarding school in England. For the first time in her life Auralie had got drunk. Feeling very strange she had made for the nearest room to lie down. Scarcely knowing where she was Auralie had wrapped herself in the silken draperies on Penelope's massive cherry-wood double bed and gone to sleep. When she awoke she found Stefan fast asleep and stark naked beside her.

Stefan had been an exceptionally handsome man with deep set, green eyes and a shock of black hair. Unlike his brothers, Boris and Petrov, he had been slim and athletic. Auralie had sat up and gazed at him. It had seemed to her that he was in a deep, deep sleep. She had looked at his body and admired it. She had especially admired his penis. It had lain to one side, inert but beautiful. Auralie had the strongest desire to touch it. To feel it. To see what would happen if she did. Slowly and carefully, with great trepidation and the lightness of a feather, she had reached out a hand and gently stroked it. Stefan remained fast asleep but his prick quivered. Auralie stroked it again. Its rounded tip pushed out from under the furrows of concertinaed flesh. Utterly entranced she touched it again along the ridges of its emerging cap. Stefan's penis continued to pulsate and grow. Auralie watched with a quiet fascination as it thickened and extended. When it was proud and upright she held it firmly along its trunk and guided its head into her mouth. Stefan lay still, his breathing never changing. Auralie, careful not to touch any other part of his body, knelt up on her haunches beside his waist. Completely oblivious to everything, she held his tool in her hands and sucked on the head. She had been so totally immersed in the pleasure of his penis that she had failed to hear the door open and Penelope enter. She was still unaware of Penelope's arrival until the older woman screamed.

Penelope had thrown Auralie out of the house and had thrown her suitcases out after her. She told Auralie she would never ever speak to her again. Penelope was true to her word and her attitude had never changed. She was implacable in her hostility but, because they were family, there were occasions when they had to meet. The first occasion turned out to be not long after the incident, at Stefan's own funeral. Penelope treated Auralie with an icy silence, which caused some surprise at the time. Now everyone knew about the feud but no one knew why. Auralie never told anybody. Neither did Penelope, and that had always intrigued Auralie. After a while Auralie decided that Penelope had kept her mouth shut because she had not wanted anyone to know what her late husband had allowed to happen that day. Auralie now realised that Stefan must have known, and enjoyed her attentions. Penelope would have realised that too and pride kept her silent. Stefan had had a reputation as an upright, clean-living man and Auralie knew that no one would have believed her had she dared to sully her uncle's memory. So she also kept quiet. But both women knew the truth and Penelope hated Auralie for possessing that knowledge. Auralie knew if there was anything that Penelope could ever do to humiliate her, the older women would have no compunction about doing it. Auralie had always seen to it that she was well protected by other members of her family, and kept well clear of Penelope. Whatever Auralie could do to hurt Jeanine she knew it would also hurt her mother, who doted on her only child. This had added impetus to Auralie's desire for revenge.

Nevertheless, she did wonder where she would be now and what she would be doing had Penelope not thrown her out that day. The simple act of playing with Stefan's penis had changed her life. Now, as she watched Terry, Jill and Mary enjoying each other's bodies, Auralie's mind returned to the events after her belongings had landed on the sidewalk of the Rue Jean Gourjon.

Still wearing her party frock Auralie had collected up her scattered suitcases. In a dazed state she had walked across the Pont des Invalides and along the Quai d'Orsay. On automatic pilot she had turned right and left, right and left until she had ended up in a tiny street behind the Rue de Bourgogne. This was where her aunt Olga had her magnificent two-tiered apartment.

Olga had gone to Hong Kong on a buying trip and this was the reason she'd been unable to attend Auralie's party. But Auralie knew instinctively that whether Olga was there or not, she would be welcome in her home.

Auralie approached the high wrought-iron gates and pulled at the ancient bell set into the plasterwork. She watched as the fat, thin-lipped, scraggy-haired concierge waddled across the cobblestones. Recognising Auralie, she undid the clanking lock and let her into the courtyard.

Auralie walked through the archway at the far end of the exclusive enclave and entered the tiny and temperamental elevator. It took her up to the second storey. There she got out and rang the bell of Olga's apartment.

The door was opened by Nin, the younger and prettier of Olga's two Vietnamese maids.

'*Mon Dieu!* You look terrible, Mam'selle,' Nin said.

'Can I stay here?' asked Auralie, attempting to wipe away the tears that had started to flow.

'Of course,' replied Nin, taking Auralie's suitcase and ushering her into the high-ceilinged and elegant drawing-room. 'But Madame is in Hong Kong.'

'I know,' said Auralie.

'How long do you want to stay?' asked Nin.

'I don't know,' replied Auralie, sitting down in the imposing but familiar salon and feeling a sense of relief and comfort.

'Perhaps Madame will telephone tonight,' said Nin, 'then we can ask her. Now, please, I will show you to your bed.'

Nin, dressed in her chic maid's uniform, guided Auralie through a maze of rooms to the guest suite at the farthest end of the first floor. The second floor was kept quite separate and private for Olga's occupation alone. Nin stowed Auralie's belongings into a beautiful wardrobe.

Auralie, who had not been in this part of the apartment before, gazed approvingly at the decor. It was based on a theme of cream, gold and rose-pink. The heavy, cream silk curtains, coloured with sprigs of roses, were draped above and around the high French windows. The panelled walls were painted light and dark pink, with plasterwork picked out in gold; the skirting boards and the high double-doors in cream. All the furniture, including the vast bed, was genuine French Empire.

'Whatever has happened to you, I think you need to sleep, Mam'selle,' said Nin. 'But first, a good hot bath and then some food.' She padded across the silk carpet and highly polished parquet flooring into the adjoining bathroom where she ran a bath for Auralie.

Some time later, refreshed and wearing a pale-green silk negligée, Auralie made her way into the kitchen. There Nin and Rea, the other tiny, small-boned Vietnamese maid, were preparing food.

'We make you a little light dinner,' said Rea, smiling at Auralie, then saying something fast in Vietnamese to Nin.

'She said you look very pretty,' said Nin to Auralie.

'Thank you,' said Auralie, sitting down at the large well-scrubbed table.

Auralie watched them wash lettuce and beanshoots, chop onions and other vegetables, thinly slice some pork then measure some rice and tip it into an electric rice cooker.

'We make for you a special dish from our country,' they said, taking down spices from a rack.

'How nice,' said Auralie. She didn't like to tell them she wasn't really hungry.

'But, first I think, a little saki,' said Nin. 'You like saki?'

'I've never had it,' replied Auralie.

'It's rice wine. You must have it hot.'

Nin heated the saki then poured it into a diminutive blue-and-white bone-china bowl.

'Drink,' said Nin.

'In one go?' asked Auralie.

'Why not,' they said. 'There's plenty more and it's very good for you, especially if you're upset.'

Auralie took a sip. Then quickly took another. Its welcoming warmth flooded through her and moments later she was holding out her bowl for more. Nin put the saki, its container and Auralie's tiny bowl on a tray.

'We will bring your dinner to your room,' said Nin, handing her the tray. 'But take this with you, it's a good aperitif.'

In her bedroom, alone with her thoughts, the image of Stefan's penis rose up in front of Auralie's eyes. She lay down on the bed and relived the touch of it between her hands, and the taste of it in her mouth. Had he really been asleep? Had he really not known what she was doing? She wanted to tell someone what had happened to her. But who would listen? Who would believe her?

Having consumed the whole container of saki Auralie was more than a little drunk when Nin and Rea brought her dinner to her room. They set it out elegantly on a table near the window. Auralie stumbled out of bed and Rea helped her to her seat whilst Nin drew the curtains. Auralie took a couple of mouthfuls of meat and beanshoots and rice.

'It's delicious,' she said approvingly. They smiled then started to leave the room.

'Don't go,' said Auralie. 'Please stay with me. You see, I need to talk. I must tell someone what's happened. But you must promise to keep it a secret. Do you promise?'

The two young maids nodded their heads.

'Then bring the rest of the saki and we'll drink together.'

When the two slim young women returned, Auralie gestured to the chaise longue. The two of them sat down, put their feet neatly together, made sure their frocks covered their knees, then, drinking primly from their small bowls, listened to the tale of Auralie's encounter with Stefan. When she had finished the broad outline of her story they began to ask more intimate questions.

'Did he have a big penis?'

Auralie was too young and inexperienced to know whether Stefan's cock was big or small. She showed them the approximate size with her hands.

'And was it nice to hold?' asked Nin, taking more rice wine.

'Yes.'

'How big was it when it wasn't stiff?' asked Rea, downing her bowlful.

Auralie showed them that too. 'Haven't you ever seen one?' she asked.

'No,' they said and giggled.

'How old are you?' asked Auralie, surprised by their admission.

'I'm twenty-four and she's twenty-five,' said Nin.

'And neither of you have ever had sex?'

'We didn't say that,' said Rea.

'But you've never seen a man's thingy! Never played with it, or had it inside you?' exclaimed Auralie.

'No, and we don't need to,' said Nin.

'How do you have sex without a man?' asked Auralie, intrigued.

'One day we will show you,' said Rea, mysteriously.

By now the saki had done its work and Auralie's head was swimming. She tried to get up from the table but her legs felt like jelly beneath her. Rea and Nin came to her assistance and helped her to the bed. There they made her comfortable.

Auralie closed her eyes and felt herself drift into a delicious nothingness. She had a dream concerning the two maids. The two women, naked, perfumed and oiled, were climbing into bed with her. They removed her night-dress, then slowly caressed her body.

In her dream Rea was kissing her lips whilst Nin picked up a jar of oils Rea had put beside the bed, and unhurriedly began massaging Auralie's breasts. Rea also coated her hands with oil and let them travel down Auralie's unmoving body, over her belly and onto her hips. Gently, Rea stretched Auralie's legs apart, her hands running up and down her inner thighs until she touched a tiny point just inside Auralie's small black mound. With this sudden and unexpected pressure on a wholly unknown spot the whole of Auralie's body sprang to life. She began to undulate and roll as the maids' sensuous movements excited parts of her she had not known were there to be excited. Rea then snaked the length of her, buried her head between Auralie's thighs and placed her tongue on that little point at the apex of her black curly mound. The feeling was so delicately exquisite that Auralie had cried out and moaned. And had continued to let out a series of long, happy, contented sighs. Then Rea's searching tongue found another deeper place but, not wanting to leave the little point without pleasure, she had put an oiled finger on that tiny protuberance. With Rea's tongue and finger gliding on her wetness and Nin's lips caressing her nipples, Auralie's hands felt at a loss until she reached out and discovered their mounds and their breasts. The three of them had then lain entwined, writhing and moaning, shaking and trembling until a moment of pure ecstasy was reached. After that Auralie had drifted away from her erotic visions and relaxed into a deep slumber.

Next morning she was too embarrassed to face Nin and Rea. The dream had made her almost too shy to face herself. She was about to leave for her tutorial at the Sorbonne when Nin stopped her.

'Madame telephoned this morning,' said Nin.

'Oh!' said Auralie, unable to look the maid in the eye.

'She said she was happy to have you here and to stay for as long as you like.'

Auralie felt an acute sense of relief and skipped off to college happy in the knowledge she had somewhere to live. Olga, complete with entourage of more maids and handsome black chauffeur, Drenga, returned a week later but was soon off on her travels again. Meanwhile Auralie's cousin, Laurence, flew in from Brazil and she fell heart-flutteringly, exhilaratingly, wonderfully in love.

They met quite by chance in a *bibliothèque* in the Rue des Ecoles on the very day he arrived. They had both reached up for the same book on plants: Laurence because he was a budding botanist, Auralie because the shapes and colours on the cover appealed to her designer's eye. There was an immediate rapport between them, and it was over a coffee in a nearby café they discovered that they were related. For months after there was no separating them.

Their elderly grandfather was so delighted to have his only grandson in Paris, he bought him a small apartment in the Rue des Fosses St Bernard. It was there, one autumn afternoon, in a room overlooking the faculty of science, that Auralie lost her virginity.

Auralie had been standing at the window of the sitting-room, staring out at the green trees and the red-daubed graffiti on the grey building in front of her when Laurence had quietly entered. He had come up behind her, put his arms around her waist and gently kissed her neck. It was something that Auralie had longed for for weeks. Each time she had turned up at his apartment she had desperately wanted him to show her some affection, but he never had. It seemed to Auralie that Laurence treated her as a sister. He didn't see her as a young woman with a sex drive, or notice that her sex drive was specifically aimed in his direction.

She had been so deep in thought that his action had come as a complete surprise. She had responded automatically, winding her arms around his neck and kissing him tenderly on the lips. Within seconds their tenderness had turned to passion as the pent-up longing of months turned into fire. Their bodies were instantly ignited. Every muscle, every sinew, every fibre sent the same shattering message to their hearts and their brains. Screw. And screw fast.

They ripped their clothes in their hurry to feel naked flesh and threw them wherever they could, not caring if a shirt, or a brassiere, flew out the window. This was no time for caution or gentleness. Standing, Laurence lifted Auralie up, then brought her down fast, impaling her on his penis. She wrapped her legs in a vice-like grip around his waist. Joined together at the genitals and at the mouth they moved with consummate violence until in one massive explosion of energy they had a simultaneous orgasm. Afterwards they lay exhausted on the cushions on the floor.

'You took my virginity,' she said, leisurely stroking his chest.

'What!' he exclaimed in alarm, throwing her arm to one side. 'You mean you've never had sex before?'

'No,' she said.

'Oh, really?' he said, sarcastically.

'Don't you believe me?' she asked, hurt by his tone of voice.

'Sure,' he said. 'If you say so.'

'You don't believe me,' said Auralie, starting to cry.

'For Christ's sake!' he said, annoyed by her tears. 'Look, if you were a virgin why did you give in to me so easily?'

'Because I wanted you. Because all of my body said it was a good thing to do.'

'You should have made me wait.'

'Why?' she asked.

'That's what women have to do,' he replied.

Auralie couldn't believe her ears. For months she had been coming home with him, and every day she had wanted him to make love to her. She had suppressed that desire until today, and now he was berating her for doing something she thought they had both enjoyed. She didn't understand him.

'Didn't you enjoy it?' she asked.

'Sure, it was great,' he replied, matter-of-factly.

Auralie rolled away from him. She had enjoyed it, but wasn't enjoying this. Now, when she ought to be feeling happy she was crying.

'Where are you going?' he asked, as she started to dress.

'Home,' she said.

'I thought you had work to do,' he said, pointing to her drawing pad.

'I'll do it at Olga's.'

'See you tomorrow, then,' he said airily.

Auralie was flabbergasted. She couldn't believe his reaction. There had been no loving, no fondness, no gentle kissing.

'Maybe,' she said, picking up her bag and heading for the door.

Utterly deflated, she decided not to take the elevator but walk the five flights of narrow winding stairs instead. That would give her time to compose herself before she was in the street and likely to meet friends or acquaintances. Once outside she would take a cab home. She hurried away from the students' quarter towards Boulevard St Germain and the nearest taxi rank. When she arrived at Olga's apartment there was a flurry of activity.

'Madame's coming home this evening,' said Nin. Olga had been in Africa for six weeks.

'At what time?'

'Six o'clock,' said Rea.

'Oh! Do you need any help?' asked Auralie, thinking physical work might stop her thinking about Laurence.

'*Non*,' said Nin and Rea in unison.

Auralie went to her room and slept, whilst over her head in Olga's sumptuous bedroom the vacuum cleaner raged.

'Auralie. *Mon enfant. Mon petit chou*,' Olga's imperious voice rang in her ears. Auralie opened her eyes. Olga was standing beside her bed. She looked as she always did, magnificent, poised and elegant.

'Nin and Rea tell me you are unhappy again, *chérie*,' said Olga, as always going straight to the point. 'What is it this time? Has that *putain*, Penelope, been bothering you?'

'No,' said Auralie, smiling. It was rather nice to hear her stunningly beautiful, but severe and prissy aunt called a *putain*. Both women knew nothing could have been further from the truth.

'Then what is it, *chérie*?' asked Olga, sitting on Auralie's bed and giving her a gentle kiss on the cheek.

Whether or not she had intended to tell her aunt, Auralie could not remember, but Olga's sudden show of kindness and affection released an honesty in her.

'Laurence,' she said.

'Laurence!' exclaimed Olga. 'Your cousin Laurence?'

'Yes.'

'Well, he is very handsome. What have you been doing with him?'

'We made love,' said Auralie simply.

'You did what? You fool!' screeched Olga. Then she tempered

her anger as she saw tears in Auralie's eyes. '*Ma petite*, that was very stupid.'

'I know that now. But I love him.'

'Oh, dear,' said Olga, taking Auralie's hand and stroking it affectionately. '*Chérie*, tell me what happened.'

'I went back to his apartment, I often do that, and we were both working. Then he kissed me and the next minute we were . . . we were . . .'

'. . . Screwing,' said Olga, finishing her sentence.

'Yes.'

'And you didn't like it? It wasn't any good?'

'It was wonderful,' said Auralie. 'It was fantastic. But afterwards . . . it was afterwards. When I told him I was a virgin and he didn't believe me . . . Then it was horrible.'

Olga gathered Auralie up into her arms and rocked her while she cried.

'*Chérie, chérie*,' said Olga soothingly. 'Come, don't cry. You love him, yes, but there are many people in this world to love. Don't be exclusive. And, *chérie*, it doesn't have to be a man.'

'Not a man? I don't understand,' said Auralie.

'Don't you think Nin and Rea are very happy?'

'Yes.'

'They don't have a man to love. They don't want a man to love.'

'Oh?' said Auralie, still puzzled.

'*Chérie*, they have each other. They love each other and they make love to each other.'

'It's not possible!' exclaimed Auralie. Then she remembered her dream.

'Oh, but it is,' said Olga. 'Now, you and I are going out tonight. First we will have an aperitif. I will have a bath and then I'll take you to my favourite restaurant. We will celebrate.'

'Celebrate what?' asked Auralie.

'Anything,' said Olga. 'My return to Paris. Being alive. Being alive is a good reason. Being rich is better. So, we will have champagne and then ... Well, we'll see what happens after that. Now put on something beautiful.'

As soon as Olga had left her, Auralie jumped up, threw off her clothes, bathed quickly then rifled through her meagre wardrobe. One by one she discarded various items of clothing. Nothing seemed up to Olga's exacting standards. She was standing naked when Nin entered carrying a tray.

'Madame said drink this now,' said Nin, handing her a very large glass. 'It's to cheer you up.'

'What is it?'

'A champagne cocktail,' said Nin, smiling, then departing.

Auralie sipped the drink. It was delicious but it went instantly to her head and made her feel woozy. It certainly didn't help her solve what she was going to wear that evening. Auralie decided further advice was needed. She would see if Olga had anything in her wardrobe she could borrow. Throwing on her silk negligée and taking her glass of champagne with her, Auralie made her way up to Olga's room. She heard some noises coming from inside and knocked hesitantly before entering.

'Oh, it's you, Auralie,' said Olga. 'Come in and sit down.'

Auralie had closed the door before she realised what was happening. Olga was sitting on a chair, sipping champagne whilst watching Nin and Rea making love on the bed.

'Aren't they beautiful?' said Olga. 'Look at them, aren't they too beautiful for words?'

Auralie was speechless. Nin and Rea were quite naked, their bodies glistening with oils as they writhed this way and that on Olga's huge bed.

Auralie started for the door.

'No, don't go, *chérie*,' said Olga, pouring Auralie a flute of champagne. 'You will see few things more beautiful.'

Auralie sat down. She watched as Nin and Rea stroked and caressed one another. They touched each other's breasts, then let their hands meander downwards over belly and hips to play with one another's sex. Then they looked up and saw Auralie.

'We said one day we would show you how we don't need a man,' said Rea.

Auralie smiled. She had been embarrassed, but was now quite drunk and genuinely intrigued.

'Join them on the bed, *chérie*,' said Olga. 'I promise you, you'll enjoy it.'

They all seemed so happy and relaxed that Auralie felt it would be churlish to refuse. Rea stretched out a hand to Auralie. Hesitatingly, she took it and Rea pulled her down beside her.

'I want you to stroke me just here,' said Rea, guiding Auralie's fingers between her legs. Auralie felt the harsh black curly hair, then the softness of the woman's flesh-opening beneath her touch. It excited her. Auralie began to feel a wetness between her own legs. 'Keep stroking me,' said Rea, taking Auralie's other hand and putting it over Nin's small breasts. 'Play with them. Take the nipples and roll them between your fingers.'

Basking in the touch of Auralie's fingers Nin's nipples hardened. This excited Auralie and she could feel herself swelling and tingling. Lewdly she edged her own legs apart; she too wanted to be touched. Because of the growing pressure inside her Rea guessed Auralie was needing to be felt.

'Now, Mam'selle, you must close your eyes and keep them closed,' said Rea.

Auralie closed her eyes. Her negligée was slipped off and her body repositioned so that her head rested on a lap. A pair of hands softly and tenderly began to massage her breasts. Another pair gently travelled up her legs. Auralie felt the touch of breasts and stiff nipples gliding along her thighs. The next moment she felt something thick and wet touching her at the top of her legs. She opened her eyes and saw Rea kneeling in front of her, her tongue finding the spot of Auralie's dream. Rea's touch was so delicate and the sensation so delicious that Auralie was immediately transported to another world. The world of sensuousness, of erotica and visions. And then she remembered her first night at Olga's, and her dream about the two maids. *Déjà vu*. The situation she was now in was practically a rerun of that.

Then a thought occurred to Auralie. Had the two women actually enjoyed her whilst she was in that drunken stupor? Perhaps *they* had taken her virginity. In that case Laurence had been right to query her assertion that she was still a virgin. Auralie had never played with herself, therefore she had no way of knowing if she was intact or not. Until recently sex had lain dormant within her. Her first inkling of desire was when she saw Stefan's penis lying at half-mast. It had been curiosity as much as anything else that had prompted her to touch it.

'You see, *chérie*, there is never any need for you to know *triste*,' said Olga. 'See how they care for you, how they love you. Now, come here to me.'

Auralie slid off the bed and stood before Olga, naked, panting and trembling with excitement. Silently, Olga admired the girl's neat, trim, almost boyish body. She narrowed her eyes, licentiously licked her lips then put out a hand to cup one of Auralie's pert, rosebud breasts.

'What would you like to do now, *chérie*?' Olga asked, drawing Auralie closer and stroking her belly. 'Would you like to stay here and play or would you like to go out? Perhaps we could find you a man. Would you like to be screwed, *chérie*?'

Auralie was swaying backwards and forwards, her pleasure intense. She couldn't answer Olga. She couldn't decide. Olga's hand trailed over Auralie's body and began to tease her between her legs. Suddenly she put an arm around the trembling girl's waist, drew her even closer and, with one quick thrust, shoved a finger hard into Auralie's willing, wanton and very swollen vulva.

'Oh, *chérie*, you do have a very wet pussy,' said Olga, jerking her finger up and down.

Auralie braced her body and pushed her breasts forward, inviting Olga to clasp her lips to their dark-brown nipples and suck. Olga sat imperiously as if playing with an obedient slave. Squirming and rolling her hips Auralie turned her head to see what Nin and Rea were up to. The two were lying side by side, head to tail, tonguing each other's swollen openness. The sight of them made Auralie's belly quicken and her muscles tense.

'Now I think we should go out for dinner,' said Olga, suddenly and sadistically letting her hand drop.

An acute feeling of disappointment swamped Auralie. 'I couldn't find anything to wear,' she said.

'That's not a problem. We will dress you,' said Olga, showing her into an adjoining walk-in closet. They searched along the rails until they came across a black-leather outfit.

'Try this on,' Olga said.

The garment was in two pieces. The boned top had a scooped neck, long sleeves and criss-cross thongs running the length of the bodice ending in a 'V' shape pointing towards her belly button. Olga helped Auralie into the garment, then fastened the zip at the back. It was a skin-tight fit.

'*Magnifique*,' said Olga, tightening the leather thongs under Auralie's breasts so that they stayed jacked up, rounded and enticing.

'Now, step into the skirt,' said Olga.

The leather skirt hugged Auralie's small waist and hips then fell in wide bias-cut strips to her ankles.

'No panties, *chérie*,' said Olga, running a hand up Auralie's legs, feeling the black mound at the top, checking to see if she was still wet. 'Not tonight. I want you easily accessible.'

Olga rummaged in her chest of drawers, bringing out a pair of fine, black silk stockings. 'Put these on. There is no need for a suspender belt, they stay up on their own. You will also wear make-up and these high-heeled shoes.'

Auralie drew the black silk over her well-shaped legs and put on the black, very high-heeled shoes. Nin and Rea sat up to look at Auralie.

'Oh, she is beautiful,' they said.

'Come, you two. While I change, you can do her make-up and hair. I think we'll have it up; it looks more sophisticated,' said Olga. 'And pay extra attention to her eyes. They are a beautiful green and we must make sure everybody notices them.'

It was an hour later when both women, looking stunning, groomed and coiffeured, stood in the courtyard waiting for Olga's white, stretch limousine to arrive. Olga wore a black, bias-cut, flowing chiffon evening gown which enhanced her underlying sexuality but left her wantonness understated. Auralie looked ravishing and totally sexual. At Olga's insistence, both women wore long, drop diamond ear-rings but no other jewellery.

'I am taking you somewhere very special,' Olga said to Auralie as the limousine drew up and the chauffeur, Drenga, jumped out and held the car door open.

'Where's that?' asked Auralie as she slid onto the back seat.

'Jacqueline's,' Olga instructed Drenga as she got in beside Auralie. Auralie was delighted. Countess Jacqueline Helitzer was a well-known society hostess who gave fabulous parties. Her name was always in the gossip columns, but only the very rich and truly privileged were invited to her salon.

Auralie sat quietly beside Olga. She desperately wanted to ask her various questions but, as usual, felt slightly overawed and so kept her thoughts to herself.

'*Chérie*,' said Olga. 'Sit up straight and don't cross your legs.'

Auralie did as Olga commanded. The leather strips of the skirt fell away to either side of her stockinged legs. Olga began to stroke her knees and then slowly moved her hand along her thighs.

'Now, put your hands neatly together in your lap. Don't move them. You will sit like this unless told otherwise. And when we get to Jacqueline's make sure there is nothing between your bare buttocks and the seat of the chair.'

Auralie felt herself blush, but she tingled at the thought. Olga pushed Auralie's legs further open and gently rubbed a finger along her soft labia. Auralie's breath came and went in short sharp bursts as she wriggled and squirmed to the tune Olga was playing on her body.

'You sound as if you're enjoying this, *chérie*,' said Olga.

'Yes,' gasped Auralie, panting, wanting more, wanting that straying finger to plunge deeper into her.

'Can you think of a better way to spend an evening?'

'No.' Auralie gulped as Olga continued to play with her. She looked out of the window. The chauffeur obviously knew the way. He drove quickly and easily across the Seine, through the sixteenth district towards the Bois de Boulogne. After that, in the darkness, Auralie lost her bearings, but eventually the car swung into the driveway of an impressive mansion.

Olga and Auralie swept up the majestic steps to the high porticoed doors. Olga took a small piece of plastic from her handbag and keyed it into a computerised plate near the old-fashioned bell. The heavy large black doors swung open. In the high marble hall beyond, an enormous blond man, resembling a body-building champion but dressed as a butler, bowed to Olga.

'Princess,' he welcomed.

'Good evening, Kurt,' she said. 'Dinner.'

Auralie followed Olga and the butler the length of the bright, spacious hall and into a huge, softly lit dining-room full of formally dressed and happily chattering people.

The Maître d' showed them to a table in the middle of the room. This, like all the others, had a most unusual centrepiece. Instead of a bowl of flowers, different coloured tall feathers were arranged in a vase. As Olga and Auralie passed by, various men and women waved to them.

'Don't forget what I told you. Bare buttocks,' reminded Olga as they approached their table. 'And no matter what happens, unless you are actually eating or drinking, your hands must stay neatly in your lap.'

The waiter held Auralie's chair back for her to sit down. She stepped in front of it and, instead of the usual action of smoothing the fabric of her skirt beneath her bottom, Auralie swiftly switched the leather to one side, giving the other diners a quick flash of her neat, bare arse and black stocking tops.

Auralie was surprised to find that the velvet plush was harsh against her bare skin and made her itch. Also, there was a ridge running the length of the seat making it awkward for her to close her thighs. She then discovered that if she sat up straight, as Olga had instructed, tensed her muscles and wiggled, the combination of the fabric and the ridge excited her, forcing her protruding wet lips to open even more.

'Comfortable?' asked Olga, smiling, knowing what Auralie was experiencing.

'Yes, thank you,' replied Auralie, wondering if Olga was sitting in the same manner. The waiter brought an ice-bucket complete with champagne and proceeded to pour the sparkling liquid into their waiting flutes.

'This used to be the ballroom,' said Olga, watching Auralie scan the decor. 'It's very art nouveau, *chérie*, is it not?'

Auralie admired the twinkling cut-glass chandeliers and the swirling shapes painted on various mirrors and on the ceiling and walls. 'It's very beautiful.'

'Jacqueline's had some changes made,' said Olga, indicating the stage at the far end where a small orchestra was playing a selection from the classical repertoire. Then she pointed to the two balconies, raised four feet off the ground, that ran down either side of the main body of the room. There were six exceptionally good-looking couples sitting at tables on the balconies, but there was room for more people at empty tables. The six couples were happily eating and chatting, and, like everyone else in the room, they were wearing formal evening dress. The women wore strapless gowns in very bright colours, making them easily distinguishable from every corner of the room. Auralie was unable to see their lower parts, which were hidden by a long curtain that hung from a rail running the length of the balcony at tabletop level. The curtains ended at their feet and Auralie could see the women's high-heeled shoes.

The waiter brought them both smoked salmon.

'No menu?' asked Auralie.

'No,' said Olga. 'The chef decides.'

Auralie had taken a couple of mouthfuls when her attention was grabbed by a number of small men wearing eighteenth-century Helitzer livery, parading beneath the balconies and looking upwards. Auralie was struck not only by the size of the men, who were all under four feet tall, but by the fact that they seemed to her to be ugly, almost to the point of being grotesque. She watched for a moment then, when nothing more happened, continued her eating and drinking.

Olga ordered another bottle of champagne. 'Is Pierre on duty this evening?' she asked the waiter.

'Yes, Your Highness,' he answered. 'But we have a new man. Carlo. I think you should see him.'

'What's he like?' she asked.

'I'll send him over,' he said.

The waiter bowed and moments later an ugly little man wearing a long frock coat stood beside Olga, grinning. He flexed his shoulders and leered at Auralie, who shivered involuntarily. With muscles bulging, heavy eyebrows hanging over tiny eyes, a squashed nose and thick lips, Carlo was an ugly pint-sized mannikin, bursting with virility and raw sex. He seemed so out of place amongst the beauty of their surroundings that Auralie wondered what on earth he was doing in the place.

'So, you're Carlo,' said Olga.

'Yes, Your Highness. At your service, Your Highness,' the man replied in a deep rumbling voice.

'I hope you are,' said Olga, sternly, unbuttoning his coat. Olga then turned the little man towards Auralie whose eyes opened wide at the sight in front of her. Carlo's very large, semi-flaccid sex was hanging free from his breeches. An astonished Auralie also noticed that his penis, even in that state, almost reached his knees. Olga turned in her seat, cupped his balls in one hand, ringed his massive prick with the other and slowly began to rub it. Auralie swallowed and squirmed, getting more and more excited as Carlo's cock grew bigger and bigger under Olga's expert handling.

'Did Jacqueline choose you?' Olga asked him.

'Yes, Your Highness,' said Carlo.

'She chose well. I am pleased,' she said.

Olga smiled and looked over to the balcony. Her eyes alighted on a stunning, tall, slim black girl wearing a silver strapless top. Taking a long silver feather from the vase she gave it to Carlo, who took it, bowed, then walked over to the balcony. Olga, as if nothing untoward had happened, picked up her knife and fork and began eating again.

Auralie's curiosity was aroused. She watched Carlo stop

beneath the black girl, raise his hand holding the silver feather and stand as if dusting the ceiling of the platform.

'What is he doing?' Auralie asked, bemused.

'He is tickling her pussy,' replied Olga.

Auralie tingled at the thought and imagined a feather touching her. She licked her lips and gave a little wiggle of her hips so that once again the chair fabric was sexily itching her. Olga picked up a black feather and handed it to Auralie.

'Put it between your legs,' Olga commanded. 'Don't play with it. Just leave it there, touching you.'

Auralie obeyed, positioning the feather so that its tip was on her clitoris. Auralie smiled at Olga then looked around the room again. She noticed various men and woman at the tables near them handing different coloured feathers to other small men. Within moments each woman seated on the balcony had a man standing beneath her holding a feather identical in colour to her evening gown and tickling her pussy.

'But how do they do it?' asked Auralie.

'There's a hole in their seat,' said Olga.

'But . . .' Auralie wanted to know more.

'Watch,' hissed Olga, cutting her short.

The Maître d' appeared and pulled a cord, letting fall the curtains covering the lower part of the balcony. Auralie was then able to see that from the waist down all the couples on the platforms were completely naked. They were sitting on glass so every part of them was visible to everyone in the room. Auralie noticed that most of the men had an erection and in some cases their partner was using a foot to play with their tool.

The Maître d' gave a signal and two waiters appeared. To a fanfare from the musicians and slowly, as if it was a dance routine, the waiters travelled down the line of small men, unbuttoning each man's coat and removing it. With a flourish they exposed the little men's large balls and massive pricks to the excited stare of the diners. Whilst they continued to tickle pussy with one hand the waiters ceremoniously took the midgets' other hands and placed them on their penises, with the whispered command 'Wank'.

At the sight of those little men rubbing their enormous cocks Auralie found herself involuntarily moving her hips in small circles. She began slipping and sliding on the little ridge between her thighs, opening further and further, getting wetter and wetter and wanting to touch herself. Carefully, hoping Olga wouldn't notice, she snaked her hands down between her legs.

'No, you don't,' shouted Olga, authoritatively, realising what Auralie was about to do.

Auralie decided to change her line of vision and looked up at the women on the balcony. She noticed that they continued to eat and chat as if nothing was happening to them. Remembering how she felt when her pussy was played with, Auralie was quite astonished and said so to Olga.

'They are trained,' Olga told her enigmatically.

Auralie would have liked to ask more but a waiter arrived with their steak tartare and the stage was cleared of the musicians and the lights went down.

When the lights went back on again a statuesque redhead sat on the stage doing the splits. Her neck, breasts and arms were all tightly encased in a bright-red slinky fabric. Her draped skirt was wrapped over at the hips. She had a long black object clasped between her legs and as she started to her feet Auralie realised it was a microphone. In a low husky voice the girl began to sing.

'The cabaret?' asked Auralie.

'The beginning,' replied Olga.

When she had finished the first verse the young woman stepped down from the stage and began to walk amongst the diners. Sometimes she bent over the men and kissed their heads, other times she sat on their laps, but as she progressed further into the room she got more daring. Auralie watched her lift her leg, put a high-heel onto a man's knee, take a piece of food off his plate, then trawl it along her well-oiled labia and pop it into his mouth. Olga watched Auralie wiggle and lick her lips and knew she was both excited and frustrated. She beckoned the girl over to her table.

'Heidi,' she said. 'I want you to meet Mam'selle Auralie.'

In greeting, Heidi wrapped one leg around Auralie's neck, so that her pussy was resting against Auralie's shoulder, bent her head and kissed Auralie's lips.

Olga stretched out a hand and undid the only button that held the girl's skirt in place. The skirt dropped to the floor revealing her bare shaved pussy and her full rounded buttocks. The other guests clapped. Acknowledging the applause, Olga smiled, turned slightly in her chair and clasped the singer's mound. As she did so the girl let out a quick gasp and Auralie felt a rush of jealousy as Olga's finger began slipping and sliding in and out of the chanteuse.

'What is her Highness's pleasure today?' asked the girl politely, swaying backwards and forwards on Olga's exploring finger.

'To watch you being screwed,' said Olga.

Olga leant across the table to Auralie who was sipping some ice-cold champagne.

'Would you like that, *chérie*? Shall we watch one of those pricks glide up in and out of this nice fat pussy?' Olga asked Auralie. Then she signalled to the waiter. 'Clear this table and tell Carlo he is wanted.'

Auralie twiddled with her glass and watched Carlo strut across the room, his massive cock swaying as he made his way to Olga's side.

'It is our pleasure to watch you stick your lovely big dick

into Heidi's pussy,' said Olga, encircling his engorged member. 'But first I'd like to see what my companion can do with it. Auralie, I now give you permission to feel him. This is a real cock. A stiff one. Carlo, let her feel you.'

Auralie put down her champagne flute and hesitatingly placed her cold hand on the head of his penis.

'You're not a virgin playing with a navvy's prick,' derided Olga. 'Rub it.'

Auralie was suddenly aware that everyone in the room was watching her. The coldness of her fingers against the warmth of his cock had made Carlo harder, even more erect. Auralie decided not to obey Olga immediately. Instead she picked up her glass of champagne and dipped Carlo's penis into it. Then she began to rub. When he started to sigh she clasped the full squashiness of his huge testicles in her other hand. She looked up from his prick to the ugly little man's half-closed but sexy eyes, tensed her wet pussy against the feather and the fabric of the chair and squirmed.

'You look as if you've got a juicy wet pussy,' said Carlo and put his large fat hands over Auralie's pert, jacked-up and rounded breasts. The feel of the little man's huge member in her hands and the touch of his hands on her tits excited Auralie so much that she moved faster and faster on the little ridge between her thighs.

'She's got a feather between her legs,' said Olga to Heidi. 'Let her find out what it's like to have her pussy tickled.'

Heidi leant across the table, took hold of the feather lying between Auralie's thighs, and began to draw it along her lustful sex. Auralie relaxed back in her chair, braced her breasts against Carlo's massaging hands, arched her hips, tensed her buttocks, rubbed Carlo's prick and balls and, with the feather exciting her still further, began to know real and heightened sexual pleasure.

'Stop that now and bend over,' said Olga, pulling the tall redhead away from Auralie and pushing her over the table. That was when Auralie noticed that the waiters had not only cleared their table but had also removed the others from their vicinity. Olga, Auralie, Heidi and Carlo were now alone in the middle of the room. They were a neat little quartet: Olga fingering Heidi's pussy, and Auralie playing with Carlo's massive thick and throbbing penis. And everybody in the room was watching them. Heidi bent over so that her full rounded bare buttocks faced the excited and waiting assembly.

'Put your legs apart,' ordered Olga. The girl parted her legs so that her swollen pink pussy was on show.

'Carlo, first I want you to suck her pussy,' ordered Olga.

Moving towards Heidi, Carlo took his massive member into his own hand and turned towards everyone in the room. He was exceptionally proud of his over-large tool and wanted them all to admire it. Some of the women gasped at its size. That excited Carlo even more and he rubbed it harder, making it even thicker, even more erect. Then he walked between the girl's long legs, where her waiting, wet sex was level with his mouth. He stood in front of her, put out his big thick tongue and began to slobber and slurp noisily at her very swollen, lascivious opening. Auralie was now tingling throughout her body. Her sex was open and very wet. She, too, wanted to be touched, played with.

'Keep your hands neatly in your lap,' said Olga to Auralie, sternly.

Auralie did as she was told but Olga's imposition made her hornier than ever. Slyly she glanced about her. She noticed that the empty tables on the balconies had now been taken by some of their fellow guests, who had divested themselves of most of their clothing and were having sex. Round about her she saw that a few of the men had taken their pricks out of their trousers and their bare-breasted women were kneeling in front of them, sucking them off. Others were playing with their women's breasts; some had raised their partners' ballgowns and were leisurely stroking between their pussies and buttocks.

In the midst of all this sexual activity Countess Jacqueline Helitzer sauntered over to Olga and Auralie's table, stood behind Olga's chair, crossed her arms and snuggled her hands down through Olga's clothing so that she was holding and tweaking Olga's nipples. Olga put up a hand, pulled Jacqueline's face down to hers and gave her a long passionate kiss on her full red lips. As she watched the two women, Auralie was struck by the Countess's beauty and understood how she had captured the heart of the elderly Count Helitzer within days of her arrival in Paris. He had married her quickly, then, three months after the marriage, had conveniently died leaving Jacqueline many millions of pounds richer.

It was rumoured she was Hungarian but nobody knew for sure. Neither did anybody know how old she was; they guessed she was somewhere between twenty-five and thirty-five. She had an unlined peaches-and-cream complexion that gave nothing away. She wore her very blonde hair piled in soft curls on top of her head, little tendrils escaping down her neck giving her a look of vulnerability. She was tall and slim and wore a fabulous Empire-style gown in flowing turquoise silk chiffon which emphasised her large breasts, although the material barely covered her nipples. The folds of the gown, and its long centre slit, were held together by a rose in the middle of her cleavage.

'Jacqueline, *chérie*, let me look at you,' said Olga, slowly parting the silk and revealing first white stockings then Jacqueline's naked and glorious body. Olga ran her hands over Jacqueline's belly, and began caressing her between her legs. Then she bent her head and licked the Countess's clitoris. Jacqueline sighed with pleasure.

'Darlink,' she whispered, looking at Auralie, 'She's absolutely divine. Everybody wants to have her.'

'They can't,' said Olga, imperiously.

Auralie felt a sharp twinge of disappointment. She was desperate for sexual release. Her bud was itching to be played with. She turned her attention to the stage. The curtains had been drawn back and a vast sloping bed had been placed in the centre. It was covered in a white, shiny satin sheet and masses of pillows.

'I've decided to change the billing,' said Olga.

'And what, darlink, have you decided?' said Jacqueline, kissing Olga full on the lips as Olga continued to caress Jacqueline's thighs.

'Wait and see,' replied Olga.

It was at that moment that Auralie heard a series of loud screams and gasps coming from one of the balconies. She looked up and, to her horror, spotted her cousin Laurence. He had the beautiful tall black girl bent over the balcony rail and was holding onto her breasts as he screwed her from behind. Auralie sat spellbound. Sexual jealousy and anger flooded through her. Olga noticed Auralie's look of anguish and followed her gaze up to the balcony. Laurence was doing what he had been doing ever since he had landed in Paris – screwing Petrov's pet slave, Leyisha. Olga's glance strayed to the man sitting at the table adjoining Laurence's. Her ex-husband, Petrov, was as naked as the day that he was born. He had a woman between his legs, her head going rapidly up and down on his cock. Olga waved to him and he returned her salutation. Auralie noticed Petrov and saw that Olga was licking her lips whilst Jacqueline possessively encircled her breasts. Olga smiled at Auralie.

'This family certainly enjoys sex,' Olga drawled, squeezing Jacqueline's buttocks.

Jacqueline smiled salaciously.

'I want to be screwed,' Auralie announced.

'Oh you do, do you?' said Olga. 'Then you shall be.'

'Are they going to draw lots for her?' asked Jacqueline.

'No,' said Olga. 'Jacqueline, take Auralie to the bed.'

Auralie stood up and willingly followed Jacqueline up onto the stage. The moment she was there the room was plunged into darkness and a spotlight was trained on the two women. The light was so strong that Auralie had to bring up a hand to shield her eyes.

'There's no need for that,' said the Countess, picking up a blindfold lying close to the bed and tying it around Auralie's eyes. Then she guided Auralie to the bed. Jacqueline sat her down and unloosed the leather thongs on her bodice. She placed Auralie's hands above her head and tied them to a post. She spread Auralie's legs wide and tied her ankles firmly to a slack rope hanging from rings attached to the side of the bed. Then she put a number of pillows beneath Auralie's buttocks so that the girl's brazen, swollen sex was exposed and clearly visible. Searching under another pillow, Jacqueline pulled out a small vibrator. She turned it on and, holding it against Auralie's clitoris, let it glide on her wetness. When Auralie began lifting her hips up and turning her legs out invitingly, Jacqueline nodded at Olga. The spotlight was extinguished.

When the spotlight went back on, Jacqueline's place had been taken by Carlo. He was running the vibrator on her clitoris with one hand and stroking his massive erect prick with the other. Then, as he changed position, the bed swivelled and tipped so that Auralie's head was facing downstage.

The sight of the slim young girl tethered to the bed with the ugly little man, looking like a goblin and hung like a donkey, standing between her legs and poised for entry, sent a wave of licentiousness through Jacqueline's watching guests.

'Screw her. Screw her,' they roared in unison.

The changeover had been so fast Auralie wondered who they were referring to. Was a man on the bed with her? If so, who was it? Olga knew Auralie knew Laurence was in the dining-room. She hoped Olga had sent him down to take her.

'Screw her, screw her.' The people in the room continued to chant.

In the spotlight, not touching any other part of her body, Carlo ran the tip of his huge cock along Auralie's juicy labia. She tensed her muscles, spread her legs wider and raised her hips to meet him. Slowly, so that everyone in the room could see him do it, Carlo edged and probed his way into Auralie's waiting pussy. With each tiny thrust Auralie gave a deep sigh and begged for more and begged for it harder. Suddenly he gave a fast lunge and began riding her like a man possessed. A great cheer went up from the room. Auralie didn't know what had hit her but she took him, every last inch of him. Her hips rose higher and higher meeting every thrust of his penis until she was squirming and writhing, moaning and sighing, turning this way and that, not knowing whether she was coming or going.

Out of the darkness hands grabbed her breasts, and a prick appeared and was shoved into her mouth. A mouth sucked on her toes. Then the whole stage was lit up, and everyone could see the little men on the bed with Auralie, using her, wielding their massive pricks against her body, creaming over her. And Auralie responding violently, enjoying every minute of it.

The lights went out again. When they went up once more Auralie was sitting alone on the bed without the blindfold. She was given a rousing round of applause. She smiled, contentedly. Then the ugly little men trouped on and took their bow. Instantly the smile disappeared from Auralie's face. Had they been touching her? Had those ugly little men been performing on her body? And which one had penetrated her? She had a suspicion, from the depth of the prick and its thickness that it might have been Carlo. She slipped off the bed as the lights went down and made her way over to where Olga was sitting with Jacqueline.

'Who was it? Which one of those horrible little men screwed me?' asked Auralie, nearly in tears.

'Does it matter?' said Olga.

'Yes,' said Auralie. 'You knew I wanted Laurence to have me.'

'Laurence!' exclaimed Olga. 'But *chérie*, you've had him once today. It was time for you to discover another cock. And you looked as if you were enjoying yourself. You did enjoy it, didn't you? Answer truthfully, Auralie. Did you enjoy it?'

'Yes,' Auralie had to admit the awful truth.

'Good,' said Olga. 'And now it's time for us to go home.'

Auralie noticed most of the guests had left.

'We look forward to welcoming you again,' said the Countess, kissing Auralie on both cheeks.

Auralie smiled wanly.

'I think she's exhausted,' said Olga.

'So she should be,' replied Jacqueline. 'You gave a wonderful performance, darlink. Remember, now you've been initiated you can come here and screw whoever you want. A man or a woman, we don't mind. Our only rule is everything is open and above board. But we don't tell outsiders, do we, darlink?'

'Never,' said Olga. 'Neither do we have secrets from one another.'

Jacqueline kissed Olga goodbye and the butler showed them to the door. Outside, Olga's limousine was waiting.

'A successful evening, ma'am?' asked the chauffeur, Drenga, as he opened the doors.

'Extremely,' replied Olga, smiling like a cat, then turning to Auralie she added, 'By the way, Drenga's my personal property. On the few occasions I want a man I have him. Nobody else is allowed to touch him. Is that understood?'

It was a couple of weeks later, after Olga and Auralie had

become lovers, when Olga told her that it was Carlo who had screwed her that first night. A furious Auralie, who was also regularly shagging Laurence and various male members of Jacqueline's salon, paid Olga back by secretly screwing Drenga at every opportunity.

Auralie returned from her memories to her office in London and the trio in front of her. Yes, she thought, if Penelope hadn't thrown her out that day she would never have discovered sex in all its variety. She would never have become Olga's lover, a constant visitor to Jacqueline's salon, a member of Olga and Petrov's sect, or, through her partnership in Olga's company, a very rich woman. But none of this lessened Auralie's desire for revenge.

Terry let out a great cry as he came, and then collapsed. The two girls looked pleased with themselves.

'Very good,' said Auralie, with enthusiasm, 'and, you must agree, very easy in those clothes.' They nodded. 'Okay, all change.' Jill and Mary put their own clothes back on. 'She's interviewing you on Monday, you said?' They nodded their heads again. 'Well, it's vital you three get taken on. Now, she's Miss Virginal so be very prim and proper. Don't let her get suspicious. Little by little you start, but wait until her nice middle-class customers are installed.

'What if Terry's not around. Should we play with each other?' asked Mary.

'Yes, but make certain somebody always sees you. The sooner her hotel is closed the bigger the bonus for you,' replied Auralie.

'Does Petrov know?' Terry asked.

'Petrov knows everything that happens to every member of his order,' said Auralie enigmatically, thinking she must be careful with Terry. If Petrov did discover what she was up to, her position within his order would be in jeopardy. 'Ring me on Monday and let me know how you got on,' she added, looking at the clock. It was almost two. She unlocked the doors and let Mary, Jill and Terry out into the bright sunlit street. Auralie heard her staff returning and retreated back inside her own office where, after clearing her desk, she lifted the telephone and called her husband.

The line was engaged. She replaced the receiver and looked around her sparse office and smiled. Petolg Holdings had once been a dream. With Petrov's financial help, she and Olga, Petrov's ex-wife, had made it come true.

Auralie and Olga ran Petolg as a beneficent autocracy, which was hardly surprising given their essentially Russian background. They'd had definite ideas when they set up the business and they had kept to them. It was a comparatively young company and so far had been very successful. This was due not only to Auralie's good designs but also to their management policy. They operated a very lean enterprise. Waste of any kind – time, telephone calls and stationery – was kept to an absolute minimum.

In their fabrics factories in France they employed only married women with children and provided nannies, a doctor and a crèche for their workforce. At their headquarters in Paris and at Auralie's workroom in London, the small staff was made up of unmarried women under thirty. Auralie and Olga paid much better than average salaries and supplied them with an excellent private pension scheme, but they never paid Christmas bonuses or gave their employees a car or other perks. All telephone calls were timed and a complete record kept; any private calls had to be paid for at the end of each week. Too many private calls and the employee was warned. Two warnings and they were out of a job. All paper, envelopes, pens, pencils and photocopying had to be accounted for; theft, however minimal, was not tolerated and meant instant dismissal. Employees were paid from nine until six and every member of staff was expected to be at work by nine on the dot. Under no circumstances were they allowed to remain in the building after six o'clock. If they were late for work once, their pay was docked by the number of minutes they were late. If they were late for work twice, they were sacked. Olga and Auralie worked on the basis that people were never late for a 'plane for their holiday so if they were late for work they must be fundamentally bored with their job and therefore they should leave. All staff were given two hours for lunch. This was so that they could eat properly and do any necessary shopping. The offices and the factories were closed completely between the hours of twelve and two. The only people allowed to stay within their doors were Olga and Auralie.

Auralie tried Gerry's number again. All lines were still engaged. Auralie replaced the receiver then went to a filing cabinet and took out some paper and different swatches of fabric. She picked up a pencil and started to draw. She thought about the top-secret project she was working on. If she was able to pull if off it would mean serious money for her and Olga and Petolg Holdings. It was a project that involved her husband, but he was unaware of that. It was the reason that she had married him.

Auralie had met Gerry at an après-ski party in Verbier. She and Olga had gone there to drown their sorrows after the death of Krakos, a Greek millionaire with a fleet of luxury liners. Petolg Holdings had held the contract to keep them refurbished. On his death, Krakos's daughter had immediately sold the fleet and Petolg had lost the contract. Now Olga and Auralie were desperately searching for a replacement. It was not an easy assignment; people were closing businesses, not starting them.

Gerry had fancied Auralie and had wasted no time in contacting her after they had both returned to London. She had taken an interest in him because there was a rumour in the city that his father, Sir Henry de Bouys, was starting up a new airline.

'This could be the answer,' Olga had told Auralie one evening as they lay in bed together in Auralie's small apartment overlooking Regent's Park. 'You must find out if it's true, *chérie*,' she added, leisurely stroking Auralie's naked body. They had now been lovers for a couple of years.

'How?' Auralie had asked.

'Let him take you out,' Olga had advised, kissing her neck. 'Then you'll think of a way.'

And Auralie had. She had managed to plant listening devices in various lampstands dotted around Gerry's apartment. She had monitored all his conversations with his father and discovered the rumour was true.

'Now what do I do?' Auralie had asked Olga during a subsequent visit to Paris.

'You must marry Gerry de Bouys,' Olga had replied.

'I can't,' Auralie had said.

'For business you can do anything,' Olga had retorted. 'And as Sir Henry's daughter-in-law you cannot fail. *Chérie*, it is a prize. A great prize.'

The prize they were after was the contract for the soft furnishings and the carpets for his aircraft and VIP suites at the various airports where he would have landing rights.

'*Mon Dieu!*' Auralie had said. 'Olga, to screw is one thing, to marry is something else. I do not want to marry. I am very happy with you. I am very happy as part of the order. There I can have sex when I want and with whom I want and walk away. Anyway, how do I manage to marry him? I know many women want him.'

'*Chérie,*' the haughty, patrician, elegant Olga had replied, 'it is easy. First understand men. You will not have to screw him, at least not for a long time. Men like to chase. The more they have to chase the more they want. Gerry will think if you don't screw him you don't screw at all. You are pure. They all want purity in their bride. All you have to do is give him the come-on, then keep your legs closed. Very tightly closed. And he will marry you. Then the contract will be ours. You are a very good designer, but that way Petolg will have the edge on everybody because you will be Sir Henry's daughter-in-law.'

Auralie had cuddled into Olga and assimilated what she said.

'Is it really true, Olga?' she had asked. 'Men still want virgins?'

'Oh yes. Ridiculous, isn't it. They don't know what they're getting!'

'No,' Auralie agreed, 'they are getting a pig without a poke.' She had laughed. And she had married Gerry.

'You can always find a reason to divorce the man after we've got the contract,' Olga had told her.

And that was exactly what Auralie was thinking of doing. She was setting in motion the next phase of her manoeuvring. But first she had to obtain the contract. Competition would be strong and swift and she knew Sir Henry acted quickly. She also knew that certain design companies kept presentation kits permanently assembled. She had spent many hours and days planning her designs and her presentation. She was only waiting for the news to burst open. The only shadow on the horizon was Gerry's bizarre behaviour that morning. It worried her. Nothing must go wrong at this stage. She picked up the telephone and dialled his number again. His new secretary told her he was in a meeting and could not be interrupted. It was the third time that day he had refused to take her call. Gerry always spoke to her when she called. She thought back to the strange event that morning. He had woken up and smacked her bottom hard, then left the house without saying a word. No 'good morning'. Not even a kiss. Nothing.

Auralie telephoned his father's secretary, Caroline, and asked her what was going on. She made sure she stayed friendly with Caroline even though the secretary had proudly told her she had screwed Gerry not long before their wedding day. If Caroline had wanted to make Auralie jealous she had miscalculated miserably. Auralie could not have cared less. Instead she had cultivated Caroline's friendship. She had made her her confidante. Or so Auralie thought.

Caroline told Auralie she knew nothing untoward. Gerry had had a series of meetings that day but to the best of her knowledge was now on his own in his office. Very worried, Auralie sat back and tried to work out the reason for his odd behaviour.

Gerry had come home the previous evening and been quite cheery. He had wanted sex, but she hadn't. He had tried to turn her on by talking about his fantasies. That had done nothing for her. Why should she listen to him when she had been acting out her own for most of the day? Besides, she had been exhausted. Between screwing Petrov's latest novice and secretly working on her presentation she had been drained of all energy.

But now, in her office, Auralie's antennae were out. She knew she had displeased her husband. Bored though she was with him, this was not the time to give him a reason to stray. She realised she would have to do something fast otherwise the whole charade of her marriage would have been to no avail. She would have to use her sexuality to put whatever it was, right. Gerry was always telling her of his fantasy to have another woman in their bed. To disguise her own desire for women she had pretended to be shocked every time he mentioned it. But it was not her only reason for pretending; she did not want Gerry to discover she was a member of her uncle Petrov's sect. Gerry had also mentioned his desire to see her taken by another man. Perhaps she should agree to that. Suggest they do it. The telephone suddenly shrilled beside her. She didn't take it. Moments later her secretary told her that her cousin Jeanine was on the line.

'Take a message and tell her I'm out,' said Auralie.

Jeanine! Now there was food for thought. She had the sneakiest suspicion that Jeanine fancied Gerry. Wouldn't it be interesting if she could get the two of them into bed. Then, as soon as the contract was hers she could divorce Gerry on the grounds of his adultery with Miss Virginal. That was an idea well worth considering. Various sexual combinations whirled around Auralie's head. But it was the thought of Gerry screwing Jeanine that lightened Auralie's mood. She settled down to an afternoon's work no longer concerned as to Gerry's strange behaviour. She was thinking out an alternative strategy.

It was long after the staff had gone home and she was still working that her private line rang and Gerry asked her out for dinner.

Auralie changed from her working clothes, her jeans and sweat shirt, bathed and put on her latest Parisian acquisition, a superbly cut Chartreuse green, slub silk suit. It showed off her colouring and her figure to perfection. She brushed her hair until it shone and applied her make-up. Auralie was going into battle with every accoutrement at her disposal.

4

'Darling Gerry,' said Auralie, as the waiter walked away leaving two delicious white peppery liqueurs in front of them, 'I want to make love to a woman.'

Gerry drew a sharp breath. Auralie knew the calculated shamelessness of her statement would excite him. She slid a hand under cover of the tablecloth, surreptitiously undid a couple of buttons on his trousers and wormed a finger into the opening so she could stroke him. They were in a public place and she knew it would arouse him. Through half-closed eyes she took a long look at Gerry, then whispered into his ear.

'You know I've never done it. We could have her together,' said Auralie, huskily, sexily and knowing she looked good.

'No,' said Gerry, resisting her. Gerry gazed at his chic, petite French wife. You lying bitch, he thought.

'No? Why not?' asked Auralie.

'You'd get jealous and make a scene.'

'I wouldn't. I promise I wouldn't,' insisted Auralie. 'You would like to watch, *non*? And would like to take her too, *non*?'

Gerry thought about this carefully. Apart from his wife, Jeanine was the only woman he wanted, and he was perfectly sure Auralie would not suggest *her*. Neither did he want to be the one to make the suggestion. He wondered who she was thinking about – who it was she had decided was to share their bed. He conjured up visions of their various friends and acquaintances. He thought of the plump young woman, Margaret, he had seen recently. Was it her? Something told him possibly not. Gerry decided to change tactic.

'Why now?' he asked.

'Because we love each other,' she replied simply. Two days ago Gerry would have believed her, taken her words at face value, but not any more. 'All fantasies should be lived, acted out and appreciated,' Auralie continued.

'Oh really? Then who do you suggest?' he asked.

'Well, there is Caroline,' Auralie said airily.

'No. I don't fancy her,' lied Gerry, remembering the imaginative session he'd had earlier that evening with his father's secretary.

'Valerie?' suggested Auralie. Valerie was Caroline's sister.

'Definitely not,' replied Gerry. 'She's too skinny.'

'Kit's got a new girl,' said Auralie.

'Oh, how do you know?' Gerry asked.

'Her name's Sally. He came round with her the other day but you were out.'

'What's she like?'

'OK. Big boobies. You'd like her.'

'Would you?' asked Gerry.

Auralie didn't answer. Instead she finished her liqueur and asked for another. Whilst waiting for the waiter to appear, Auralie's cold fingers played inside Gerry's trousers. Gerry's thoughts began to drift back to the scene with Auralie and the girl tied to his bedpost. Against his will his penis started to twitch and grow.

'So that only leaves her,' said Auralie, her voice cutting across his increasingly sexual thoughts.

'Who?' Gerry asked.

'Jeanine.'

'Jeanine!' exclaimed Gerry. He couldn't believe his ears. The woman he most wanted. The woman he thought of as out of bounds. And here was his wife suggesting they made love to her. Had Auralie plugged into his psyche? Jeanine had seemed almost passionless since the death of her husband but recently Gerry had sensed something new about her. As if a part of her had been unlocked and her underlying sexuality had risen to the surface. Had Auralie felt the same thing? Had she too twigged the difference in Jeanine?

'No, not Jeanine, darling,' he said emphatically.

'Why not?' demanded his wife. 'She's pretty.'

'Is she?' He continued the pretence. He picked up Auralie's hand and kissed it. 'Darling one,' he added, 'You know I like my women dark, earthy and vibrant.'

'Well, I quite fancy her,' said Auralie.

The audacity of her statement overwhelmed Gerry. He was shocked. He was also excited but was not going to allow Auralie to see how excited he was. There was all to play for here and he intended to savour every minute.

'Can't you think of anybody else?' Gerry asked, guessing his very lack of interest would be a spur to his wife's desires.

'Gerry,' said Auralie, in her best 'be reasonable' voice, 'Jeanine has a lovely figure.'

'Has she?'

'Yes. And she fancies you.'

'How do you know?' Gerry asked, genuinely intrigued.

'I can tell.'

'Don't be ridiculous.'

'I am not being ridiculous,' she insisted. 'I have seen her looking at you. Sometimes she narrows her eyes and licks her lips.'

'And that means she fancies me! No, that's too absurd.'

'She doesn't know she's doing it. Look Gerry, I bet you could seduce her.'

'I don't want to,' he lied.

'But I bet you could. Gerry darling, let's have some fun. You seduce her then let me play with her and . . .'

'Yes, darling and . . .?'

'Then I will let you find a man to screw me,' she added teasingly.

His other fantasy. This was too much. Was his wife a witch? She was sitting beside him, brazenly stating all his fantasies. Why? From time to time whenever he had mentioned wanting to watch her being made love to, wanting to watch another man entering her, lying on top of her, kissing her, sucking her, Auralie had been shocked. Or so he had thought. What had changed? Had she enjoyed the hard slap he had given her bottom that morning? Was she worried because he had refused to take her calls? Did she really love him, and he had misread her?

Auralie watched, delighted at the perplexed expression flitting across Gerry's face. She was confusing him. She also felt the strengthening of his penis. She was arousing him. She remembered how she had had to pretend to be so shocked by his fantasies, then had gone to Petrov's where Gerry's fantasies had become her reality. One day she might tell him. But men were odd about their wives. Especially men who wanted purity before marriage. Fantasy was one thing. Reality something else. There was no way she would give Gerry the ability to divorce her. She would divorce him after the contract was signed and settled. Yes, she would divorce him for screwing Jeanine and obtain a major settlement. But now she was going to let him think that if he wanted to watch her being fucked, he could, but only after she had got him into bed with Jeanine.

'My choice of man?' Gerry asked.

'Definitely,' she said. 'As long as you seduce Jeanine.'

'And whatever this man wants to do with you, you'll let him do it?'

'What do you mean?' There was a slight tremor in Auralie's voice.

'Exactly what I say, my darling.' Gerry was having visions of his wife tied to the bedpost whilst an unknown man whipped her pretty little bottom then screwed her.

'Do you have anybody in mind?' she asked.

'Not at the moment,' he said. 'First things first. First you promise me, then I'll try to seduce Jeanine.'

'I promise you, Gerry.'

'In that case we'd better work out a plan of action.'

'No time like the present,' said Auralie.

'Tonight?' exclaimed Gerry.

'Yes, why not?' replied Auralie. 'You see, I happen to know that today was her last day at work. Next week she opens her hotel.'

'But it's late now, what if she's gone to bed?'

'We'll wake her up.'

'And if she doesn't answer the door?'

'She doesn't have to,' said Auralie. 'I have a key.'

'You have a key! Why?'

'I designed her place, remember. And it was so that I could get in and out when she was at work.'

'Of course,' said Gerry, adding, 'but she might not take too kindly to being woken up, to being invaded. She might not be totally acquiescent.'

'Darling, let's take her a couple of bottles of champagne and say we've come as her first guests.'

'Why would we do that when we've a perfectly good home of our own?' queried Gerry.

'We'll say we've had an accident; a plumbing accident and we can't use our own bed.'

'Sometimes, my dear, you can be most inventive,' Gerry said sarcastically, although his sarcasm was lost on his wife. He smiled indulgently at Auralie. He took her hand and squeezed it affectionately. Yes, he would enjoy seducing Jeanine. He thought he would enjoy watching her being touched by Auralie. He tried to visualise it but those thoughts did not come easily. Uppermost in his mind was himself screwing Jeanine. His kissing Jeanine, and sucking Jeanine. He was still slightly taken aback by his wife's other suggestion – that he could find a man to screw her whilst he watched. That was a revelation. Two days ago he was thinking his wife was almost frigid and now she was sitting beside him in one of London's top restaurants making outrageous suggestions. He smiled. Ignoring the bitch had paid off. He must do it more often. But who would he find to have sex with her? Kit?

She liked Kit. Gerry knew that. Kit fancied her, he knew that too. Kit had told him so. Gerry would blindfold Auralie then take her to Kit's place. He had taken various women there in the past. He would watch Kit touch her, probe her, tie her up and screw her. Then Gerry would take a great delight in spanking her. He would take a wooden paddle to her bare bottom and spank her for her lies, for her disobedience, and for her dishonesty. The next few weeks could prove interesting, even adventurous. But he wondered if it was true that Jeanine really fancied him, or was it only a product of Auralie's fertile imagination? He was determined to find out. His cock was frisky. He wanted sex. He was incredibly horny and the idea of seducing Jeanine appealed to him no end.

'You are right, as ever, my darling,' Gerry said. 'There is no time like the present. Let's get a couple of bottles of champers and the bill.'

Armed with two bottles of Möet they left the restaurant and hailed a cab.

As the taxi drove up outside Jeanine's house Auralie told Gerry that perhaps it would be better if she left him to seduce Jeanine on his own.

'Make some excuse for me. Tell her I'm mopping up water or something. I will come in later and find you in bed. Then I will join you,' Auralie said, kissing his lips. 'See what utter faith I have in you as a seducer, *mon amour*.'

Gerry told the cabby to wait while Auralie let him into Jeanine's house. Then Auralie stepped back into the taxi and it drove away.

The house seemed empty as he stood in the hallway. A slight noise coming from the top of the stairs made him look up. From his vantage point Gerry watched, unseen, as Jeanine came slowly down the stairs wearing her basque, seamed stockings, ankle-length boots and the long flowing leather cape. He had never seen a sight so lovely, so tantalising or so unexpected. Then Jeanine caught sight of Gerry standing in the hall and almost fainted. The face, the very face that had been the object of all her fantasies was staring up at her. She fastened the cape tightly around her body and tried to compose herself. Auralie's husband, so tall and handsome, so tanned and muscular, so deeply sexual. Jeanine was bitterly ashamed of her attraction to Gerry but wondered perversely if it was this forbiddance that had increased her desire.

'Jeanine,' said Gerry, holding out his arms to kiss her cheek as he always did. 'I didn't recognise you for a moment.' That, he thought, was an understatement.

'What are you doing here?' she said, flustered, dodging away from his embrace. 'How did you get in?'

'Auralie has a key. I've bought a couple of bottles,' he said waving the champagne. 'Came to see you, wish you luck and ask to be your first customers.'

'Oh, why?' said Jeanine, warily.

'We've had a bad leak. Can't stay at the house. Have to go somewhere, so thought why not here?' Gerry held out the two bottles and Jeanine was careful to avoid any contact with him as she took them.

'Where is Auralie?'

'At home, mopping up. She'll be along later,' replied Gerry. 'Well, is that all right? I mean, can we stay?'

This was not what Jeanine had envisaged. In her imagination her first guests had always been middle-aged, middle-brow, mid-west Americans. Never had she thought that this man who made her tremble, whose sexuality overwhelmed her, who made her instantly open and wet just by his presence, would arrive, wanting to stay under her roof.

'Yes, of course,' said Jeanine, looking into his strong blue eyes then swiftly turning her head in case he read the invitation written there. 'You have a choice of rooms. I will show them to you.'

'In a moment,' said Gerry. 'Why don't we have a drink first.'

Drink! She had already drunk a whole bottle of champagne and was slightly unsteady on her feet. Could she take another drop? She looked into Gerry's face. He was smiling. She would have to; she couldn't possibly let him know how much she had already drunk. That was a secret, a confidence, and one confidence might lead to another.

'Come and see what I've done to the house. I have made my own private apartments downstairs. Follow me,' she said, clearly enunciating each word lest he should think she was slightly tipsy.

Clutching the cape ever more tightly to her body Jeanine led the way to her garden-level apartment. Gerry walked behind her, noticing her erect carriage and how her luxuriant fair hair bobbed on her shoulders. It had always been primly pinned back into a bun. This new style, he decided, was a great improvement. The smell of leather from her cape drifted up to his nostrils and excited him. Was it just the leather, or was there another smell. He couldn't be sure, but whatever it was it stimulated him and he found himself not just vaguely attracted to her but desperately wanting to seduce her. And he still could not quite believe what he was seeing. Jeanine, sweet mousy Jeanine, wearing black silk stockings, her feet enclosed in high-heeled, ankle-length boots and the most sensuous black leather cape he had ever seen. This was not a Jeanine he had ever seen before. A thought struck him. Perhaps she had a lover. A secret lover who was perhaps still upstairs.

'Have I disturbed you?' he asked.

'No,' Jeanine said firmly, thinking 'Yes. Yes, Gerry, you always disturb me. You disturb my peace of mind. You make me think wildly sexual thoughts. You've made me think wildly sexual thoughts all evening. You make me have to confess those thoughts.'

'Which way now?' Gerry asked as they came to the bottom of the stairs.

'Sharp right,' she said.

'What's that room there?' he asked.

'My bedroom.'

'And that one?'

'That's a nothing room at the moment. It's too large for a study and I don't need two bedrooms so it lies carpeted but empty. This is my sitting-room.'

Jeanine opened the large double doors onto a room that had been exquisitely decorated. The walls were hung with silk, and large baroque mirrors and well-framed paintings were highlighted. They sat down in deep armchairs either side of the white marble fireplace. There was an awkward silence between them. Jeanine was trying not to tremble. Aware she had no knickers on and that her sexual juices were flowing, she endeavoured to keep her legs together. Unfortunately the dildo she had been using all evening had stretched and enlarged her opening so that her body now wanted more. She wondered what Gerry's penis was like. Was it big and fat, or long and thin? Was it short or . . .? She closed her eyes and imagined her hand in his trousers. God, where had she left the dildo? She tried to think and then remembered she had dropped it on the stairs when she saw Gerry. She must find an excuse to collect it before he saw it. Gerry was looking at her, a look that discomfited her. Was it only in her mind, something conjured from longing, or was there electricity between them? She must make certain she never stood too close to him. He must not touch her or all her vows would disappear. She looked at his lips and drifted into wondering what they would be like to kiss. No. Nothing must be allowed to happen. He must never know her secret, must never guess her fantasy.

'Champagne?' he offered.

Jeanine jumped at the sound of his voice. To quickly cover her embarrassment she stood up and opened a wall cabinet, taking out three champagne flutes.

'One for Auralie when she arrives,' she said.

Gerry uncorked the champagne. He was wondering which approach to use. The gentle seduction or the full-frontal attack. She seemed to him to be sexually aroused. Perhaps he could put out a hand and touch her hair. He looked at her again. As she moved the cape gaped and he caught a glimpse of leather and lace.

'Jeanine,' he said, standing beside her as she held two of the flutes in her hand, 'it's hot in here. Shall I help you with your cape?'

'No,' she said, but she was too late; he had taken hold of the collar and pulled. Jeanine stood before him, glorious in her semi-nakedness and utterly unable to move for shame. Rooted to the spot, she felt her hands grip the twirling stems of the blue-tinged crystal flutes. Her face flushed pink as he stared at her.

Jeanine's flaxen hair tumbled over her shoulders, her high white breasts welled up over the leather and lace of her basque and he noticed her knees tremble slightly as his gaze travelled down to just above her stocking tops. No knickers. His penis shot instantly to its full length. No knickers and hair so pale and fine she looked as if she had shaved.

'God, you are beautiful,' he said. He put out a hand and touched her face. For the first time in minutes she regained control of her limbs and tried to pull away.

'No, don't do that,' he said, a note of command in his voice that made her obey instantly. He held her eyes and said, 'I think you need to be screwed.'

Jeanine's mouth parted, her tongue came out and she licked her lips. But before she could answer, before she could protest or acquiesce, Gerry had put one arm around her waist, bent her slightly backwards and put his middle finger along the inside of her swollen secret opening, leaving his forefinger and ring finger holding firm to the outer lips of her vulva and pressing. Jeanine gasped. His grip on her waist tightened as he put his mouth over hers and kissed her. The tingling sensation that was let loose throughout her body threatened to engulf her. With controlled slowness Gerry's middle finger pressed further in, feeling her softness and the ridges and the juices and the muscles taking him, sucking him upwards. He pushed his tongue past her teeth, drinking in the sweet taste of her. Still maintaining the pressure between her legs he searched for her tongue.

Jeanine thought she was existing in a dream. A dream better than her fantasy, for this man was doing things to her that her fantasy had never thought of. She opened her mouth to receive his tongue and wound her arms around his neck. His hand slid from her waist, grabbed her buttocks and squeezed them hard. She could feel his penis stiff in his trousers. She straightened slightly and his finger inside her shot up to the top of her vagina, dancing in her juices. The feel of his hand gripping her bare arse and his finger moving deeply inside her, electrified her. Her mouth opened wider to take more of his tongue and her shaking legs braced themselves open. He let another finger slide inside her and his thumb began to gently ease backwards and forwards on her clitoris, another finger travelling round seeking the area between her labia and her anus. He pulled her closer to him so that his fingers could gradually massage that now-wet virgin hole. Slowly, with infinite care, he entered her back orifice. When her whole body was impaled, dancing on his fingers and thumbs, he undid his trousers and let his penis graze her thighs between the stocking tops and her bare flesh. Kissing her lips, he pulled down the lace and leather of her basque, exposing her breasts. Then, with the artistry of years, he fondled her erect nipples. He turned her so that his cock was rubbing between her legs at the top of her thighs, making her squirm with desire.

Jeanine lost all control. Her entire body was vibrating. The only thing she was aware of was the touch of Gerry's hands on her breasts, the touch of his lips on her mouth, his tongue winding, stabbing at hers, and the tip of his prick sliding beside his hand between her legs, touching the outer lips of her sex. She was breathing faster and faster, inhaling and exhaling in short fast gasps. She moved her legs, her hips, her muscles in a desperate effort to grip him, to take him, every bit of him, right up to the hilt, but Gerry had every intention of suspending that moment of intense pleasure. She wanted to lie down with her hips arched, her legs open, and feel his cock entering her, feel its stiffness, its throbbing hardness pushing through and past her soft juicy open wetness, touching every tingling, quivering nerve ending; every ridge, every crevice, filling up every space, every nook, within her body.

'I am going to take you,' he said, and she almost came at the sound of his voice, 'but not yet.' And with that he pinioned her arms behind her back and lowered her into the armchair. He removed his shirt and trousers, then stroked her body. Kneeling between her legs, making sure her hands were fastened tightly under her buttocks and forcing her hips to remain raised, he bent his head and began to lick the top of her legs.

Jeanine took short sharp breaths of joy as the stiffness of his tongue explored her softness. She closed her eyes in delight, enjoying the fusion of their flesh. Sensations she had never known washed in waves over and through her body. Then, without warning, giving no signal whatsoever, he took her. His prick charged through her fiery, sweet-smelling, enticing flesh and the whole of her body lifted. Rigid with desire she clasped her hands around his neck, her legs fastening around his hips, and she raised herself higher. She met him, leaving no gap between his belly and hers. They were completely one, meeting wherever they joined and every pore, every vibrant particle of themselves, exploded simultaneously.

So did the flashbulbs. Both of them were so lost in their excitement, their exquisite feelings of complete oneness, they had not seen the stranger enter. Dressed in paramilitary clothing and wearing a balaclava to hide his face, the man carried on taking photographs until Gerry, realising what was happening, jumped up naked. Jeanine fell to one side in a crumpled heap. The man, taking his camera with him, sped from the room, up the stairs and through the main door which he had left open.

'Jeez!' exclaimed Gerry. Then, noticing Jeanine crying, rushed over and gathered her up in his arms. Gerry wiped her eyes, noticing how beautifully rounded they were, and how the tears increased their luminous blue.

'My God,' she said. 'Oh Gerry, I am sorry, very sorry.'

'Are you?' he said. 'Why? I'm not. I wouldn't have missed that for the world. Why are you sorry, Jeanine? Because we made love, or because we were found out?'

Jeanine said nothing, suspecting his assessment was correct. She was not sorry he had touched her, stroked her, sucked her, entered her. She had loved and squirmed and moaned happily through every minute of it. And, though trembling with the shock of discovery, a part of her longed to do it again.

Gerry stood up and poured out belated glasses of champagne. He handed one to Jeanine. 'Drink,' he said.

Gingerly, with a shaking hand, Jeanine sipped at the bubbles while Gerry stroked her hair. 'What am I going to tell my Confessor?' she asked.

'Your Confessor!' He had no idea she was religious.

'Yes.'

'You'll think of something,' said Gerry.

Gerry had no idea she was referring to Petrov. If he had, he might have given her different advice.

Jeanine turned her tear-stained face towards him and shivered. 'Unfortunately that won't be good enough. It has to be the truth. I have to tell him the truth.'

Gerry was not to know she shivered from fear, not from cold. He covered her with the black cape, then kissed her lips.

'What was that man doing here?' she asked. 'And taking photographs. For what reason?'

'I don't know,' Gerry replied, 'but I think we'd better get dressed fast. And Jeanine, put something less sexy on.'

Jeanine went into her bedroom, washed, then wrapped herself in her pure silk, deep-yellow dressing-gown.

In sombre mood, Gerry dressed. He thought the whole

episode very strange. A mass of thoughts whirled around in his brain. The topmost one was that perhaps Auralie had organised the photographer. But why? He was still pondering on this when he heard his wife's voice calling out to him.

Gerry turned as if nothing had happened, greeted her with a kiss and offered her a glass of champagne. 'I'm afraid I woke Jeanine,' he said cryptically.

Gerry was angry. He had a strong feeling he had been outwitted. He knew how, but he didn't know why. He was determined to find out. Auralie was up to something. He felt he had for the moment lost his bargaining position. Now, more than ever, he was determined to watch her being screwed. And he would spank her bottom, not just for having the plump young nun, not just for depriving him of the pleasure of seeing her make love to Jeanine, but for having so rudely and crudely had the photographer crash in upon him and Jeanine. He would have his revenge. But first thing in the morning he would telephone a firm of private detectives his father often used. He would have Auralie followed night and day. He would find out what she was up to. Jeanine wandered into the sitting-room.

'Ah, Jeanine, I was just telling Auralie that we couldn't stay here,' said Gerry, downing his drink.

An amazed Auralie was about to protest when she saw the set of Gerry's mouth. She thought it wiser to say nothing.

'It's OK,' said Auralie, 'because I came to tell Gerry that everything has been done. All the little nonsense has been cleared up and we can go home.'

Gerry took his wife's elbow and guided her from the room. He did not attempt to kiss Jeanine goodbye. Auralie waved as husband and wife departed. Jeanine poured out the last glass of champagne. She drank it quickly, then burst into tears again.

5

It took Jeanine a couple of weeks to recover from the events
of the night when Gerry turned up unexpectedly and made
love to her. Jeanine thought of it as making love; it seemed to
her so much more than a quick screw, or lust grabbed at and
satisfied. The poignancy of that evening hit her constantly. It
caught her unawares in the daytime, but at night she curled
up in her lonely bed, put her hands between her legs, held her
golden mound and dreamed. In her mind she revisited the
touch of Gerry's hand. The feel of his mouth. The exquisite
thrill of his penis travelling upwards between her thighs, then
suddenly entering her swollen, tingling lustful sex. She let her
fingers drift inside her vulva and gently play herself to sleep,
banishing all thoughts of the photographer who had so rudely
interrupted their enjoyment.

Although she had been deeply involved in the running of
the hotel she often wondered what would happen if the photographs suddenly turned up and somebody she knew, or
somebody who knew her, saw them. It was a constant worry.
The thought of her Confessor ever seeing them caused her
great angst. 'Stay in the world and be tempted,' he had said.
And she had fallen at the first hurdle. The experience had left
her divided; part of her was joyful, another part deeply
ashamed. Gerry had telephoned a couple of times but she had
made excuses not to talk to him. She longed for him more than
ever now that she had been possessed by him, but she knew
it was a sin. Far worse than coveting her neighbour's wife, she

coveted her cousin's husband. And she dreaded telling Petrov.

Neatly dressed in a soft, deep-apricot linen suit, her hair once again curled back in a bun, Jeanine stood at reception checking the bookings. She looked elegant and calm. Nobody would have guessed the passion, the eroticism or the angst that raged within her. She smiled. She was pleased. Open three weeks and the hotel was nearly full. She watched the three Misses from Nebraska leaving for their sight-seeing. They were followed by a Mr and Mrs Harry Kreitz from Brooklyn, talking about Buckingham Palace and the Tower of London, and a rather snooty young English couple discussing shopping in Knightsbridge.

She noticed Terry, the handsome floor waiter who, for the moment, was acting as doorman. He was carrying suitcases, closely followed by a pear-shaped woman with a loud American voice. Terry directed her towards the desk. A smile of satisfaction crossed Jeanine's face. The place looked wonderful and she had managed to find the most attractive staff. In particular Terry and the two young chambermaids, Jill and Mary. She had taken them on two weeks' trial and they had shown themselves to be hard workers. The rooms were extra well cleaned; shining and polished exactly as she wanted. Of all her staff, Jeanine decided that in these three she had found absolute treasures. She made a mental note to discover which agency had sent them; they would receive a letter of thanks. Her next priority was to find a husband and wife team to work as cook and head porter. She was making do with a temporary chef who was passable but not wonderful.

The wide-arsed American woman with tightly permed, dyed blue hair approached the desk. 'I'm Mrs Maclean,' she said to Jeanine, while smiling at Terry.

It was obvious to Jeanine that Mrs Maclean had taken a fancy to Terry. He was good-looking and charming and managed to be neither servile nor pompous. Mrs Maclean was totally captivated. Terry was good for business.

Jeanine settled the formalities with Mrs Maclean, then Terry took her luggage and escorted her to her room. Jeanine asked Terry to return immediately as she wanted him to help on reception. She retreated into her office but found it difficult to settle. She had urgent calls to make but thought of reasons not to make them. She walked to and fro, from filing cabinet to desk, doing nothing in particular. She thought she was thirsty and made herself a cup of coffee. She drank it but was still unsatisfied; her feeling of wanting, a feeling akin to frustration, lingered. She thought she was hungry but could not decide what it was she wanted to eat. There was a knock on the door. Terry came in.

'There's a gentleman, a Mr Sawyer, outside,' said Terry. 'Says he hasn't booked, but wants the first-floor front room. You've got a query beside it in the book, so I thought I'd better ask.'

Jeanine checked her watch. It was almost one o'clock. She had been asked to hold the room until noon for one of Petrov's clients. He had neither arrived nor confirmed. Jeanine peeped out to assess the guest for herself and saw a tall, beautifully dressed, distinguished-looking man.

'Exactly our sort of client,' Jeanine said to Terry. 'Let Mr Sawyer have it,' she added, noticing how well Terry's uniform fitted him and at the same time observing that his crotch appeared to be bulging. As he turned and left her office she was suddenly aware of the neatness of his backside. Jeanine chided herself. She did not normally look at men's crotches or the shape of their bottoms so why should her attention have drifted in that direction? She seemed to be seeing sex everywhere. And then she realised she was tingling between her legs. Her feeling of frustration was sexual. That was the last thing she wanted to feel in the middle of a working day. Had Terry made her feel sexy or was it merely left over from the night before and dreams of Gerry? She sat down, squeezing the muscles of her legs together. This did nothing to abate the tingling. It increased it. Perhaps, she thought, if she lifted her skirt and gave herself a little rub that would satisfy her craving. Or should she go downstairs to her own apartment, find her dildo and give herself a good going-over? No, there was not enough time for that, but she made a mental note that in future she would leave a vibrator in her desk drawer so when she felt like it she could play with herself.

Jeanine lifted her skirt and twined her fingers under the elastic of her white silk panties. She was swollen and aching. The feel of her cool fingers against her tingling sex was exactly what she needed. Her thoughts began to sail away. Happy thoughts. Sexual thoughts. Gerry with his head between her legs, sucking where she was now stroking. She saw his shaft upright beside her. She saw herself take it in her mouth. She felt his hands touching her breasts, rolling her nipples between his fingers.

She was very near to coming when the telephone rang beside her. She picked up the receiver.

'Yes,' she said, in as formal a voice as she could muster.

'Jeanine.'

It was Petrov's voice. With her hands still inside her knickers, Jeanine froze.

'Yes,' she answered, breathlessly.

'Jeanine, I am looking at some photographs of you being screwed.'

Jeanine's heart dropped like a stone. Petrov was looking at the photographs. And he was not mincing his words. Petrov, usually so urbane, was using the vernacular. And she found it thrilling.

'I can see a large prick going up inside your very wet pussy,' he said. 'I can see you wearing outrageous clothes: high-heeled boots and black stockings, and a leather and lace basque which is not covering your breasts. Your naked breasts, Jeanine, are spilling out over the top and being sucked. Your nipples are in a man's mouth, Jeanine. His cock is rammed up inside your pussy, Jeanine . . .' Petrov paused for a moment.

Jeanine thought it extraordinary. She had been terrified of Petrov discovering those pictures, but now, as he was talking, she found that his words were stimulating her. Far from remaining frozen, as he spoke she began to fondle herself again. She let the tips of her fingers edge along her labia, exciting her clitoris.

'I told you to tell me everything,' Petrov continued. 'I told you to tell me if you felt carnal desire. Why didn't you?'

'I don't know,' said Jeanine.

'That is hardly an answer, Jeanine. I think you did know. You are dressed in highly erotic clothing. In fact, it looks as if you were prepared to be screwed. Waiting for it. What worries me is why you didn't tell me.'

'I don't know. Oh, I'm sorry, Petrov. I'm sorry.'

'Sorry. You are sorry. That is not good enough, Jeanine. I told you I would know if ever you had those desires. And I suspected they were beginning to form within you. I needed to know. And I told you I would know if you gave into those desires. And I told you you would have to be punished.'

'Punished?' Jeanine whispered, hoarsely.

'Yes. Punished for having a cock inside you, ramming you, screwing you, and for not telling me you wanted it.'

'What sort of punishment?' she asked.

'I will decide after you have been to confession,' said Petrov. 'But as your sin was sexual your punishment will have to be, too.'

Jeanine's mouth had gone dry, but her sex was not. It was soaking wet. She began to squirm, working the muscles in her buttocks up and down, as her fingers went round and round. Petrov spoke again, enunciating clearly, describing in his deeply hypnotic voice the photographs he was looking at. It made her more sexual, more alive, more wanting. She let out a series of short, sharp excited gasps.

'What are you doing, Jeanine?' he asked.

Jeanine paused. She had to think of something quickly.

'Drinking hot coffee,' she lied.

'Are you? It doesn't sound like that,' he said.

Jeanine noisily picked up and put down her coffee cup.

'I am,' she said.

'Now, aren't you ashamed of yourself?' he asked.

'Yes,' she replied, pushing her fingers deeper within her own body.

'I want to see you,' said Petrov. 'You must come to confession.'

'I'm very busy,' she replied. She did not want to face him. Not yet.

'Jeanine, do you want to be a member of my order or not?'

'Yes,' she said.

'Then you must do as I say. You must come to the monastery today. This is a serious situation, Jeanine. I have recognised the man in the photograph. It's Auralie's husband, Gerry. It is, isn't it?'

'Yes,' she whispered.

'Sin! And sin must be punished.'

'Petrov, I can't come today. I can't.'

'Why not?'

'I have interviews. More staff to take on. I've still got to find a cook and head porter.'

'Don't worry about that. I'll send you two people from here.'

'Thank you, Petrov.'

'Thank yous are not necessary. You're forgetting that I have a stake in your business. I want it to succeed. So you'll come to confession today?'

'No, I can't come until the end of the week. The weekend, I promise.'

'Very well. And you can expect Leslie and Pierre some time this evening.'

Petrov put the telephone down. Leslie and Pierre? Who were they? She didn't know them. How long had they been at Petrov's? She had so wanted a nice roly-poly female cook and a big burly man as head porter. Now she was getting two men. Ah, well, at least he had not decided to send her his manservant, Jackson, or his housekeeper, Mrs Klowski. They both terrified her. Jackson so big and bold and black and imposing; Mrs Klowski so grim and curt and efficient.

She was greatly relieved that she didn't have to face Petrov today. What could she say to him now that he knew everything? She could not make excuses. He had the evidence in his hands. Punishment. What had he meant by punishment? Sexual punishment? Her mind conjured up a number of bizarre visions. She remembered punishment at school. That had meant bending over; having a cane across her bare bottom. Surely he could not mean that. She felt a strange thrill at the idea of bending over for Petrov. She conjured up an image of being made to lie face down unclothed on his long refectory table: of him touching her, his large hands spreading over and fondling her naked arse. He had something in his hand. What was it? The image was fading. Jeanine tried desperately to hold on to it, to recapture what she had seen in his hand. What was in his hand? It appeared to be a leather dildo. It had things hanging from it. Leather strips. Leather thongs. Then she realised it was a whip that Petrov was holding. He was caressing her bare bottom and murmuring, 'Punishment . . . Punishment.'

He was stroking her with the leather. He was trailing it along her body. He started at her feet, tracking her ankles, calves, knees, thighs; the wisps of leather touched feather-light along her sensitive skin between her knees and her . . . She hesitated. Even in her mind she hesitated . . . *her pubis*.

Petrov parted her bottom-cheeks and let her feel the fine slip of the leather on her soft hidden flesh. He trailed it between her legs. Her sex responded to its touch. She tried to grab the thin strip of leather with her muscles. And then searing, delicious pain swept across her rounded cheeks. Across her raised bare bottom. He stroked her, and with his tongue licked the mark he had left. He seared her again. She lay open, excited, and wanting more.

Was this his danger? Was this the feeling about him that always left her bewildered? Was it the threat of physical punishment and the possibility she might enjoy it? She wondered whether Auralie knew that she had made love to Gerry. She hoped not. She would let Petrov do anything to her rather than have Auralie know what she had been up to with her husband. But how did Petrov get the photographs? A terrible thought occurred to Jeanine. Had Gerry organised it? Was he secretly in league with Petrov?

There was another knock on her office door. Jeanine hurriedly pulled down her skirt. It was Terry. Spruce, neat Terry, smiling at her through his heavy-lidded, half-closed eyes. He was, she decided, definitely sexy. But he was smiling at her as if he could see through her clothes, see her nakedness, and feel, almost smell, her sexuality. Terry asked her if she would take over on reception as there were more arrivals and suitcases needed to be taken upstairs.

What Jeanine hadn't realised was that Auralie had been standing beside Petrov when he made the telephone call. Dressed in her skin-hugging black leather suit, Auralie leant against the refectory table in the main hall of Petrov's magnificent Tudor manor house. She was feeling extremely pleased with herself. Auralie looked at Petrov as he replaced the receiver but he gave no indication as to how he felt.

He was a bull of a man, commanding and impressive, with a great barrel chest and a big-featured impassive face. His black hair, greying at the temples, was beautifully cut. His long fingers were well manicured. Petrov was head of the order of which he was the founding member. The manor house was his headquarters as well as his home. He was wearing a dark-green flowing cassock and, like every other member of his order, he was naked beneath his cassock.

It was Auralie who had shown the photographs to Petrov. It was her first opportunity, as most of her recent time had been spent either placating her husband or in completing the presentation for Sir Henry. The announcement of his new airline and invitations to bid for the design contract had been made the day after Gerry had seduced Jeanine. The contract became her priority and everything else had been put on hold. The presentation to Sir Henry would take place the afternoon of the following day. Now Auralie's concentration was able to wander in other directions.

Auralie spread out the whole series of twenty-four colour photographs on the table, where Petrov and eight of his acolytes, four men and four women, were seated. Each man, except Petrov, had his wrists and ankles bound by leather thongs to his chair whilst the women sat completely unrestrained. Everyone wore their habit hoods up and sat very upright. To see the photographs properly they had to bend forward. The women found this easier to do than the men. One by one Petrov asked them what they thought. One by one they made comments on the beauty of Jeanine's breasts, the size of Auralie's husband's cock, and the ease with which it appeared to be entering Jeanine's pussy.

Auralie was feeling turned-on despite herself. They were very good photographs. Her husband and her cousin had performed well and it was quite obvious that they were totally involved with each other's body. So much so that Terry had been able to take a whole roll of film before either of them had realised he was in the room. Terry was a very clever young man. Auralie smiled maliciously. She enjoyed the idea that Terry was now employed as Jeanine's waiter. Every time he looked at Jeanine, so nice and sweet and prissy, he would remember her as he had seen her the night he took the photographs. Erotic and abandoned, her legs open, her sex on display, her breasts being sucked. For Auralie's purposes the photographs had proved ten times better than she had anticipated. Her sweet virginal cousin was dressed like a high-class harlot. Leather and lace, stockings and boots. Auralie wondered what had possessed Jeanine to wear them. And how long had she had them? Who had she got them for? Did Jeanine have a secret lover that Auralie was unaware of? Auralie thought it unlikely; her cousin seemed far too straightforward for such a devious notion to have entered her head. On the other hand, Jeanine had refrained from confessing anything to Petrov for weeks. Had she bought those clothes for herself? Surely not.

Auralie searched Petrov's face as he looked at the photographs. She tried to discover some essence of feeling there – pleasure, anger, disappointment. Auralie knew Petrov took a keen interest in Jeanine but she did not know how far that interest extended.

Petrov's face remained impassive. He had no intention of allowing Auralie, or anyone else, to know that he had wanted to introduce the virginal widow to the delights of his love-making. He was therefore not at all pleased by the sight of Jeanine being screwed by Auralie's husband. Nevertheless, it had given him an instant erection. Petrov reached out a hand to the nearest female acolyte and indicated her to stand beside him. He slid a hand under her dark-green habit, grabbing her naked pussy.

'Made you wet, eh, Sister Chloe, seeing these photographs?' he said.

'Yes,' said his young novice.

'Good. Now get down and suck my cock,' he ordered.

He was sitting in the main chair at the head of the table. He spread his legs. Sister Chloe let down her hood, revealing a mass of tumbling, softly curling, red hair, then removed her habit. Petrov ran a hand over her tiny rosebud breasts, her neat waist, her slim boyish hips, lingering on her titian-red pubes. Looking at the other acolytes but not at her he let a finger trail into her vulva, toying with her clitoris. The novice wiggled her hips, her arms hanging limply by her side. Her breasts were thrust forward and there was a slight smile of triumph on her thick pouting and painted lips.

Today she was the chosen one. She wanted everyone to watch Petrov play with her. She licked her lips as the others stared at her. She knew they were becoming aroused; she could see by the way they began squirming. Petrov's finger never fully entered her, just kept beckoning her sex to open wider and wider. Sister Chloe moved her hips forward in tiny concentric circles as her inner lips unfurled. She was very excited.

Petrov dropped his hand. Without saying a word she knelt down between his knees, went under his cassock and took his large, thick, stiff shaft into her mouth.

Petrov turned his attention back to the photographs and, apart from jerking his cock in her mouth from time to time, ignored her.

'What did Jeanine say?' Auralie asked Petrov.

'She'll come at the end of the week,' he replied. 'But I think I'll make sure she comes before then.'

'How will you do that?' asked Auralie.

'I'm not sure. But I'll start by sending her Pierre and Leslie,' Petrov said. He pressed the intercom bell beside him and instructed the pair to come to him as soon as they had finished what they were doing.

'They won't like that,' said Auralie.

'I would remind you, Auralie,' said Petrov giving her a withering look, 'that my word here is law. Pierre and Leslie will be quite happy as long as I don't part them.'

Petrov was peeved. Gerry and Jeanine. That had not been a combination he had thought of. He was so utterly convinced that he would be the first person to take Jeanine that the photographs had taken his breath away.

Petrov had been waiting a long time to hear Jeanine's confession. Waiting to hear her tell him how her body was opening. How she was feeling lust and how she had rediscovered her sexuality. He had felt a change in her. He knew she had been masturbating. He wanted her to admit it to him. He wanted to hear her lovely soft voice, fearful, explain it to him. He wanted to make her use crude words. He wanted to hear her say, 'I was wanking. I put a finger in my pussy and played with myself.' He got harder just thinking about it and gave the girl who was sucking him a hard jab with his prick. All the things he had planned had been ruined by Auralie's jealousy. He was annoyed with her and would have to think up a punishment for her, too.

The girl between his legs was softly stroking his thighs as he had trained her to do. He inched forward so that he could feel her fingers trace round to his bottom-hole. He thought of Jeanine again. He had wanted to invite her to understand the needs of the body. Her body and his body. He would get Jeanine to feel his prick. Get her to take it in her mouth and suck it.

The girl under the table was now kissing his balls. She had got his large loose sac in her hands and was massaging his testicles between her fingers. It was bliss. Her tongue was licking along his thick shaft; exactly as he wanted Jeanine to do. He pressed his hand onto the hidden girl's head so that the whole of his cock was suddenly rammed to the back of her mouth. He moved his knees so he could feel her naked breasts rippling along his skin.

He had planned to open Jeanine's legs, run his tongue along her thighs, push it between her labia then lick her clit. He was still going to do it. He was going to suck her, screw her, and then tie her up and whip her. He was going to enjoy giving Jeanine her punishment.

'Is there anybody you want to screw now you're here?' Petrov asked Auralie.

Auralie looked down the line of male acolytes.

'Who's that?' she asked, eyeing a tall thin young man with pale eyelashes who was busy studying a close-up photograph of Jeanine.

'Brother Geoffrey,' said Petrov. 'Beautiful, isn't he? Enigmatically beautiful. I found him on a recent visit to Russia. He's come here in place of Brother Terry.'

Auralie said nothing. Terry had been one of Petrov's favourite acolytes but at her instigation he had announced his intention to take an extended leave from the order. Under

Petrov's rules everyone was free to come and go as they chose, but Petrov's word remained law. Petrov did not know of Auralie's little subterfuge to use Terry for her own devious purposes. If Petrov had known he would not have approved. Auralie was paying Terry, Jill and Mary good money to achieve Jeanine's downfall.

'I'll have him,' said Auralie. She moved Geoffrey's chair a little further back from the table. As he was unable to do it for himself, Auralie slipped back his hood and a mop of pale gingery hair fell forward over his pale-blue eyes and fine aquiline nose. She lifted his cassock and saw that his penis was short and thick and quite erect. Then she hitched up her short leather skirt, revealing her naked body and the dark triangle covering her sex.

Petrov looked at Auralie and decided what her punishment would be. He would make her shave her pubis. She had told him that Gerry did not like the feel of a stubbly pussy. But Petrov decided he would insist, and make her keep a thin closely-cropped line along its lips. She would have to explain that stubble to Gerry. That, thought Petrov, would go a little way towards reducing his anger. He knew how devious Auralie could be. He had long suspected that she was jealous of Jeanine. Now the photographs proved it. For all her protestations of innocence, Petrov supected that Auralie had engineered Gerry's seduction of Jeanine. She had organised it, just as she had organised a photographer to burst in upon them during their lovemaking. He did not believe that Auralie herself had taken the photographs. She was a very clever designer, but put a camera in her hands and either the flash did not work or the whole thing would be out of focus. No, the photographs he was looking at were highly professional. He wondered who had taken them. Sooner or later he would find out. Auralie was a compulsive liar but after her objective was achieved she forgot which lie she had told. It would be then that he would discover the truth.

Petrov watched Auralie straddle Geoffrey. With her back to the novice she positioned his cock against her sex. She hovered over his prick, then noticed Margaret sitting opposite.

'Come here, Sister Margaret,' said Auralie. The plump girl rose from her chair. 'Stand behind him!'

Margaret did as she was told.

'Put your hands over his shoulders and whilst I screw him play with my breasts,' said Auralie.

Still hovering, not allowing his cock to enter further than an inch, Auralie undid the buttons on her leather jacket. Margaret took hold of her exposed breasts, tweaking Auralie's nipples between her fingers. With his wrists and ankles still bound to his chair Brother Geoffrey was unable to do a thing except allow his stiff member to be teased by Auralie's sex-lips gliding backwards and forwards. Auralie positioned her hands so that she was clasping the insides of her open thighs whilst kneading Geoffrey's balls with the backs of her fingers. Tensing her buttock muscles, then relaxing them, Auralie lowered herself a fraction. She squeezed Geoffrey's throbbing prick and felt it wanting to thrust inside her. Then, with one violent and fast gesture, she took the whole of him up to the hilt and screwed him furiously.

Petrov leant over and grabbed the breasts of the girl who was sucking his cock.

'Get up,' he said, 'and sit on me.'

Sister Chloe did as she was told. She sat with her back to Petrov and lowered herself on to him. He pointed to the other girls, indicating which girl should go to which man, and told them to take up the same position. Then his hands came up and fondled Chloe's pert little breasts. Soon every tethered man around the table had a woman on his lap. Every woman was riding each man like a horse. Up and down. Up and down.

Auralie left in her German sports car half an hour later. She unkeyed her dashboard, put on a tape and let loud music flow over her. She was disgruntled. Petrov had finally shown his feelings. She had sensed that he was not pleased with the photographs of Jeanine and Gerry. Not that he had said anything up front. No. But he had ordered her to shave her pussy, knowing full well Gerry hated that. He also knew it was not the moment to upset Gerry. It was Petrov's command that she shave her pussy that made Auralie realise he was annoyed with her. The contract was not yet hers. But Petrov was head of the order and what he said went. She knew she would have to do it but it could wait for a day or so. Olga arrived tomorrow and Olga liked a naked mound. But would she like a thin line of stubble close to her mouth? Perhaps not. But to hell with him. To hell with Gerry, too. Tomorrow she would be in Olga's arms. And tomorrow they would be making their presentation.

Brother Leslie stood in the main hall waiting for Petrov. He was a pale, puny little man who was going bald and the habit he was wearing looked far too big for him. It exposed a studded collar fixed around his neck, but covered the chains that fell from a ring on the collar front, down his chest, around and under his balls then up to a fastening ring at the back of the collar. Brother Leslie's many tattoos came into view. He had been a merchant sailor, and once a ship's cook.

Idly, he picked up the photographs still on the table.

'Nice,' he said, when Petrov appeared.

'Put them in that large black envelope over there,' said Petrov.

'Looks like Jeanine,' said Brother Leslie, clanking slightly as he moved.

'It is,' said Petrov.

'Oh!' exclaimed Leslie, 'And I thought she was so . . . what's the word? Pure.'

'She's your new employer,' said Petrov.

'What!' exclaimed Brother Leslie.

At that moment a heftily built black woman with short cropped hair sashayed into the hall. She had a bunch of keys on a chain round the middle of her habit.

'What's he looking at?' she said to Petrov.

Sister Pierre was from Martinique. She had the lilt of the island in her booming voice. 'If it's a picture of a naked woman I'll give him a good whipping.'

Brother Leslie dropped the photograph hurriedly. 'No, madam, no it's not,' he said quickly.

Sister Pierre picked up the offending picture.

'You know what this means, Brother Leslie, don't you?' said Sister Pierre.

Brother Leslie cowered away from her.

'Sister Pierre,' said Petrov. 'Brother Leslie will have to wait for his punishment. He has been looking at a picture of your new employer.'

'Why? What've we done?' asked Sister Pierre.

'You've done nothing. It's what I want you to do,' said Petrov. 'Have a look at these.'

He showed her some more of the photographs.

'It looks like Jeanine,' said the big woman.

'It is Jeanine,' replied Petrov. 'And I am very angry with her. What I want you to do is go to her hotel. She needs a cook and a head porter. You, Brother Leslie, will be her cook . . .'

'But Petrov . . .' protested Brother Leslie, 'you know I'm the worst cook in the world.'

'Exactly,' said Petrov. 'I did say I was angry with her. And you, Sister Pierre, will become her Head Porter. She will get what she wants but not what she's expecting. She will protest of course. She will say you're not suitable but you will have to persuade her otherwise. If she proves difficult, as I suspect she will, you will show these photographs. She will have no option but to employ you.'

'What has she done?' asked Sister Pierre.

'This is what she's done,' said Petrov, pointing to the snaps. 'Screwing. Screwing Auralie's husband. She was supposed to tell *me* when she felt sexy. Confess. But she didn't. Not only that but she is now making excuses not to come and confess. She says she'll come at the weekend but I want her to come sooner. You will be instrumental in making her do that. I suggest you bide your time and punish Brother Leslie, as appropriate, in the kitchen of Jeanine's hotel.'

Sister Pierre smiled salaciously. Brother Leslie lowered his head. He knew there would be no mercy tonight. Petrov gave the two of them some further instructions, then they changed from their habit into ordinary clothes. Brother Leslie wore a polo-necked jumper and a smart black suit, but it managed not to look smart on him. It was too baggy. It had to be to cover his chains. Sister Pierre also wore a suit. At first glance it seemed fairly normal and would do perfectly as a head porter's uniform. It had a long frock coat which covered most of her short white shirt and trousers, the latter more like fishermen's waders. They ended at the top of the thigh and were held up by long elastic suspenders. Beneath the coat, from waist to thigh, she was completely naked. Her massive dark-brown buttocks wobbled free. Her black, tightly-curled hairy sex was unconfined. Whenever she chose, Brother Leslie had access to her pussy. She chose often and in the most unlikely places. If Brother Leslie desisted for any reason other than her order then his red-striped bottom received more red stripes at the earliest opportunity. Petrov drove them both to the local station and put them on the London train. Sister Pierre was looking forward to their train journey.

It was more than an hour later when they arrived at Jeanine's hotel. Jeanine was sitting in reception. Terry was off duty when they walked in, which was just as well because Leslie and Pierre had no idea he was working there. They, like Petrov, thought he was on holiday in Paris.

'Petrov sent us. We're Leslie and Pierre,' they announced to Jeanine's instant horror. She stared at them both and wondered which was which. They were hardly her idea of a roly-poly couple. More like the Odd Couple. Or Laurel and Hardy. At any other time Jeanine might have found them amusing, but not when she saw her business under attack. The woman looked more like a slave overseer than a cook, and the man looked barely capable of anything, let alone carrying heavy suitcases. What had Petrov sent her?

Sister Pierre could see what Jeanine was thinking. She considered them unsuitable. Exactly as Petrov had predicted. A couple of smartly dressed guests passed by. They looked askance at the odd pair standing beside Jeanine. Jeanine thought it better to take them into her office. There she could tell them nicely that neither of them were what she was looking for.

'Follow me,' said Jeanine.

'I'm Pierre,' Sister Pierre announced in her booming but lilting voice when safely seated in Jeanine's office.

'And I'm Leslie,' squeaked the other.

Jeanine wanted to die. She thought back to earlier in the day and her feeling of self satisfaction with her staff. But these two were a joke. There was no way she was going to hire them. They looked odd. They felt odd. There was something distinctly peculiar about them. Jeanine did not know what it was but she felt it in her bones.

'We've come for the jobs. Cook and head porter,' said Sister Pierre. 'I'm the head porter. He's the cook.'

Jeanine stared at them. Why had Petrov sent them, when they seemed so unsuitable? He had a stake in the business. He wanted it to succeed. That's what he had said. And now he sends her these two clowns. Perhaps he didn't realise but Jeanine knew instinctively that to employ them, either of them, would be a disaster.

'I'm sorry,' said Jeanine, 'but . . .'

Sister Pierre did not give her time to finish the sentence. She stood up to her full six foot and laid the black envelope on Jeanine's desk.

'Petrov said you might need some persuading,' the big woman said. She opened the envelope and one by one laid the photographs of Jeanine being screwed by Gerry on the table.

'They're very good, aren't they,' said Brother Leslie, innocently.

Jeanine wanted to disappear. She would have been grateful if she could have vanished into thin air. Her secret self was unveiled. Her secret fantasies had been recorded on film for all to see. Yes, the photographs were good. Every nuance of her body, her sex, Gerry's cock, was captured. Intimately, perfectly focused.

'Petrov said he didn't think you'd want Auralie to see these,' said Sister Pierre, menacingly.

'No,' said Jeanine with a composure she was not feeling.

'We can start straight away,' stated Sister Pierre, simply. 'I've got my black suit and that'll do for now. Do you have a cap for my head?'

'I might have,' said Jeanine. She knew she was beaten. She would have to take these two whether she wanted to or not.

She unlocked a cupboard and took out a variety of doorman's hats. Auralie had had a number made in different sizes. 'You'd better try these on. Find one that fits you.'

'I don't really need a uniform,' said Brother Leslie, cheerfully. 'Just an apron and an ordinary chef's hat will do me.'

Sister Pierre found a hat that almost fitted her large head. 'This is fine,' she said.

'You'll show me the kitchen,' said Brother Leslie.

'Yes,' said Jeanine. She tried to smile. She must put a good face on it. Perhaps her instincts were wrong. They might turn out to be brilliant. Unorthodox but brilliant. Some small voice within her doubted it but she had little option but to take them.

Sister Pierre went out into the hall and took up her position by the door. Jeanine took Brother Leslie to the kitchen. He looked at all the paraphernalia and declared he was delighted. Jeanine looked at him and wished she were somewhere else. For one night of pleasure she was taking a lot of punishment. Punishment. Was this what Petrov had meant? No, surely not. He said it would be sexual. Jeanine suddenly felt alone and isolated. She could not talk to Auralie about this. Nor could she talk to Gerry or Petrov. And her mother was still on her Mediterranean cruise. Well, the place was running quite smoothly. She would go to bed and by the morning everything would look very different.

6

Auralie put three bottles of Krug into the office refrigerator. It was her favourite champagne and she knew today she would have something to celebrate. Having done that, she glanced at the clock, saw the time and slipped out of the jeans, sweater, bra and panties she wore in the workroom and took a quick shower. She had had the bathroom put in so that she could transform herself at a moment's notice.

Hanging in the closet was her new, fabulously expensive white cashmere suit. She had bought it especially for the occasion. Today was the day she and Olga would make their presentation to De Bouys Airlines. Today would be the day she would get the contract. She couldn't fail. Her designs were the best, the very best she had ever done. They were bright and innovative and, besides, she held the ace: she was Sir Henry's daughter-in-law. The telephone rang. She let it ring. Moments later there was a knock on the door.

'Mrs de Bouys. Mrs de Bouys.' It was her secretary's voice. She sounded extremely agitated.

'Yes?' queried Auralie.

'Madame Olga is on the phone. She says it is very important.'

Auralie leisurely picked up her extension.

'Auralie, today is postponed,' said Olga, mysteriously but with a hint of mischief in her voice.

'What!' exclaimed Auralie.

'I've just heard from Sir Henry's secretary. Apparently he's stopped off in Rome. Some urgent business.'

'But . . .' said Auralie.

'The girl said he'll be ringing her later. She expects him in England tonight so there's a possibility of tonight or tomorrow morning. We just have to wait.'

'That's terrible news,' said Auralie.

'Not really, *chérie*,' purred Olga. 'I'll pick you up in ten minutes and we can go to the apartment. I've given Sir Henry's secretary the number. She can ring us there.'

Auralie immediately dispensed with her panties, brassière and the white cashmere suit. She took down another set of clothes and over her bare, pert, upright breasts she put on and buttoned up a heavy, translucent slub-silk blouse. She stepped into a black leather skirt which hugged her hips then fell in graceful bias-cut folds over her slim, suntanned thighs. She sat down to apply some extra lipstick, enjoying the feel of the leather against her bare bottom. She put on her highest high-heels. Auralie possessed neatly pinched-in ankles and the height of her shoes accentuated their shape. She knew what Olga wanted. She knew what Olga liked. She also knew what *she* liked and wanted. Auralie wondered if Olga had brought her entire entourage with her, or only her chauffeur. If it was only the chauffeur she wondered if it would be the same one as last time.

Picking up her handbag and notebook, saying goodbye to her secretary with a reminder to put on the burglar alarm, Auralie stepped out into the smart Mayfair street as Olga's blacked-out white limousine drew alongside the kerb.

Auralie noticed the chauffeur was new, young and very beautiful. He was also very black. He held the door open for her. She smiled, inwardly. Wantonly. A certain familiar feeling, an anticipation, a sudden welcome juiciness flowed through her loins. She could feel a tingling gripping her belly, finding its release in the delicious wetness that began to flow as her sex unfurled.

Olga, attractive and patrician, was perfectly coiffured and made-up. With her long, almost beak-like nose, and eyes that slanted as if way back in her ancestry there was Mongolian blood, there was something magnificently savage about her. She held her straight mouth with a disdainful air. Tall, in her late thirties and elegantly swathed in flowing chiffon, Olga lounged back with the ease and haughtiness of the very rich and waited for Auralie to get into the car. Olga stretched out a bejewelled hand. The two women smiled at each other – a secret conspiratorial smile. The chauffeur closed the door. Before she could sit down Olga ran her hand up and over Auralie's thighs. She squeezed her bare buttocks.

'Good girl,' she said. 'Immediately accessible. I hope you are wet, *chérie*.'

Insolently, with no foreplay, Olga pitched her long and elegant forefinger into Auralie's moist, lascivious pussy. Auralie gasped audibly with the sudden rush of pleasure. Moving that finger backwards and forwards Olga quickly found the entrance to Auralie's anus and penetrated that with her ring finger. Excited and willingly impaled by her lover's fingers, Auralie squirmed. Olga gripped the whole of Auralie's black mound, forced her back against the leather seat and kissed her mouth. With every orifice plundered Auralie let out squeals of bliss. This was what she liked, what she had been waiting for. Olga's touch. Olga, who knew exactly what to do and how to do it. Olga, who could make her feel first sexy, then erotic and sensual, and finally completely abandoned.

'Miss me?' Olga asked.

Auralie turned slightly and smiled. Olga's fingers were making her wetter with every second. Auralie pushed back her shoulders so that Olga could see her erect nipples straining through the fabric of her blouse.

'Yes,' replied Auralie.

'Then show it,' said Olga.

Auralie knelt between Olga's legs, parted her chiffon skirt, revealing lacy stocking tops then Olga's total nakedness to the waist. Olga put her own hands between her legs and displayed herself, allowing Auralie to see how much she desired her. She moved her hips from side to side. Auralie rubbed a finger along Olga's swollen sex lips, softly touching the stiffening bud at the top. Olga tensed her muscles, silently asking for increased pressure on her clitoris. Auralie obeyed, and Olga gave a tiny gasp of delight and began kneading her own breasts. Auralie, looking at Olga lying lewdly on the leather seat, her legs apart, her hips raised, her sex being played with, thought she bore a greater resemblance to an expensive strumpet than the boss of a multi-million dollar industry. Auralie began to ease her fingers inwards, feeling the delight of the soft ridges, the tender juiciness of Olga's beautifully made mound.

Olga undid the buttons of Auralie's blouse. Auralie pushed her flat little tongue through her neat pearly white teeth and wiggled it suggestively. Olga narrowed her eyes and smiled like a cat. The two women stared at one another, playing a familiar game of excitation. Olga reached out a hand and grabbed at one of Auralie's hard nipples. Auralie bent her head. Olga raised her hips but Auralie did not do as she was expecting. She didn't put her tongue to Olga's ripened opening; instead, she took her legs and, with a sudden harshness, spread them further apart and stroked and kneaded the sensual flesh at the top of Olga's thighs.

Olga, panting, raised her hips higher, offering herself to Auralie who finally buried her tongue in Olga's sweet perfumed, rosy flesh. She licked her. She teased her. Olga stroked herself, letting Auralie see how wet and open she was, how much she desired the other woman. She began sliding her hips from side to side and rubbing her fingers along her swollen vulva.

Auralie moved her tongue along Olga's pussy, her nose devouring her smell. Then she bit gently on the engorged clit. Olga lay back, her hands playing with Auralie's breasts, and moaned with abandonment. Auralie put her fingers beside her tongue at Olga's private opening and waited. She felt Olga's muscles quicken with anticipation. She felt her quiver and tremble. Auralie quickly, sharply and suddenly penetrated Olga's sex with the forefinger of her right hand, her other forefinger invaded her anus. To the roar of the traffic, to the sound of engines and car horns, Auralie continued to suck on Olga's clitoris while fingering both her orifices. Then they rolled onto the floor of the car and touching each other, feeling each other, sucking each other, wallowing in each other's soft, creamy sensitive, wet, pliable sex, they played until the car came to a halt.

'Madam, we are here,' came the chauffeur's voice through the intercom.

'Two moments,' replied Olga, giving them time to adjust their clothing before alighting at Olga's short-rent apartment.

Olga did not keep a London home. When she was in England she usually stayed at Petrov's mansion in the country, but if spending more than two days in town she took short-let accommodation. The owner of her present apartment was a long-time friend. He let it to Olga, at a price, on a fairly regular basis. It suited her needs more than a protracted stay at a hotel where all her comings and goings could be watched and spied upon.

'Leave nothing in the car,' Olga told the chauffeur imperiously before she and Auralie swept into the lobby of one of Kensington's prime mansion blocks and entered a waiting elevator.

'How new is he?' Auralie asked, referring to the chauffeur.

'Kensit? Very,' said Olga.

'Has he been . . .?'

'No, *chérie*. Not yet,' Olga said wickedly as the elevator reached their floor. Nicole, the maid, opened the door before Olga rang the bell. She must have known, must have watched our arrival, thought Auralie, but then she had been with Olga for a couple of years. Olga would have given her a time. Nicole would have known exactly when to open the door.

The pretty maid in her little outfit, a black frock with frilly white apron and a little white lace cap, curtsied. Her frock was brought in tightly at the waist with a wide elastic waspie belt. She was wearing high-heeled, lace-up shoes that made her arse jut out curvaceously, emphasising her very full breasts.

'There is someone waiting for you, madam,' Nicole said as the two women entered the terracotta-coloured hall, their foot-steps echoing on the parquet floor. Olga and Auralie exchanged glances. Auralie deliberately walked behind the maid looking at her gait, her shape and her frock. She could see through the split from waist to hem loose-fitting, pink satin knickers. Auralie had a strong desire to run her hands up the maid's legs and feel the girl's bottom under the pink satin.

Olga suddenly rounded on her maid and checked that every button on her uniform was securely fastened. 'And may they stay that way, Nicole,' she added, menacingly.

'Yes, madam,' said the girl, as Olga's hand splayed and each finger pressed softly over the maid's breasts. Nicole took in a short sharp breath of pleasure and anticipation then, swallowing over a lump in her throat, she glanced shyly away and blushed deeply.

'But why is she wearing knickers?' asked Auralie maliciously.

'You're wearing knickers, Nicole!' exclaimed Olga.

'Sorry, madam,' said the maid, contritely.

'Sorry is not good enough. Let me see. Bend over and show me this instant,' ordered Olga.

Nicole bent over obediently. Her frock parted revealing the pink satin drawers.

'You know that is against the rules,' said Olga, 'and you'll have to be punished. Auralie, pull down her drawers.'

Savagely, and with some satisfaction, Auralie pulled the girl's panties down to her ankles, leaving her beautifully rounded bare bottom exposed. At that moment the new chauffeur entered the apartment. He stopped in amazement, then quickly tried to cover the sudden bulge in his trousers with the bags he was carrying. He was not quite quick enough. Both Olga and Auralie had already noticed his reaction.

'Take those bags through to the kitchen,' commanded Olga, pointing along the corridor. The chauffeur did as he was told and Olga's attention returned to Nicole.

'A bare bottom, Nicole,' said Olga, giving the maid a swinging swipe as if to reinforce her statement. The girl's cheeks immediately flushed pink. 'A bare bottom at all times.'

'Yes, madam,' said the maid, not moving from her position.

'Miss Auralie will punish you in a moment. First I want a cocktail. A Bellini. What'll you have, *chérie*?'

'The same,' Auralie replied, licking her lips in anticipation, but not for the cocktail. She desperately wanted to touch the maid's body, her breasts, the top of her thighs, between her thighs, and her bare bottom. She knew she would have her pleasure very soon.

'Go,' said Olga.

'But, madam,' said Nicole. 'You're forgetting that there is someone waiting to see you. Her name is Margaret. She's come from Monsieur Petrov. I've put her in the study.'

'Margaret? From Petrov?' queried Auralie. 'What's she like, Nicole?'

'Not very tall,' replied the maid, 'plump, quite pretty.'

A smile of recognition crossed Auralie's lips.

'You know her?' Olga asked Auralie, giving the maid a dismissive wave.

'Yes,' said Auralie.

'You have had her?' asked Olga.

'Oh, yes,' said Auralie, smiling, remembering with salacious pleasure a recent afternoon at her home.

'And . . .?' said Olga.

'She has definite potential,' replied Auralie.

Olga and Auralie walked into the drawing-room. It was magnificently furnished with exceptionally high windows leading onto a balcony overlooking the park. Auralie sat on a sage-green, velvet-covered chaise-longue. Olga stood against the black marble fireplace, absent-mindedly playing with an arrangement of brightly coloured exotic flowers and bamboo canes.

'Your designs are beautiful,' said Olga, approvingly. '*Très chic, chérie, très chic.* I am sure we will get the contract. The designs, the colours, the fabric, everything. We will win. It is impossible for us to fail. And we mustn't fail, *chérie.* Because, well you know the consequences! The de Bouys contract has to fill the gap left by Krakos. Why did he have to die? The fool! Even more of a fool to leave everything to his spoilt-brat daughter. What a thing she did to sell her father's lifetime's work. Sell all those liners. You know, not one did she keep. Not one. Not one for us to redecorate, redesign, refurbish. So we have to have Sir Henry's contract. Without it, Petolg Holdings, the factory, the company, everything is, how you say in English? A dead duck. *Finito.* Finished.'

'I know,' said Auralie.

'That girl is taking a long time to make two cocktails!' said Olga.

'Isn't she!' Auralie replied enigmatically.

'So, *chérie*. Tell me, how is your little cousin?' asked Olga.

'Fine,' said Auralie. She didn't want to think or talk about Jeanine.

'And her hotel; is that fine too?'

'I believe so,' said Auralie. She had never let Olga know the depth of her hatred for Jeanine. Nobody had any idea that she had sent two of her old lovers to be chambermaids at Jeanine's. And nobody had any idea what she had told them to do whilst they were there. 'Yes, Olga, everything with Jeanine is absolutely fine.' Auralie felt the need to reassure her.

'Petrov tells me she hasn't been to see him recently. Do you know why?'

'No.'

'Ah well, business I suppose. Perhaps you and I should pay her a visit . . .' Olga stopped abruptly and rang the bell pull. A moment later the maid appeared bringing in their cocktails. 'What have you been doing, Nicole?'

'Making the cocktails, madam.'

'Making the cock's more like it,' said Olga.

'Oh no, madam. No,' said the maid, trembling. With lowered eyes she placed the two glasses on the table.

'Nicole, I asked you a question. What have you been doing?'

'Nothing madam. Nothing.'

'You expect me to believe that? Where is my new chauffeur?'

'He's in the bathroom, madam.'

'In the bathroom! And what's he doing in the bathroom?'

'I don't know, madam.'

'You don't know! Come here.'

Shaking slightly, Nicole stood in front of Olga.

'You don't know! I think you are lying, Nicole. I think he's waiting in the bathroom to screw you.'

'No, madam, no.'

'Nicole, I think you have been showing my new chauffeur your nice fat arse. I think . . .' Olga took a bamboo cane from the vase beside her and staring into Nicole's big blue eyes began to lift the hem of the maid's frock with the stick. 'I think you have been letting him lift the hem of your skirt.'

'No, madam, oh no,' replied Nicole earnestly, wondering what else her mistress was going to do with the cane.

'Oh yes, I think you have been letting him lift your skirt, and . . .' said Olga. 'I think you have been letting him play with your pussy.' Very slowly and with great assuredness Olga let the cane trail along her maid's sex-lips, teasing, pressing on, but never entering, the girl's willing wetness.

'No, madam, no. I wouldn't,' said Nicole, breathless and squirming, making tiny little rolling movements wih her hips. She was trying to make Olga let the hard pencil-thin cane accidentally glide into her silken warm opening.

'And I think you let him undo the buttons and let him feel your tits.'

'No, madam, no.'

Olga ran a finger down the front of the girl's frock, counting as she went. She got to button number three and found it gaping open.

'No?'

'No, madam,' the maid whispered tremulously.

Olga continued counting and checking, finding numbers four and five undone as well.

'Then what's this?' said Olga angrily.

'Oh no . . . no . . .' the maid's hands flew to her breasts in a vain attempt to hide the offending opening in her clothing.

'One, Nicole. One I could have forgiven, but three!'

Almost before the maid realised, Olga thrust Nicole's hands away and forced her own hands inside the girl's frock. She squeezed Nicole's stiff, excited nipples. 'Auralie, see, there is a gap here big enough for me to put my hands inside. And if I can do it, he can too. Nicole, aren't you ashamed of yourself?'

Enjoying the erotic sureness of her mistress's touch, Nicole lowered her head as if admitting her disgraceful behaviour. Olga tweaked the girl's nipples again. Auralie sipped her Bellini. Every minute that went by, every minute that Olga chastised her maid, humiliated her, touched and felt and played with her private places made Auralie hornier and hornier. She was still waiting to caress the girl's fat bottom. She wanted to feel its lusciousness quivering beneath her touch. And she wanted to smack it. Slap it. She also wanted to feel between the girl's legs. Touch the open wet juiciness at the top of her thighs.

'Auralie,' said Olga, grabbing the maid's wrists and pinioning her arms behind her back, 'did I or did I not check that all her buttons were done up when we arrived?'

'You did,' said Auralie.

'And she wants us to believe that she hasn't let the chauffeur touch her. *Chérie*, lift her skirt. Feel her. Feel her pussy. I think you'll find it's very wet.'

While Olga kept the maid's hands locked behind her back, Auralie snaked her way across the room then lifted the maid's frock. Nicole let out little gasps of pleasure as Auralie's fingers slid all too easily into her extremely moist sex.

'Very wet indeed,' Auralie pronounced, shoving her fingers up and down, making Nicole dance and squirm.

'*Chérie*,' said Olga, 'would you say that while we were sitting here, thirsty, waiting for our drink, this slut was being felt and screwed by my new chauffeur?'

'I would say there was every chance of that,' replied Auralie, knowing how well the maid's soft flesh was responding to her moving fingers.

'No, madam, I didn't,' protested the maid.

'You know my rules,' said Olga. 'You do not touch a man, or allow him to touch you unless we give you permission.'

'But I didn't, madam, I didn't.'

'We think you did, and you know what happens when you break the rules don't you, Nicole?'

'Yes, madam.'

Olga undid the remaining buttons on the top half of Nicole's frock, letting her full breasts spill out. Olga brought her mouth down, allowing her tongue to flick across the soft brown nipples.

'You have to be punished,' Olga said sweetly. 'Auralie, tuck the hem of her skirt into her belt.'

Reluctantly Auralie withdrew her fingers from the girl's sex and did as she was told. Olga reached into the flower arrangement and picked out another bamboo cane. This one was extra thin and extra long.

'Your pleasure, *chérie*,' said Olga, testing the cane for spring then handing it to Auralie, who smiled wickedly, licentiously.

'Bend over, Nicole,' commanded Olga.

'No, madam, I didn't. I didn't touch him. Please, no, don't cane me, please.'

'Bend and take your punishment!' said Olga, ignoring the girl's pleas and pointing to the raised end of the chaise-longue. Nicole bent over. Auralie placed a cushion between the arm of the chaise-longue and Nicole's belly, raising the girl's bottom higher. Smiling, Auralie now had the maid exactly how she wanted her. She massaged her rounded, expectant bottom. Then, pulling the girl's arms out ahead of her, made sure her voluptuous breasts were hanging free. Auralie thought Nicole was ready for her punishment, but Nicole knew what really aroused her mistress. She gave a tiny sigh then let her fat white buttocks go loose and floppy. Later she would have her reward. She would be allowed to crawl between her mistress's legs and suck her pussy. And she knew the more Olga enjoyed the spectacle of her being caned, the longer her fat little tongue would be able to slurp at her mistress's juices. Meanwhile, she was longing to feel the harsh sharp bliss of that strip of thin springy bamboo scorching and marking her white buttocks.

Olga smiled her cat-like smile as the girl bent over; so wet, so willing, and waiting for the stripe to sear down across her bare bottom. Auralie trailed the thin cane up between the maid's legs. Then, with tiny circular movements, poked first at her arse then at her soft open sex. The maid quivered with excitement as the thin hardness of the cane touched her hidden, rosy, creamy-wet flesh.

'Six, Auralie,' said Olga sternly.

Nicole caught and held her breath as Auralie brought the cane swishing down over Nicole's buttocks. Between each stripe Auralie rammed her fingers into the girl's sex. The exquisite mixture of pain and pleasure almost brought Nicole to the point of orgasm. She tried to contain herself, not wanting Auralie to see how much she was enjoying her punishment. Each time the cane came down Nicole cried out, begging Auralie to stop, but to no avail. Auralie knew exactly what she was doing. She loved the feeling of control and the sight of the deep-red weals on Nicole's tender fleshy bottom. After the sixth stripe Auralie threw away the cane and sat on an easy chair. Wetter than before, more excited than before, Auralie lifted the black leather of her own skirt and began to rub her fingers along her own sex. Olga glanced at her enjoying herself. She knew Auralie's fingers had found their fountain of pleasure. Olga smiled as Auralie sighed deeply with satisfaction. Then, Olga inspected the criss-cross of red weals on Nicole's bottom. She gently kissed and caressed the marks left by the cane.

'Now, what do you say, Nicole?' said Olga walking away and sitting on a chair in the far corner of the room.

'Thank you, madam, thank you.'

'And how are you going to show your thanks, your true thanks?'

Auralie, who now had her own legs wide apart, her thumb on her clitoris and two fingers inside herself, watched lecherously as the maid crawled to where Olga was sitting.

Nicole knelt between Olga's outstretched legs. She removed Olga's shoes, then her stockings and, as she did so, she stroked the soft erogenous zone of Olga's inner thighs. Nicole bent her head and, parting Olga's chiffon skirt, and with due reverence, sank her fat little tongue into her mistress's pussy.

'Thank you, madam,' said Nicole, remaining on her knees and greedily licking and slurping between her employer's legs.

Olga lay back, her arms over the side of the chair and her legs spread wide apart, doing nothing except lapping up the feeling of total abandonment and the precise touch of her maid's expert little tongue. From time to time she glanced at Auralie, who was still playing with herself, sighing and gently enjoying her clitoris, but not allowing herself to come.

'You may get up, Nicole,' said Olga after a while, 'but your dress stays where it is. We want to be able to see those delightful buttocks. You won't break the rules again, will you?'

'No, madam.'

'Now, you wanted to screw my chauffeur?'

'No, madam.'

'But isn't he beautiful? Isn't he desirable?'

'Yes, madam. But I don't want to screw him, madam.'

'Then you will have to do something you don't want to do.'

'No madam, please. No.'

The maid fell down to the ground and crawled towards Olga again. Olga watched her impassively.

'Nicole, do you want to remain my maid?'

'Yes, madam.'

'Well, then you understand what that means, don't you? You do everything for my pleasure,' said Olga, bending the girl over her knees and making gentle affectionate circular movements over her marked bare bottom with both her hands. 'It is my pleasure to watch you being screwed. I want to see you sitting on him. I want to see his big black prick going up inside you, making you shudder. And I hope it is a big black prick,' mused Olga, almost absent-mindedly.

'It is, madam, it is.' The words were out before Nicole realised what she had said.

'What!' Olga brought one hand down on the girl's backside with a loud resonant slap at the same time as the fingers of her other hand expertly jabbed into her sex and anus, impaling her wickedly and deliciously.

'You lied to me. I knew you'd been playing with him,' said Olga. 'I knew it. So, where is he now?'

Nicole stayed silent. Olga teased her maid's clitoris. Nicole was making exquisite little movements of enjoyment with her hips.

'Come on, tell me.' Olga jabbed her fingers viciously into her maid's lewd pussy.

'I left him in the bathroom, naked,' Nicole finally admitted.

'Completely naked?' said Auralie, coming over and stroking Olga's breasts whilst Olga continued to play with the maid. 'Nothing on?'

'Nothing except a blindfold,' replied Nicole.

'A blindfold?' asked Auralie.

'Yes.'

'You are a wicked girl,' said Olga. 'A very wicked girl to tell me such lies.'

'I wanted to watch him wanking.'

'Wanking! Wanking!'

'Playing with himself.'

'You deserve a good whipping,' said Olga, and she felt the girl's muscles twitch in anticipation. 'But now you are going to screw my chauffeur. You are going to screw Kensit.'

Olga pushed the girl off her lap. Auralie pulled her up and grabbed her hand.

'Now do it, and don't you dare disobey me,' said Olga, taking an elbow-length pair of black leather gloves from her handbag and putting them on. Then she followed Auralie as she dragged the reluctant maid out of the room.

They found Kensit in the bathroom, sitting on the ebony lavatory seat facing the door. He looked superb, and Auralie's eyes narrowed as she smiled greedily. In the 1930s bathroom, which still had the original black-and-white tiles and white porcelain furniture, his black body glistened harmoniously. With her designer's eye Auralie decided he looked perfect. In fact, he was breathtaking. He was naked except for a bandanna covering his eyes. Auralie took a deep breath. He was sinuously beautiful and his muscles rippled as he sat playing with his very erect penis. Auralie wanted him. She wanted to feel his shaft inside her. It was hard and upright, a penis in full glory. It was neither too big nor too small. It was, thought Auralie, the perfect shape and size. She stuck out her tongue and wiggled it in lustful approval. Kensit heard the movement at the door.

'Is that you, Nicole?'

Olga curtly shoved her maid into the room, indicating she straddle the naked Kensit. Nicole gave her employer a 'do I really have to' look and then obeyed her mistress.

'Yes, it's me,' Nicole whispered into Kensit's ear.

'You were a long time,' he said, with one hand stroking his cock and the other cupping his balls.

'Yes, there were things I had to do for them,' Nicole replied enigmatically.

Kensit reached up and felt for Nicole's pendulous breasts. Nicole closed Kensit's legs and stood facing him. She turned her head to look at Olga, who gave a nod of encouragement.

Holding on to Kensit's shoulders Nicole hovered over his stiff prick then, very slowly, let him feel the merest whisper of her wet sex on his swollen tip. Kensit gasped. He wanted to shove it straight up and ride her, but Nicole had other ideas. Nibbling at his ear, she pulled up and away from him.

'No, not yet,' she whispered, hovering again. Nicole was determined to take a number of pleasures instantaneously. She was going to make her mistress and Auralie wait for as long as possible before they enjoyed the sight of his black prick entering her juicy pussy. She knew the thrill they would get from watching his cock slide into her, watching that hard knob push her open, then its black shaft inch its way upwards further and further into her squashy, pink, swollen, lustful flesh. She also knew what those two bitches would be doing to each other the moment she had Kensit's cock rammed hard inside her. They would start playing with each other's pussy and tits. Well, they could wait. This time she was in control. And besides, she wanted to feel the full impact of Kensit's pleasure, taking her, stretching her, screwing her. Screwing her fast and furiously, his anticipation finally realised.

Pressing her hands down on his shoulders so that they were taking her full weight, Nicole very gradually let his prick feel its way inside her horny sex. Kensit gasped and moulded her breasts with his hands. Then, just when he had got used to her gliding rhythm, suddenly, and with one quick movement, she thrust down, taking his engorged prick up to the hilt. She devoured him, she took every inch of him until there was no gap between his belly and her belly, no gap between his body and her body. With one fast jerk she had taken him completely. She rode him like a horse.

He was still unaware of Olga's and Auralie's presence. They watched lasciviously from the doorway as Nicole's reddened bottom rose and fell. They were enjoying the vicarious pleasure of seeing Kensit's proud cock penetrate Nicole's lush wet opening. The beauty of Kensit's erect black penis sliding deeper and deeper into the maid's eager sex was not lost upon them. With her hands encased in the fine black leather gloves, Olga began to undo the buttons on Auralie's silk blouse. Lifting Olga's chiffon skirt, Auralie lent back against the doorpost and gently rubbed Olga's clitoris as Olga massaged Auralie's breasts. Teetering on her high-heels Auralie braced herself as Olga's hands travelled over her body. She tensed her buttock muscles as she felt the gloved hand slowly slide up her legs. Auralie swayed from side to side as the seams of the gloves touched the delicate malleable flesh beyond her pubis. Aware of the need for silence Auralie held back the gasp of delight as Olga rammed her leather-covered fingers harshly inside her. The two women, stimulating each other, continued to watch Kensit thrusting harder and harder into the maid. They watched with pure pleasure as they saw him stretching her sex and his large black hands holding her fat white bottom whenever Nicole took an upward motion, forcing it back down again. Auralie stroked Olga's inner thighs as Olga's gloved hand penetrated deeper and deeper, imprisoning her on the moving shaft of black leather. Kensit's prick was moving faster and faster too. Up and down. Fast and furious. Auralie began to want the cock. Wanted Kensit's cock inside her. She wanted to take that beautiful prick into her and enclose her flesh around its hardness.

Kensit was almost on the point of orgasm when Nicole, turning and seeing Auralie's wanton expression, suddenly stopped moving.

'No,' cried Kensit.

'One moment,' Nicole whispered. And before the man could realise what was happening Nicole had withdrawn and Auralie had taken her place. Olga and Nicole left the room. Auralie sat on Kensit's penis, used her muscles to squeeze him back to extra hard, then removed his blindfold.

'Jeez!' he exclaimed, 'I thought you were the maid. She left me here, said she was coming back to screw me. Told me to play with myself and said to put the blindfold on, it's more sexy.'

'So it is,' said Auralie, starting to ride the slightly bemused young man. 'You like to screw?'

'Sure,' said Kensit.

'Then you're in luck,' she said, confusing Kensit even more by removing herself from his hard cock.

'But . . .'

'No buts. Follow me,' said Auralie, and led the naked man through to the study across the hall.

Auralie opened the study door. There was Margaret, the girl sent from Petrov, dressed in a black habit, her face hidden by the hood. She was kneeling in supplication on the floor.

'This girl,' said Auralie to Kensit, pointing to the figure whose clothed bottom was raised up and facing them, 'has secret desires. Unbecoming desires. She has told her Confessor she has been dreaming about sex. Sex with men, sex with women, sex with strangers. Wicked dreams, Kensit, wouldn't you agree? Do you know why she's kneeling like that? I will tell you. She wants to be screwed. She's waiting for it. And we would like you to take her.'

Auralie stood astride the girl, facing Kensit and gazing lasciviously at his prick. Keeping her eyes on the man, Auralie rolled back the girl's black habit, revealing her plump, white bare legs with chains attached to her ankles, which were attached to a large ring on the wall. Long, navy-blue serge drawers covered her raised bottom.

'Pull down her drawers,' ordered Auralie.

Kensit's cock quivered. He bent over and pulled her knickers down to her knees. Auralie, excited by Kensit's hard prick, leant forward and took it in her mouth. Sensual, incredible and very erotic thoughts flooded through Kensit as he felt Auralie's lips tightening around his stiff cock. Kensit began to shake. The exquisite sensation of her mouth on his prick was almost too much for him to bear. He could feel his sap rising. He wanted to come. But, expertly, Auralie gripped his penis at the base and held his orgasm back.

'Smack her bottom,' commanded Auralie. 'Smack it hard.'

Kensit brought his hand down on the soft flesh of the unknown girl.

'Again, and harder,' ordered Auralie.

Kensit did as he was told, his hand stinging from the contact.

'She belongs to a special sect,' explained Auralie. 'She must experience pleasure and pain. And pleasure with pain. And the pleasure of pain. She must live out all her secret desires. Feel her. Feel her pussy.' Auralie took the forefinger of Kensit's right hand, hooked it around her own, then trailed it along the top of the girl's legs. 'She's wet. This bitch is very wet. Kensit, bend down and put your tongue just where I've got my finger.'

Kensit did as he was told and licked at the outer rim of the girl's labia. Auralie splayed her vulva lips wider so that Kensit's tongue could move easily and slurp in the girl's soft juiciness. There was a mirror opposite and, from where he was kneeling, Kensit could see Auralie's naked pussy as she bent forward. This gave an added impetus to his already stiff prick.

'Madame Olga wants you to screw her. Yes, your mistress has given permission,' Auralie reassured him, 'and this dirty bitch wants to be screwed. That's what she's been dreaming about, haven't you, slut?'

The girl's head gave a slight nod.

'You see, Kensit, that is why she kneels so still, so open and so wet. She wants to be taken by a stranger, and you and I are going to give her her heart's desire. Take her. Take her fast.'

Kensit stood up and positioned himself. Auralie took hold of his cock and, leaning across the girl, whispered in his ear: 'Take her. Take her now, but use her arse. She's here to be improved. To know the pleasure of each orifice. Except her mouth. Tody her mouth is gagged. Today she won't have that pleasure. Today she has to know the pleasure of a cock, a beautiful stiff cock in her anus. And, her anus needs to be stretched.'

The girl on the floor said nothing and remained utterly motionless. Auralie played with her wet pussy, taking some of its juices to lubricate her other opening. The girl's hips began to sway with a licentious roll. She was offering herself to Kensit. She was talking with her body, silently consenting to everything that was being done. Kensit came up between the girl's legs.

'This man is going to screw you now,' Auralie told the girl. 'He is going straight up into your pretty little arse.'

Kensit placed his hands on the girl's hips, aimed, and penetrated. With the force of his enthusiasm she shot forward. The habit covering the top half of the girl's body slipped awry and Kensit saw that not only was her mouth gagged but her hands were bound together and fastened to a long chain. She rolled back on to his penis, then jerked forward. He pulled her hips back hard, penetrating her deeper then smacked her plump, fleshy buttocks. Auralie smiled, lifted her own skirt and began to stroke herself with soft tantalising strokes. Kensit penetrated the girl again and again. And smacked her again and again.

The girl rolled and heaved, and rocked and swayed, taking every last inch of him.

'Kensit, what are you doing?' roared Olga, walking into the study.

Kensit could not believe his ears. He had been seduced by the maid, taken by the niece, told that his employer wanted him to screw the chained girl and, thinking it was a condition of employment, was happily doing it. Yet now he was being asked what he was doing. Well, *screw her* because all he wanted to do now was come. He had been interrupted twice and this time he was going to manage it. He didn't care if he did lose his job. He wanted his orgasm.

'Screwing this young lady's arse, madam,' he replied boldly, continuing to jab, penetrate, hold and smack the girl, whose only sounds were muffled gasps of enjoyment.

Olga looked across at Auralie with a smile of amusement on her face.

'Impertinence,' said Olga. She walked over and ringed the base of his cock with her hand as Auralie juggled his balls.

'We wouldn't want to stop your pleasure . . .' said Auralie.

'Or ours,' added Olga. 'But . . .'

Kensit held his breath. Auralie was rolling his balls between her fingers and his mouth had gone completely dry.

'Don't look at her face,' Olga commanded, 'and when you've finished come into the drawing-room. We have a proposition to make to you.'

Auralie and Olga left the study, closing the door behind them, leaving Kensit on his own with the chained girl

Kensit flicked his cock with his hands, making certain it was as stiff as it could be, then he penetrated the girl's anus once more. He rode her hard, enjoying her delighted moans. He was going to come in a way he had never experienced before. He was excited beyond anything he had ever known. The gagged and chained girl with only her sex on show was opening, expanding under his thrusts. His whole body shuddered. He was reaching heights, pinnacles of desire and lust he had never known, never thought existed. And the covered girl continued to sway and moan, accepting, wanting, loving every jerk, jab and thrust he gave and her total compliance was taking him higher and higher, beyond himself into unknown territory.

Olga and Auralie went back to the drawing-room. The maid, having properly fulfilled her role in the charade of seducing Kensit, was now in the bedroom sorting out Olga's clothes and hanging them in the closet. The telephone rang. Nicole answered it. It was Sir Henry de Bouys's secretary. Nicole buzzed through on the intercom for Olga. Auralie listened to the conversation with a growing sense of disquiet. Annoyance was spreading across Olga's face and she was answering in monosyllables. There was a tone in Olga's voice that was odd. Auralie tried to analyse it. It was slightly put out, slightly petulant but conciliatory, not the usual Olga imperiousness.

'Yes, yes of course we understand,' Olga said. Then she turned to Auralie. 'Sir Henry's sorry, he can't make London today. He's stayed in Rome.' Olga turned back to the caller. 'Yes, of course. Of course he must have a honeymoon, if only a short one.'

'Honeymoon!' said Auralie. 'Who's he married? Olga, who's he married?'

'And who is the fortunate lady?' Olga asked airily. Her airiness changing dramatically with the answer. 'Who?' she screeched. 'Who did you say? Penelope Vladelsky!'

Auralie blanched at the news. Olga continued talking. Auralie avoided her glance. She was distantly aware of Olga murmuring the usual congratulatory platitudes then ending the conversation, but her mind had gone into a spin. Jeanine's mother, her enemy, had married the man who could save the company. Who could give them one of the biggest furnishing contracts in the world. Her father-in-law had married her aunt! God, how incestuous! And she had been thinking of divorcing Gerry. She could not do that now. She would have to hold on to him with everything she had and with everything she could do.

'Well . . . ?' said Olga.

'Disaster,' said Auralie.

'Disaster?' asked Olga.

'Yes, we'll never get the contract now,' said Auralie. 'That woman hates me. Really hates me.'

'I've never understood why,' said Olga.

'You really don't know? Did Nin and Rea never tell you?'

'No,' said Olga. 'Auralie, Sir Henry's coming to London in four days and wants us to do the presentation then. So, *chérie*, I think I should know everything. Everything. But first tell me, your relationship with Jeanine, that's OK, isn't it?'

Olga watched Auralie's face fall.

'I see,' said Olga. 'Well, why does Penelope hate you?'

'She found me sucking Stefan's cock.'

'What!' shrieked Olga, then burst out laughing. 'Stefan! *Merde!* Her husband. Your uncle . . .'

'So's Petrov,' said Auralie.

'True, but Petrov is Petrov. Stefan. Holy bloody Stefan. But when, when did you do it?'

'It was on my eighteenth birthday. He was lying on his bed. He was naked but asleep and his prick looked so pretty I thought it would be nice to touch it. So I did. He didn't wake up, just sighed, so I touched it a bit more and it grew. Then I wondered what it'd be like if I put it in my mouth. So I did. I was enjoying myself so much. He had a very big prick, you know. Well, I thought so at the time. Anyway I didn't hear Penelope come in.'

'What happened?'

'She screamed and threw me out of the house. That's when

I came to stay with you. As you know, she said she'd never speak to me again, and she never has.'

'Umm, well I think we'd better discuss the whole thing with Petrov.'

'Petrov?'

'Yes. Perhaps he'll have some ideas. You see, *chérie*, it's quite simple. With the state of the market at the moment, without that contract as a company we are finished. We must have it. Now, of course, there is one simple way. We de-hire you as our designer.'

'What! You couldn't! You wouldn't.'

'*Chérie*, this is business. Business is a jungle. There are no friends or relatives in business, not if it means failure. But I don't want to do that. So, we go and see Petrov. Perhaps he'll have another, and better, idea.'

Olga rang the bell for Kensit who quickly appeared, naked and expectant in the doorway.

'All our plans have been changed,' Olga said, all thought of sex erased from her mind. Now there was only money and survival, and the change in her attitude showed in her voice. Kensit felt it keenly, stood to attention and almost saluted.

'Put your clothes on. You're driving us to my husband's house in the country,' Olga added.

Not one of the three spoke as they made their way down in the lift to the limousine parked outside. And the silence continued to reign until they were safely ensconced with Petrov, when all hell was let loose.

7

Jeanine woke at dawn, jumped out of bed and drew back the heavy gold silk curtains from the French windows. It was a beautiful morning. She stood staring out into her small walled garden enjoying the sight of the honeysuckle and the ivy, the pink begonias and the white geraniums. There was, she thought, a special quality to the early morning summer light. It had a soft blueness to it that no other time possessed. She stretched lazily and smiled. Then she remembered the two odd-balls Petrov had sent the evening before. A shadow crossed her brow. No, she would not think negatively. They could turn out to be a blessing in disguise. She went to her wardrobe, sorted out the day's clothes, tidied her room then bathed and dressed. Her body felt alive, healthy and cleansed. She felt good. She had no inkling of what was to lie ahead.

Downstairs, she collected her post then went to her office to sort out the daily routine. Sister Pierre was on the door and wished her good morning. The murmur of voices and the sound of tinkling china came from the dining-room. Obviously all was well and Jeanine's fears of the night before seemed utterly groundless. She made a few telephone calls, then noticed that a message had come through on the fax. It was dated late the previous evening and written in her mother's elegant scrawl. *'Darling, married Sir Henry de Bouys in Rome today. Arriving in London the day after tomorrow after our brief honeymoon. Will telephone. Love Mother.'*

Jeanine could not believe her eyes. She was gob-smacked.

Her mother married again! And to Sir Henry de Bouys. She couldn't contact her mother because there was no address on the fax. They must have gone off on Sir Henry's yacht and there was nothing more Jeanine could do except wait for her mother's call. The shock of the news made Jeanine hungry. She would take breakfast. She would sample Leslie's cooking.

The dining-room was fairly full. Rose, the plump little waitress, came over and took Jeanine's order of scrambled eggs, toast and coffee. The Brooklyn couple passed her table and Jeanine bade them good morning. They smiled and took their seats. The three Misses from Nebraska were drinking coffee with sour expressions. Jeanine sipped at hers. It was passable. She'd had worse, but Jeanine made a mental note to buy an espresso machine. There was no sign of Mr Sawyer or Mrs Maclean. She nodded to the English couple who gave her a curt nod in reply. She bade them good morning and the couple managed a wan smile in return. This alarmed her slightly.

Sally looked apologetic when she brought the toast, which was burnt. She was nearly in tears when she presented Jeanine with flaccid bacon lying forlornly beside a rubbery yellow concoction floating in greyish liquid. A precarious thread that had already been stretched to breaking point suddenly snapped within Jeanine. She was mute with fury. She gripped the table top to stop herself from throwing the offending plate at the girl.

'May I go home now?' asked Rose.

'You may,' replied Jeanine between clenched teeth.

The girl scarpered. Jeanine pursed her mouth and stormed into the kitchen.

As she entered, the sight that confronted her stopped her dead in her tracks. Pierre, wearing only a pair of thigh-length waders supported by braces criss-crossed over her huge breasts, was perched on the edge of the kitchen table. Kneeling between her open thighs was Leslie, absolutely naked except for his chains and chef's hat, which bobbed up and down. Pierre turned her large head towards Jeanine.

'He's being punished, madam,' said Pierre.

Jeanine watched in horror and amazement as Pierre raised a long black whip and brought it down on Leslie, who instantly howled from the harsh strike of the lash.

'Now you'll do it properly,' Pierre said to him.

Jeanine, believing Pierre was referring to Leslie's cooking, moved further into the room.

'It's not necessary to whip him,' said Jeanine.

'I know my business, you'd better learn yours,' said Pierre, maliciously.

Jeanine was stunned by the venom in the woman's voice.

Pierre brought the lash down again, then she changed her stance and spread her legs wide.

'Properly!' repeated Pierre, sending the chef's hat flying across the room.

Jeanine's own anger returned.

'What are you doing?' she screamed at Pierre.

Leslie raised his head from between Pierre's massive thighs and looked up at Jeanine. Jeanine gazed at him in a mixture of awe, fascination and alarm.

'The truth is he's sucking my pussy, honey, and he's taking too long to make me come,' said Pierre. Holding the whip in her hand she lifted Leslie up by his hair. As he stood up Jeanine saw that the little man had the most enormous cock. It was erect and huge and the chains going under his balls accentuated it.

Pierre took hold of his stiff member. Gripping it with one hand she wound thin strips of leather from the whip around it with the other.

'Now he's going to suck my titties, aren't you?' said Pierre.

Leslie nodded obediently. Pierre turned back to Jeanine.

'Why don't you hold his cock,' she said. 'You'll never hold

another one like it.' She turned back to her puny lover: 'I'm giving her permission to rub your cock, Brother Leslie. That okay with you?'

Leslie didn't answer fast enough. Pierre quickly unravelled the whip and flicked it hard across his backside.

'Thank you, madam,' said Leslie as Pierre thrust a nipple in his mouth.

Leslie began to stroke Pierre's legs, his fingers entering her swollen sex. She began to sway backwards and forwards as his impressive cock trailed up and down along her inner thighs.

Jeanine felt a tingling between her legs. Against every instinct she possessed she found herself becoming more and more excited. The sight she was witnessing was unbelievably sexual and her initial reason for going into the kitchen was momentarily forgotten. Leslie's cock seemed to be pointing, large and inviting, straight at Jeanine. She had to force herself not to grab hold of it.

Pierre was sighing and moaning as the man's fingers thrust into every fold and crevice of her vulva.

'Put your dick in *now*,' ordered Pierre, 'and give it to me hard.'

She flicked Leslie's arse with the tail of the whip. Then put her great legs up and on the little man's shoulders.

'Yes, madam,' he said obediently.

Rooted to the spot Jeanine watched as Leslie's huge cock penetrated the large black woman. Her whole body rolled and heaved. She was squirming and holding him, embracing him and kissing him. He was screwing her as if the demons of hell were after him. He went at her like a madman, sighing and moaning, holding on to her great rolls of flesh and screaming that he loved her. Suddenly they both exploded in mutual orgasm.

'You're fired,' said Jeanine as the odd couple collapsed in a heap on the kitchen floor.

'No way, honey,' shouted Pierre after her departing figure.

In her room, Mrs Maclean, the American guest, had been awake for some time. She was very happy to be in such a beautiful hotel. It had given her a good night's rest. Mrs Maclean was a comparatively rich widow from Pepper Pike, Ohio, where she lived in a modern Japanese-style house designed by her late husband's company. She had protested when she first saw the plans but her husband had overruled her by informing her that they both felt real comfortable with all things Japanese. Her husband had been posted to Japan on business and she had joined him there, but she had not adapted to Japanese life. She preferred Europe. Mrs Maclean felt real good with European culture. That was why she had come to London. To visit the opera, the theatre and the art galleries. Mrs Maclean was lonely. She had lived a lot of her life through her husband. Since her husband's sudden death from a heart attack Mrs Maclean had not had any sex. Not that she'd had much sex when he was alive; her husband had been very business-orientated.

Mrs Maclean was feeling truly rested because she'd had a most invigorating dream that she was having sex with Terry the waiter. It was, she told herself, much better to have a dream like that in a foreign country. Mrs Maclean looked at her watch. Soon her early morning tea would arrive. She wondered if Terry would be the one to bring it. She nipped out of bed, brushed her teeth, combed her hair and smeared some lip gloss on her lips. Perhaps she'd been stupid to rinse her prematurely grey hair with blue. But then all her neighbours did something with their hair, and she could hardly go black at her age. Mrs Maclean was forty-five, going on fifty. She had a young skin but had eaten herself out of shape; a little less so since her husband's death.

Mrs Maclean told herself they'd had a good marriage even though her husband hadn't paid much attention to her body.

'I love you, honey, whichever way you look,' he'd told her. And she had accepted that and joined the opera society and various other cultural clubs to keep busy and stop herself from worrying about the house. Mrs Maclean never worried about sex. It was something she didn't think about and hadn't thought about for years. Until yesterday, when the waiter had smiled at her. Smiled provocatively. Suddenly she became aware that she was a woman with desires. These desires, dormant for years, had come through and been played out in her erotic dream; the handsome waiter lying on top of her, his member inside her, his hands exploring her body. The dream had quite excited Mrs Maclean. She looked in the full-length mirror and wondered if she should change from her nice serviceable, cosy pyjamas into her frilly cotton night-dress. She decided she would and only just had enough time to cover her body before there was a knock on the door. Mrs Maclean hurried back into bed.

'Come in,' she called out.

Terry came in carrying a tray set with a silver teapot and water jug and pretty white china covered with sprigs of roses. Some biscuits lay on a plate. She signalled for Terry to put the tray on the bed beside her. As he did so Terry's arms brushed Mrs Maclean's breasts but neither drew attention to it.

'Shall I pour for you, madam?' he asked.

'Thank you,' she said, leaning slightly forward so that her breasts touched his arm again. Mrs Maclean let her hand fall so that it was close to his leg. Terry moved his position so that her hand was against the fabric of his trousers.

'You're a very pretty woman to be travelling on your own,' said Terry.

Mrs Maclean glowed. It had been many years since any one had complimented her in this way.

'I'm a widow,' she said simply.

'I'm sorry to hear that, madam,' said Terry. 'How long is it since your husband was taken?'

'Three years,' answered Mrs Maclean.

'So you'll be stopping your mourning now,' said Terry, handing her the cup of tea.

'Yes,' said Mrs Maclean, taking a quick sip of the Darjeeling tea then putting the cup back on the tea tray.

'Is the tea not to your liking, madam?' asked Terry.

'It's a little too hot,' said Mrs Maclean, not looking at Terry's face but at the bulge in his trousers. She had an irrational and almost uncontrollable desire to touch that bulge. She moved her hand away to stop herself at the very moment Terry picked up the milk jug.

'Allow me, madam,' he said and began to pour extra milk into her tea cup whilst his bulge was accidentally pressing on her hand.

Mrs Maclean sat transfixed. She dare not move. If she did she would be touching him, touching him more than she was at the moment.

'There now,' said Terry. 'You drink that and I'll be back in a while to see if you'll be wanting anything else.'

Terry left the room. Mrs Maclean drank her tea quickly to cover her confusion. She lay back on her propped-up pillows. Mrs Maclean's heart was racing; blood seemed to be coursing at a great speed through her veins. She realised she had not felt such excitement since she first met her late husband at high school.

There was another knock on her door.

The chambermaid, Jill, came in. Mrs Maclean's heart, which had risen expectantly, dropped like a stone when she saw the girl. She had so hoped it would be Terry.

'Good morning, madam,' said Jill. 'Terry apologises but he forgot your morning papers.'

The chambermaid put them on the bed then departed. Listlessly Mrs Maclean began to read but she couldn't concentrate. Mrs Maclean felt foolish. At her age and feeling sexually aroused. She nestled into her pillows and thought about what had occurred. Mrs Maclean concluded that Terry must have realised his bulge was resting against her hand. It was a large bulge and had felt quite stiff to her. He must want her. Of course, she reasoned, he could not do anything about it. He was an employee. It would be up to her to make the first move, but that was impossible. In her cotton frilly night-dress, Mrs Maclean blushed. She must have been influenced by her erotic dream. She was not accustomed to dreaming of sex.

She was about to get out of bed but then thought better of it. She suddenly had an idea. She would ring room service and order breakfast in bed. This time, if his bulge landed on her hand she would accidentally move that hand and see what happened.

Mrs Maclean dialled the number. Terry answered.

'Yes, Mrs Maclean, what can I do for you?'

'I'd like breakfast in bed,' she said, her loud voice down to a whisper and shaking slightly.

'Yes, madam,' said Terry, giving the thumbs-up sign to Jill who was standing beside him. 'And what would you like?'

'A full English breakfast with coffee,' Mrs Maclean replied.

'It'll be done in the wink of an eyelid, madam,' said Terry. 'And did you get your papers?'

'Yes, thank you,' said Mrs Maclean.

It was twenty minutes later when Terry brought in Mrs Maclean's breakfast. By now she was full of trepidation. The audacity of her idea frightened her. She wasn't quite as sparky as she had been when she first made the call.

Mrs Maclean sat bolt upright as Terry came into the room. He held the tray high, higher than was usual, Mrs Maclean thought, as he padded over the carpet to her bed. Mrs Maclean was made very aware of the bulge at Terry's crotch.

'Here we are, madam,' said Terry, putting the folding tray over her legs. Then he picked up the table napkin and, with a flourish, let it fall across her bosom without his hand touching her. A sense of acute disappointment swept over Mrs Maclean. 'A full English breakfast.' Terry triumphantly removed the silver plate cover. In doing so his bulge managed to brush against her opened hand. 'Now madam, is there anything else I can do for you?' Terry asked. Mrs Maclean's fingers held his bulge and she squeezed.

'Is it my cock you'll be wanting, Mrs Maclean?' Terry asked. He didn't wait for an answer. She withdrew her hand as he undid the flap of his trousers, exposing his large penis. It stood proud and upright before her. This was not quite what she had imagined. She had thought that the man would kiss her, seduce her slowly, make love to her.

'Excited you, did it?' Terry asked. 'And now you want to hold my cock. Then hold it, Mrs Maclean.'

Mrs Maclean put out an unsteady hand and took hold of Terry's prick. She felt nervous. She had very rarely held a man's cock. Her husband had liked to turn her over in the dark, spread her legs, shove it up, come, and fall asleep. Mrs Maclean was ashamed to admit she didn't really know what to do with a man's penis.

'Get your hands round it and give it a rub. It likes a good rub. I do it myself all the time,' Terry laughed. 'Well not *all* the time. Sometimes it gets a good screwing. Would you like to be screwed, Mrs Maclean?'

The extraordinariness of the moment hit Mrs Maclean. Her mouth had gone dry. She nodded her head as she continued to hold and rub Terry's cock.

'Tell it to me then, Mrs Maclean,' said Terry. 'Say it. Say "I'd like you to screw me, Terry".'

'I'd like you to screw me, Terry,' she whispered hoarsely.

'I can't hear you properly,' Terry said. 'I think you've got to say it louder. Shout it out, Mrs Maclean. Shout it out.' He covered up the untouched breakfast plate and put the tray on the floor.

Mrs Maclean was aroused as she had never been aroused before. She felt a tingling somewhere deep within her that needed to be satisfied. She desperately wanted to be screwed. She wanted to feel Terry's rock-hard tool inside her body.

'Shout it out, Mrs Maclean. I want to hear you.'

'I want you to screw me, Terry,' she shouted.

'And I will, Mrs Maclean, I will. But first I want you to suck my cock.'

'S-s-suck . . .?' she exclaimed. She had never done such a thing in her life.

'Don't let your teeth scrape on it, though,' warned Terry, sensing her apprehension. 'It's me own; I can't get another, and it's precious.'

Mrs Maclean leant forward and took Terry's prick into her mouth. It had a sweet taste and she quickly realised what she had to do.

'Now, Mrs Maclean, I'd be grateful if you'd turn over and raise your lovely big arse in the air,' said Terry after a few moments of her inexpert sucking.

'What are you going to do?' she asked tremulously.

'I'm going to screw you,' said Terry. 'I'm going to stick my shaft in your pussy and make it feel like it's never felt before. So turn over now.'

Mrs Maclean obligingly turned over. Terry lifted her night-dress and knelt between her legs. He put his cock at the top of her thighs and rubbed.

'Can you feel my cock between your thighs, Mrs Maclean?'

'Yes,' she whispered.

'And are you wet and wanting it, Mrs Maclean? I wouldn't be doing it unless you wanted it,' he said, continuing to excite her by the feel of his cock touching the lips of her pussy. 'So you have to tell me you're wet and wanting it. You'll have to say, "I'm wet and wanting your cock in my cunt." '

Mrs Maclean had never used the word 'cunt' in her life and had never expected to use it. Her husband had never used words like that. Terry gripped her hips and began to move faster between her legs. He could feel her juices easing out and oiling his prick.

'I won't screw you until you tell me and you've got to shout it loud,' said Terry.

Mrs Maclean swallowed hard. She had never raised her buttocks to her husband and had never thought of having sex doggy fashion. She had thought she did not like sex but here she was with a stranger kneeling between her legs, his cock rubbing backwards and forwards along her pussy. She was very excited. He wanted her to talk dirty. Mrs Maclean gave a wiggle of her hips and a short cough to clear her throat.

'I'm wet and wanting your cock in my cunt,' Mrs Maclean shouted, without hesitation.

Terry gripped her hips harder, positioned his shaft and then entered her. He rode her gently at first, gradually gaining speed until he had established a fast rhythm. Her big bottom moved sexily in time with his thrusts. Mrs Maclean was gasping. She had never known such an experience. She kept wondering when he was going to stop. Her husband would have finished a long while ago but Terry continued taking her, making her wetter and wetter, making her wider, more open and wanting more.

Then she came. With a great force Mrs Maclean's body heaved rigid, shook, and she had the first orgasm of her life. Terry came moments later.

'Will you be wanting anything else, madam?' said Terry, buttoning up the flap on his trousers.

'The same again tomorrow morning, please,' Mrs Maclean said boldly. Terry smiled and left the room.

'Did you get it on tape?' Terry asked Jill, once he was back in his pantry.

Jill played the tape back to him. There was Mrs Maclean's voice shouting that she wanted to be screwed and have Terry's cock in her cunt.

'Poor bitch,' said Terry, feeling unusually contrite. 'I think that was the first decent screw she's ever had. And I'll swear to God she's never played with a cock.'

'You're joking,' said Jill. 'Sounds like she needs a few lessons.'

'Wants me back tomorrow,' he said chirpily. Terry lifted Jill's skirt, his fingers exploring the top of her legs. 'You don't need lessons, that's for sure. By the way, did you find a guy to screw?'

'Yes,' said Jill. 'That Mr Sawyer.'

'And where's Mary?'

'She's still screwing him.'

'Did you both go in there, then?'

'No, I went first, then Mary came in and joined us. I thought he would like that – he looked a kinky bastard.'

'A possible for Petrov's order?' asked Terry.

'Wouldn't be surprised if he's already joined and we didn't know about it. You should have seen the things he had in his briefcase,' said Jill, squirming pleasurably to the touch of Terry's fingers.

'What things?' asked Terry.

'Oh the usual. Whips and manacles, canes and gags, blind-fold and chains,' said Jill. 'By the way, have all the guests been served breakfast?'

'Mrs Maclean took it in her room,' replied Terry, slyly. 'The others have gone to the dining-room.'

'So we can start, can we?' asked Jill.

'I think so,' said Terry. 'They'll be coming up any minute now. What about Mary?'

'She'll be here soon,' said Jill.

'Go and lean against the landing wall and show them your pussy, Jill,' said Terry roguishly.

Jill stood on the landing at a point where she couldn't be immediately seen from the bottom of the stairs and lifted her skirt. Terry came out and began playing with her. They heard footsteps on the stairs. Terry leaned out to see who it was. It wasn't Jeanine, so they were safe to carry on.

'It's the couple from Brooklyn,' said Terry, undoing his trouser flap. 'Go down on me. Suck me.'

Jill knelt down, lifting her skirt so that her naked bottom, stocking tops and bare shaved pussy were on show. She held Terry's balls and put the tip of his throbbing prick in her mouth. Terry held onto its base and rubbed himself.

Suddenly there was a startled scream. 'Harry! Harry, look. Look what she's doing!' the Brooklyn woman shrieked. Her husband gawped in amazement.

'Oh my God!' he exclaimed. 'Don't look, honey, don't look.'

'But Harry, he's beating off his Peter in her mouth!' gasped his wife.

But the couple had to pass Jill and Terry to get to their room. Jill stood up, lifted her skirt.

'Screw me,' she said to Terry in a loud voice. He shoved her roughly against the wall and rammed his cock into her.

The outraged American couple ran past them as fast as they could. Jill and Terry laughed as Mary came down the stairs endeavouring to stuff her breasts back into her brassiere.

'No need for that,' shouted Jill. 'We've started.'

Mary smiled as she watched Terry's cock in action.

'Yes, I heard the scream,' she said, adding, 'Well Terry, did I win my bet?'

'You did not,' he said. 'And you owe me a grand.'

'A grand!' Mary exclaimed.

'Sure,' said Terry, groping her breasts as he continued to screw Jill. 'That was our bet. Five hundred for screwing Mrs Maclean and five hundred for getting it all on tape. It was only the bet that made it worthwhile. You didn't think I would do it otherwise, did you?'

'Did he really do it?' asked Mary, turning to Jill.

'He did,' replied Jill. 'And I recorded it.' She imitated Mrs Maclean's voice 'I want you to screw me, Terry. I'm wet and wanting your cock in my cunt.'

'Jeez,' said Mary, 'who'd've thought it! I'd never have bet so much if I'd thought you could really do it.'

'With the money our dear High Priestess Auralie is paying us to close down this hotel, you can afford it,' said Terry.

'Terry thinks it's the best screw the poor cow's ever had,' said Jill.

'He would,' said Mary.

'Did that Mr Sawyer use any of his gadgets on you?' asked Jill.

'Yeah, look at my bum,' said Mary, raising her skirt and showing the blue paddle marks and the red stripes.

'Just as well you like it,' said Terry, stroking her bottom.

They heard another couple coming up the stairs.

'Mary, keep your skirt up,' said Jill, bending down and sucking Mary's white, juicy shaven mound. Terry stood to one side rubbing his erect prick. The English couple walked quickly past them, talking about the weather and pretending to see nothing. They would be the first down to reception with their swiftly-packed suitcases.

'What now?' asked Terry.

'I'll lie down and you can screw me,' said Mary.

She lay on the carpet as Terry went straight up. Jill cupped her hands round Terry's balls, feeling his cock entering Mary.

This is how they were when the three Misses from Nebraska came up the stairs. In unison the three screamed 'Jeez' and fled to their respective rooms.

'Hey, this is fun,' said Terry. 'What now?'

'It's doggie time,' said Jill, bending down with her arse in the air. Terry moved from Mary to Jill. Mary leant against the wall and played with herself. One by one the outraged guests fled past them carrying their suitcases.

Mary lay down on the floor and positioned her pussy under Jill's head. Jill bent her head and began to suck Mary. Terry continued to screw Jill.

Mrs Maclean opened her door. She couldn't believe her eyes. She shut it quickly then slowly opened it again. Dressed in her formal summer dress, carrying her handbag and an umbrella she stood and stared.

'Hey, Mrs Maclean,' said Terry, laughing. 'Want another screw?'

Mrs Maclean was incapable of movement. Not one limb would move, nor her mouth. She was utterly shocked.

Mary moved her head and looked up at the startled woman. 'Ever had a woman suck your pussy? Ever had a woman feel you, put her hands between your legs and touch you?' she asked.

Mrs Maclean was too scandalised to answer. She felt humbled, used and debased. She had been feeling so happy, so elated. For the first time in her life she had felt sexually alive. Now all that enveloped her was intense humiliation, and a rush of anger flooded through her. Before she knew what she was doing Mrs Maclean gave Terry's bottom a sound whack with her umbrella.

In the foyer Jeanine was suddenly faced with a number of disgruntled guests, all with their suitcases beside them. Jeanine looked at them bemused. Angrily the Brooklyn couple, Harry and Linda, turned on her.

'We're all leaving,' said Harry.

'Why?' asked Jeanine.

'We didn't expect to stay in a brothel!' said Harry.

'What are you talking about?' said Jeanine.

'And that breakfast was just awful,' said his wife.

'A brothel,' said the man again.

'I don't understand,' said Jeanine, looking towards the English couple for help.

'And none of us will be paying,' said the Englishman in his clipped, hot-potato-in-his-mouth tones.

'Please . . . you'll have to explain,' said Jeanine, flabbergasted. 'I'm sorry about the breakfast. The cook's been fired . . .'

'We could just about have lived with the breakfast,' said Harry from Brooklyn. 'It's what they're doing up *there*.' He pointed upstairs.

'Who's doing what? Where?' Jeanine asked frantically.

'Your chambermaids and your waiter are having group sexual intercourse on the first-floor landing,' said the Englishman. 'Now, if you'll excuse us . . .'

He picked up his and his wife's suitcases and walked out of the hotel. They were briskly followed by the Brooklyn couple. Then the three Misses from Nebraska came trotting down the stairs.

'We'll be reporting you to the tourist authority,' said one of them as she fled past Jeanine to join the others in the street.

Jeanine, by now at the end of her tether, ran up the stairs. She passed Mr Sawyer, complete with his suitcases, on his way down.

'I will not be returning,' he said, without stopping.

She heard the noises first. The grunts and the groans, the sighs and the moans and the thwacks were very loud. Horrified,

Jeanine ran faster up the stairs, looking upwards as she neared the top. She nearly fell backwards as the tableau on the landing came into view.

Mary was lying on the floor, Jill was bending over her and Terry was bending over Jill. They were all, as the Englishman had put it, engaging in group sexual intercourse. And Mrs Maclean, a hotel guest, was beating Terry's naked bottom soundly with her umbrella.

Everything Jeanine had worked towards had fallen apart. Her beautiful hotel's reputation was a shambles. She couldn't allow these terrible things to happen all around her; she had to fight. Jeanine grabbed the umbrella from Mrs Maclean.

'Get out!' she screamed. 'Get out!' And threw the umbrella down the stairs.

Mrs Maclean was about to say something, then thought better of it. She walked back to her room and began to pack her suitcase. Jeanine looked at the three on the floor who continued their activities regardless of her presence.

'Stop it!' she shouted. 'Stop it! You're disgusting. You're fired. All three of you are fired!'

'That's what you think,' said Terry.

'It's not what I think, it's what I know,' Jeanine said. 'Leave this place immediately.'

'We'll leave when we want to and we don't want to just yet,' answered Terry.

Things could not get worse, Jeanine thought to herself. But she was wrong, quite wrong. She wanted to cry but felt now was not the moment to show weakness. She must be strong and not allow anyone to see that they had hurt her. Demolished her. She straightened her shoulders, held her head high and gracefully descended the staircase. She needed every ounce of self control she possessed when she walked into her foyer. Her instinct was to collapse and scream. Instead she stood quite still, only moving her head to survey the scene spread out before her.

All twenty-four photographs of her making love to Gerry were on display. Explicit. Blown up extra large. Even larger than the ones Pierre had shown her. Graphic, every nuance of her hidden self, wet and open, captured on film. Gerry's prick, large and entering her, preserved for everyone to see. Her in her secret clothing, her breasts spilling out over her basque with Gerry's lips on her nipples. Her stockinged legs high in the air. Her succulent, rounded bare bottom held by Gerry's hand. Every moment of their love-making captured on film. Jeanine stood staring at the photographs, devastated. Then she heard a noise behind her. She turned quickly. There stood Jill, Mary and Terry.

'Now that's what I call a good screw,' said Terry, admiring the prints. 'I thought so at the time.'

'You!' exclaimed Jeanine. '*You* were the photographer!'

'At your service,' said Terry, making a sweeping bow. 'Mrs Maclean could take a few lessons from you.'

Jeanine's mouth dropped.

'We're going now. Enjoy yourself,' said Terry, linking arms with Jill and Mary and walking towards the front door.

'Why?' said Jeanine. 'Why have you all done this to me?'

'Now that'd be telling,' he said and all three departed.

Jeanine felt broken and broken-hearted. She looked again at the photographs. Who would have such a grudge against her as to do this? Who was her enemy? Surely it wasn't Gerry. That evening was special. Special is not the province of one. It takes two. No, it couldn't be Gerry.

Jeanine felt deflated and sad. She sat at her desk, dejection written all over her face. The whole place was quiet. Eerie almost. Was nobody left in her beautiful hotel? Do something, she told herself. Be positive. Go to the kitchen and check if the odd-balls have gone. Jeanine found it hard to believe that she had witnessed those two screwing. And that it had actually got to a point where she had wanted to touch the man's prick. Not out of desire. Out of wonder.

Jeanine made her way to the kitchen. Everything was now silent. No one was there. She returned to the foyer, tears were now beginning to trickle down her face. Pull yourself together, she told herself. Slowly, one by one, she ripped the offending pictures off the walls.

She went upstairs and checked every room. They were all empty. She noticed that Mrs Maclean's door was locked. Surprised, almost worried, Jeanine knocked hesitantly. Jeanine felt a sense of relief as Mrs Maclean opened the door.

'I'm sorry,' said Mrs Maclean. She had been crying; her mascara was smudged and she looked a mess.

Jeanine stared at her and then burst into tears. Those were the first nice, genuine words she had heard all day. The two tearful women stood looking at one another.

'Would you like a cup of tea?' asked Jeanine.

'I'd prefer coffee,' said Mrs Maclean.

'Then we'll have coffee,' said Jeanine, suddenly cheering up. Mrs Maclean and Jeanine went down the stairs together. Jeanine locked the front door and took Mrs Maclean into her own private apartment. She made them both coffee and gradually the two of them began to talk. Mrs Maclean decided to tell Jeanine her secret, how Terry had come to her room and had sex with her. And how she'd had the first orgasm of her life.

'And then when I saw the three of them on the landing I was . . . Oh, I don't know. Shocked. Humiliated. Angry. I thought it was some sort of punishment.'

Punishment. Mrs Maclean's voice rang in Jeanine's ears. Punishment. Was this Petrov's punishment? Was *he* responsible? He had sent her the strange couple. She recalled what he had told her on the telephone. 'Your sin was sexual, so your punishment will have to be, too. Confess. Come to me and confess.'

'Mrs Maclean,' said Jeanine, 'would you mind staying here and watching the place. I have something to do. Somewhere I must go and I might not be back till late.'

'Sure,' said Mrs Maclean. 'I'll answer the phones. It'll give me something to do.'

'Thank you,' said Jeanine. 'Oh, my mother might telephone. Don't tell her what's happened here. Just say I haven't opened yet. And let her know her fax arrived safely and congratulations. She got married again yesterday.'

'That's nice, real nice,' said Mrs Maclean, but then wondered if it really was. She had decided she was never going to marry again. She had discovered freedom, and today she had discovered sex. Crying in her room before Jeanine had knocked on her door, Mrs Maclean had made a secret vow. Far from returning, tail between her legs, to Ohio, she was going to stay in Europe and was going to find some more sex. It was never too late to make discoveries. And she had made one big one. She liked sex. Mrs Maclean now understood sex was not a quick fumble, a two-minute shove-up in the dark. It was more, much more, and she had every intention of finding out exactly what it was she had been missing. And she was going to set her own record straight.

Together Mrs Maclean and Jeanine went back to the foyer. Mrs Maclean sat at the reception desk. Jeanine picked up the discarded photographs. They were very good. She thought fondly of Gerry. She would like to see him again. She would like to screw him again. She remembered his touch and a shiver went down her spine. No, she mustn't think sexual thoughts. He was Auralie's husband. He was out of bounds. The tears that had stopped began to flow again. Petrov. She had to go to Petrov's and confess. He knew, but now she would have to tell him in her own words.

And he would ask what she was doing dressed in such erotic clothing. Well, perhaps she should shock him, perhaps she should show him how wonderful she looked in them. He had punished her but perhaps she should get her own back. Instead of the sweet simpering girl he was expecting she should be her own woman. Jeanine threw the photographs down on the nearest chair and marched downstairs to her own apartment. She undressed, put on her basque and her stockings and some very high-heeled shoes. She let her hair fall free and made up her face to its best advantage. She painted her lips with a deep glowing red. Then she covered up her naughty underwear with a long, soft, blue crêpe-de-chine button-through dress.

Leaving Mrs Maclean in charge, Jeanine locked the doors of her hotel and walked down the steps towards her car. It was then she saw Gerry and panicked.

Not now, she thought. Not you, not now. And stepped back in an effort to avoid him.

'Darling,' he said, his arms outstretched to embrace her.

'Don't, Gerry,' she said, agitated.

He carried on up the steps. He wouldn't take no for an answer. He told her he loved her. She pushed him away. He grabbed her, said he wanted them to go inside the hotel for a talk. She broke out in a sweat. The photographs of them making love were still in the foyer. He mustn't see them. He said he wanted to marry her. Was he stupid? He was already married. Jeanine screamed at him not to be ridiculous. She wrenched her arm from his as he shouted that he'd found out things.

'So have I,' she shouted back as she fled along the pavement.

She had to get to Petrov's. Gerry would never follow her there. He had too much work to do. As she ran, with a fast-beating heart and shaking hands, Jeanine rummaged in her handbag for her bleeper. She found it and pointed it at the vehicle.

She jumped into the driving seat and turned on the ignition. Jeanine left Gerry nonplussed, staring at her as she drove away from him and Kensington. She raced towards the A40, Buckinghamshire and Petrov's Tudor mansion.

8

'Hotsie Totsie, that's what she is. I don't think you're going to like what it says, sir,' said Mr Norris, handing Gerry a most official-looking document.

'No?' said Gerry. He had decided to collect the private detective's report in person.

'She's been a bit of a naughty girl, your wife,' said Mr Norris. He was a shabby nondescript man who merged perfectly with his seedy surroundings – a dingy office in a run-down back street in Fulham. 'Actually, sir, I'd go further than that. I'd say she's been a very naughty girl and looks like she's been that way for some time.'

'That way?' queried Gerry.

'You'll see what I mean, sir, when you start reading. And if you'll take my advice, you'll find somewhere cosy and quiet before you do.'

'Cosy and quiet?' said Gerry.

'Yes, sir. No disturbances. I think you need to be by yourself, sir, when you read that. Somewhere fresh. Nice and fresh with good clean air.'

'Mr Norris, what has she been up to?'

'Filth, sir. Real filth. Disgusting. I couldn't believe my eyes, sir. Popping out of my head, they was. I've seen a few things in my life, sir, but I can honestly say I didn't think anybody carried on like that. Sex. She's sex mad, sir.'

'My wife!' exclaimed Gerry.

'Yes, sir, your wife, sir. Sex mad.'

'But . . .' Gerry was dumbstruck.

'Pretended she didn't like it, sir? Well, you wait till you read what's in there, that's all I can say,' said Mr Norris unctuously, handing Gerry a large squashy package.

'What's this?' asked Gerry.

'Clothes for the job,' he said.

'Clothes for the job?' queried Gerry.

'You'll understand after you've read my report,' said Mr Norris. 'And I had to get it made special.'

Gerry began to pull at the Sellotape binding the parcel.

'Not here, if you don't mind, sir. I suggest you open everything together. Except this.' Mr Norris gave Gerry a small envelope. 'It's my expenses. You can open that now 'cos I would appreciate immediate settlement. And here, sir, is the grand total. I like that paid within seven days sir, otherwise I start charging interest.'

Gerry settled his account with the obnoxious Mr Norris, then left as quickly as he could. He drove to Hammersmith and then out on the M4. He followed the road to Windsor, turning off for Bray. He didn't really know where he was going but enjoyed driving near the river. He had to think. Auralie sex mad? He'd had an inkling that she was not quite what he'd thought she was. The fact that she'd had one sex session with a woman did not make her sex mad. She was deceitful for not telling him, but not sex mad. Gerry found a hidden spot close to the river-bank where he could see the moorhens, the ducks and the swans. He sat for a moment watching them go bottoms-up in the water in their search for food.

He opened the parcel and saw that it contained a monk's habit. He held it out and looked at it, a smile hovering over his lips. He turned the garment this way and that with some amusement. There did not seem to be anything very peculiar about it, except it was dark green. Brown, white and black habits he had seen before but never dark green. He could not think why Mr Norris should have needed it. He lay it on the seat beside him.

Then Gerry opened the report. It was Auralie's daily routine, detailed and itemised. Mr Norris was boringly thorough. Each day had its own page. What time Auralie left the house and where she went. It was accurate, but verbose, with many idiosyncratic observations. Gerry skimmed through it and decided that Mr Norris must be slightly unhinged, definitely a sandwich short of a picnic. Auralie was a workaholic not a sexaholic. Then, on the tenth day the report said something quite different. She had left home at the normal time but had not gone to her workshop. Instead she had headed west and had taken the A40 out to Buckinghamshire. Gerry began to read more carefully.

'I tailed your wife on the A40 as far as High Wycombe. She turned off the main drag and I followed her through the narrow, winding country lanes. There is nothing in the world like the English countryside in summer. The sound of birdsong, the green of the hedgerows, the sunlight dappling through the trees.'

God, thought Gerry, why does the man have to start painting pictures. He was irritated with him. Wanted him to get to the point.

'Your wife was heading towards Lower Wycombe, along a pretty leafy lane. I noticed plenty of blackbirds and thrushes in the hedges and lots of dandelions (we used to call them dandelions-wet-the-bed when I was a kid) in the grass verge. Then she turned into a private road with a sign that read "Monastery. Trespassers will be Prosecuted." Following her now was quite tricky so I left the car and proceeded a mile or so on foot. I eventually reached some very high security gates. I deduced your wife must have gone inside as neither she nor the car could be seen.

The gates were firmly closed, and there was nowhere else she could go. The gates had a number of buttons to press to gain entry. As I did not have the code to enter in this manner, and I could think of no reason for going inside a monastery, I thought I had better devise another way of having a look. There was a high wall covered in well-established Virginia creeper. I managed to climb up it at a point where there was a horse chestnut tree on the other side. A tree provides excellent cover during surveillance activities. Climbing does not present me with much difficulty as I attend the local gym and keep myself very fit.'

Gerry stifled a yawn. The man was such a bore. Gerry read on.

'From my perch on a branch overhanging the gate, I observed a well-kept drive leading to a rather grand house, Tudor, by the looks of it, with fine lawns and plenty of good oaks dotted about. To the west of the house a number of young poplar trees stood in a row. This looked to me very continental. I deduced two things from this. That the order was foreign, or the abbot was, and that the prevailing wind was from the west. And the west wind can be quite vicious in the Chilterns.

'I saw your wife's German sports car standing in the driveway outside the house. I glanced around and saw people in the garden. They looked like monks. They all wore dark-green habits. One monk was riding a power-driven lawn mower. The others were weeding.

'Suddenly a person clothed head to toe in one of the aforementioned monk's habits appeared out of nowhere with a pair of secateurs in his hand and began snipping at the lower branches of the tree I was in. I sat as still as I could and was able to get a good look at his habit. As it turned out this was quite handy. I sat in this tree for a good few hours, and very uncomfortable it was, too. Eventually I saw your wife coming from the house. She got into her car with a man. They drove to the gate where they stopped. I could overhear them as they spoke. "Show me the new combination, Jackson," your wife said to the man, who was very large and black and dressed as a butler. A butler in a monastery. I thought that was a bit rum. "It's 5991FO," said the man called Jackson. "I'll remember. See you next Wednesday back here," your wife replied as she drove away. Owing to the nearby presence of the butler, Jackson, I could not get back to my car to pursue her. However, I am a supremely optimistic person and I counted not my losses but my gains. I had now learnt she was returning to the monastery the following week. This would leave me time to get my own monk's habit made as soon as I returned to London (which I did – see enclosed bill for said item). Then I would be able to follow her inside with no questions asked. As I had also made a note of the combination I would also be able to open the security gates.'

Gerry yawned and stretched his arms. He wondered when it was going to say something that interested him. Something sexy. He had been geared up to believe his wife was a sexpot and all he had discovered so far was that she worked hard and had visited a monastery. He flipped through the following pages of Auralie's days. Work, work and more work. She left home, went to her workshop, stayed there all day and went home again. On one occasion she had three people visit her during the lunch hour. One young man and two young women. Mr Norris noted that this was unusual because, 'Normally, apart from your wife there is no one in the building from twelve until two.'

Gerry was singularly disinterested in the comings and goings of Auralie's working life. He turned to the page for the next Wednesday.

'Your wife left her home at the usual time, then took the A40 to Buckinghamshire. I shadowed her all the way to the monastery. I did not leave my car where I had before, but further down the lane, before the private road begins. I had previously ascertained that there was a certain spot where, if needs be, I could jump over the wall, climb into my car and make a quick getaway. And that is where I left my car. I then put on the green monk's habit which I'd had made the previous week. I climbed up and over the wall. This had not been my original intention. I had planned to go in by the gate but thought better of it. I might be seen. I climbed the wall and looked over.

'Unlike the previous time I did not see any monks mowing the lawn or weeding. But the gardens did look very nice. I am a bit of a gardener myself so I noticed that. I also noticed that in amongst the red hot pokers in the herbaceous border they had some exotic plants, the likes of which I had only ever seen in the Royal Botanical Gardens at Kew.

'It was a very sunny day. Keeping close to the old wall I walked to the back of the house, which is north facing, so is darker than the front.

'I tried a few of the doors. Two were locked and one was a shed full of coal. I tried another door. I have to stress here that I am an expert at opening doors with great caution and utter quiet. And this door was no exception. It gave way to my gentle pressure on the old-fashioned latch. It opened. I was finally inside the house and in what seemed to me to be the larder; cheeses, hams and salamis were hanging from hooks. It was quite cold in there. Nobody was about. The next room was a huge kitchen. Nobody in there either. The kitchen led on to a long corridor. I had my best rubber-soled shoes on and was able to creep extremely quietly along the flagstones. I didn't see anybody and I didn't hear anything. I kept walking. I came to an arched oak door with a very heavy latch. Well, sir, I must just have walked through the servants' quarters because all of a sudden the whole place changed. It was hot for starters. Very good central heating and it was going full blast. It might be summer outside but it was freezing inside; quite the proverbial brass monkey's in that old house. There was lots of panelling and thick carpets everywhere and I could hear music and voices. Immediately I thought there was something strange about that music, but I did not realise straight away what it was. I was in a monastery but it wasn't hymns or chants, it was not religious music. Somebody was playing very loud rock and roll. It was not your nice Cliff Richard songs either. This was that noisy disco dance stuff.

'Still I had not seen anybody. Then I come to a load of different doors. They were all the same. Big and heavy with iron clasps on them. I had a choice. I could not think which one to choose, so I did what I used to do when I was a kid – eeny meeny miney mo. Very carefully and slowly I lifted the latch and peeped round the door. What I saw, sir, made my eyes pop.

'The door opened on to a huge hall. And I realised it would not have mattered which door I had chosen as they all opened onto this hall. It had a high-vaulted and beamed ceiling and plenty of panelling. And, although it was mid-morning, the very thick curtains were drawn closed. I must say the curtains were very good quality with lots of nice gold tasselling. The room was lit by candles. Hundreds of them everywhere in cast-iron candlesticks. A right old fire risk I'd have said if I'd been a fire officer. And even more so when I looked up and saw loads of tapestries hanging from the walls. What I could see of them in the candlelight, they all seemed to be scenes of naked nymphs cavorting in the countryside. Down the centre of the hall was a long table, the sort used for banquets. In front of an enormous fireplace were three or four very nice antique armchairs with heavy carving on the legs. Jacobean, I'd say, but I'm not a connoisseur. And some nice Victorian footstools. I knew they were Victorian because an old client of mine left me a couple just like them in her will. At one end of the room there was a dais. On this dais there was what looked to me like a throne but it was very strange. It had arms, a wide seat and extra high long legs. I call it a throne but really it looked more like a commode on stilts. This was the only chair in the room not occupied. Now, sir, it wasn't any of this what made my eyes pop. No, sir, it was the people.

'The whole room was awash with people. And it was what they were doing that made my eyes boggle. Most of them were wearing the monk's habit, but some of them were stark naked. Your wife was wearing a bright red PVC suit. I call it a suit for want of a better name. This article of clothing had cut-outs where her breasts, buttocks and her front privates stuck through. She wore long leather gloves and thigh-high leather boots with very high heels. She was whipping a naked, plump young girl. Yes sir, whipping. The girl she was whipping had a very large white bottom and your wife was leaving some very red marks on this girl's bottom. I also noticed that the girl was blindfolded and her hands were manacled and chained to a large hook hanging from the beams. Crouching in front of the girl was a skinny, hatchet-faced older woman in a black dress, a large bunch of keys dangling from a leather belt around her waist. She was sucking between the girl's legs every time your wife stopped with the whip.

'There were various people in action on the long table. They were all naked. The men and women who were lying down had either a man or a woman sitting or lying on top of them. It did not seem to matter to anybody if it was woman to woman or man to man or woman to man. Everyone was playing with someone else's privates.

'I noticed a heavily built, middle-aged white man lying on the table. He had a young slim red-haired woman going up and down on his pelvis. Yes, sir, up and down as if she was playing ride a cock horse to Banbury Cross, sir. A pale, thin young man with ginger hair stood beside them. The heavily built man had his head turned towards the younger man. Sir, I almost hesitate to write what I saw but in the nature of my job I have to record many things. The young man's member was in the older man's mouth and he was jerking it backwards and forwards as if he was on the point of ecstasy. I averted my eyes fast.

'A man sitting in one of the armchairs had his legs draped over the arms. A young woman knelt in front of him sucking his manhood whilst at the same time another man lay on the floor beneath her, his penis embedded inside her.

'I was peering round the door ready to run like hell if anybody caught me. The incidents I am relating I saw with my own eyes, sir. I saw every variance of the sex act between men and women that I could think of, and many that had never crossed my mind.

'I saw a particularly handsome, dark-haired young man lead one of the naked women over to the wall. He pressed a button and part of the panelling slid away to reveal a tiled recess. He stood the girl in the recess and then proceeded to urinate over her. Yes, sir, urinate. Pee, sir, and paying particular attention to her vagina, sir.

'I turned my eyes quickly away from such filth only to see a woman lying outstretched on the floor, another woman on her knees in front of her. She had her mouth between the other's legs and appeared to be slobbering over her belly and thighs. Jackson, the black butler, with all his assets on show, was spanking the kneeling woman's buttocks.

'I saw the heavily built, middle-aged man take up a large ornamental mallet and strike a copper gong. Suddenly your wife stopped whipping the plump young girl. As if it were part of a pre-ordained ceremony, the occupants of the long table slid to the floor as your wife slowly progressed past the kneeling initiates. Two of the monks then lifted her onto the table and proceeded to spread her legs open wide. She seemed to be on display, sir. I then watched everybody in the room stand in line before her. One by one they paid homage by kneeling in front of her and sucking and licking her privates, sir. I deduced from this that she was some sort of High Priestess of this disgusting order.

'When they had finished they returned to whatever practices they had been up to before the gong sounded. The fat young woman that your wife had been whipping climbed onto the table and, hovering on her haunches, lowered her genital area onto your wife's mouth. The handsome young man that only minutes before I had seen urinating on a young girl now stood between your wife's outstretched legs. He took hold of his member and, rubbing it until it was very stiff, began to probe your wife's privates. A few movements later he suddenly stuck it into her hard and as far as it would go. All this time your wife's arms were outstretched over the edge of the table. Two young men came and stood beside her, putting their manhoods into her hands which closed over their upright offerings. Your wife was sucking a woman whilst having intercourse with a man and at the same time masturbating two other men. Sir, this has to be one of the most disgusting scenes I have ever witnessed.

'Couples changed their coupling. Nobody seemed to care which orifice was plundered or which sex did the plundering. It was a free-for-all. Sir, I have to report that your wife was attending a sex orgy. An orgy of sex, sir, and in the middle of the day!

'As I stood there the music got louder and louder and the participants seemed to get more and more adventurous. There were bowls of fruit and vegetables lying around. I noticed that bananas, carrots, cucumbers and courgettes were being used for purposes not originally intended. One man was addicted to mushrooms. He had a bowl beside him. He kept lifting the habit of the nearest young woman and dipping a mushroom between her legs before eating it.

'Sir, this was when I decided that I had seen enough. I quietly closed the door and quickly made my way back. I climbed over the wall, removed the habit, got into my car and drove to the top of the lane. There I waited.

'It was four hours later, sir, when your wife passed me in her car. I followed her back to her office in London. There she stayed until the time she normally went home.

'Since then your wife has paid one further visit to the monastery, lasting only an hour and a half. But on this particular occasion she did not look at all happy when she left. I did not pursue her back to London this time, but decided to make enquiries about the monastery in the local village. I was told that everybody roundabout thought it was a "funny place" and that the people there belong to a strange sect run by a man called Petrov Vladelsky. Signed M. Norris.'

Gerry's initial instinct was to hurl this abomination into the river. To be rid of it forever. He was appalled and furious. He felt tainted. Everything about it was hateful. The place, the people, how it was written, the horrible little man who had written it, Auralie and himself. Most of all Gerry hated himself for opening up this can of worms. It was he who had contracted the wretched Mr Norris to spy on his wife in order to discover who had taken the photographs of him making love to Jeanine. But there was no mention of this in the report. He was no nearer the truth now than he was five hours ago. He still had no idea whether his wife was responsible for that little incident. Throughout the whole ghastly document there was not one mention of a photographer, a camera, film or photographs. The entire exercise had been a costly mistake.

Or had it? Gerry tried to calm down and think more rationally. No, he would not throw the report in the river; he would use it as evidence of his wife's adultery and divorce her. Gerry carefully stowed the report into the glove compartment, turned on the ignition, released the handbrake and put the car into gear. He could not live with a woman so depraved. She would have to move out of their home immediately.

Gerry was perplexed. He had thought his wife was frigid, didn't like sex. Now he had discovered that she enjoyed sex on a grand scale. She had been unfaithful to him to a degree he found hard to swallow. He wondered just why she had married him? Could it have been business? She was pretty sharp off the ground when it came to applying for the contract from his father's new airline. Could it have been that? Gerry dismissed the thought. Everything to do with the airline had been a closely-guarded secret that his wife had known nothing about.

As he drove along the by-ways Gerry was torn by conflicting emotions. Jeanine's face appeared before him. He tried to banish her image from his mind. He did not want to think about her or their little episode together.

Gerry was filled with righteous indignation. How dare Auralie have the gall to marry him whilst belonging to a sex sect run by her uncle? Gerry had never thought much of Petrov. He had found him smarmy. Women liked him. Gerry was aware of that. He had noticed how they flocked to his side at his and Auralie's wedding reception. But Olga had divorced Petrov and it was no wonder. Not that Gerry cared much for Olga either. She was too arrogant, too haughty and . . . He searched for the right word. Too authoritative? No, too masculine.

Gerry, like his father, preferred gentle women. Auralie wasn't gentle. She was dark, mysterious, a firebrand. Why had he married her if she was not his type? Because she had seemed unobtainable and pure. In the light of Mr Norris's report, that was a nasty joke. And the joke was on him. That hurt most. What had the private detective called his wife? Sex mad? She had played frigid with Gerry and screwed everything in sight at her uncle's so-called monastery. And Petrov had encouraged her. Gerry visualised the scenes that Mr Norris had described, and nearly burst a blood vessel. His wife, Auralie, the dominatrix in red PVC with cut-outs, allowing herself to be screwed and felt by all and sundry. It was too much. She would have to go. Gerry's anger exploded. He would have liked to have hit out at something. Instead he slammed his foot on the accelerator in a burst of rage. A man who wanted to become a Member of Parliament, who was a respected person in society, could not have a wife who was a sex maniac. It was only recently that he had put himself forward for a safe Home Counties constituency and had already been told that his application was being favourably considered. A whisper of scandal, especially a sexual scandal, now, or in the future, and any political aspirations he might have would be scattered to the four winds.

Auralie's fate was sealed on the M4 outside Windsor. Gerry would not tolerate anything or anyone who might curtail his ambitions. By remaining his wife Auralie was no longer an asset but a hazard. He would have to divorce her quickly. A fast cut, with no damaging repercussions. Nothing in the press. Nothing leaked, nothing to hamper his political career. His private life did not affect his position within his father's company. The old man had himself been a gadabout in his time. Since Gerry's mother's death Sir Henry had had two divorces and a vast number of mistresses.

Gerry began to think about his father's relationships and realised that no woman had been on Sir Henry's horizon recently. He decided that all his father's energy must have gone into devising his latest venture, which was odd because nothing had stopped his sexual activities before. Sir Henry had a penchant for beautiful women and he activated that penchant whenever he could. Gerry thought his father must be feeling old. But he was rich and riches were a tremendous aphrodisiac, especially for young women. Gerry had discovered this at an early age. It was Auralie's hard-to-get response to his own overtures, her not wanting to know, that had increased his desire for her. His father liked Auralie but Gerry hoped his father would understand if there had to be a divorce. Emotional mistakes were forgivable, financial ones were not. However, the thought crossed Gerry's mind that a divorced, aspiring Member of Parliament was not an advantage. He would need another woman. That was when he allowed his thoughts to turn back to Jeanine.

Sweet, soft Jeanine. He recalled that special evening he found her dressed so sexily, and wondered how he could ever have thought her mousy. He had always been attracted to her, an attraction he had suppressed. His thoughts had drifted in Jeanine's direction each time Auralie had repulsed him. Wondering what it would be like to touch Jeanine's luscious ample breasts and to put his hands between her legs and feel her sex. That was the special evening he had found out. Jeanine had inflamed him.

The flowing silkiness of her luxuriant blonde hair, the soft pliability of her skin, the sight of the black stockings, the boots and the basque. Her unique erotic smell had mingled with the smell of her leather cape. The touch of her moist, soft, squidgy sex as his fingers delved into its depths. The feel of her enlarged clitoris as he went down on her, sucking her juices, his mouth and tongue gliding on her tender, tingling, unfurling inner opening. Her sex had behaved and used muscles he did not know any woman possessed. He relived the exquisite sensation of her cool hands on his prick. This was superseded only by the sublime moment of entry and the sense of coming home, of belonging. The oneness of their flesh; hardness and yielding uniting. Gerry decided that having sex with Jeanine was one of the most exciting things he had ever done. And he wanted to do it again. Thinking about her had made him stiff. He suddenly noticed that he was as upright as a ramrod. He needed to take her. To feel her squirming beneath him. He wanted her badly, felt addicted to her body.

He had telephoned her on several occasions but she had always made excuses not to take his calls. He realised that it was because she was ashamed. She had screwed a married man. Not only a married man, but a man married to her cousin. But he would very soon not be a married man. He would be free, free to screw Jeanine whenever he wanted. He would marry her. He would make her his. The thought came to him so quickly he did not have time to deliberate on it or work it out. It was a flash of inspiration – she would make the perfect wife. She was pliant and sexy and unobtainable. It was the obvious solution. He would divorce the sex-mad bitch, Auralie, and marry gentle, malleable, loving Jeanine.

Gerry drove towards Jeanine's hotel. He must see her. He must tell her. He must hold her in his arms, kiss her, explain that he had fallen madly in love with her and would do anything for her. And she must marry him.

He could barely contain himself. His lust, his ego, his penis were all sharp, upright and raring to go. He cursed every red light and mentally thanked every green one. He turned into the smart Kensington street where Jeanine's hotel was situated. The first person he saw was Jeanine, standing on the steps and looking stunning in a grey-blue crêpe de chine dress. This was real luck. She could not avoid him or have a flunkey say she wasn't in. He brought his car to a shrieking halt and double parked. He jumped out and ran towards her.

'Jeanine. Jeanine,' he said, thinking how beautiful and vulnerable she looked. She had her hair loose again, sexily loose. He wanted to run it through his fingers. Feel its blonde silkiness.

'Gerry!' she gasped.

'Darling,' he said, running up the steps, his arms outstretched.

'Don't, Gerry,' she said, taking two steps up and away from him.

She seemed agitated. He wanted to hold her in his arms and soothe away her agitation.

'I love you,' he blurted out.

'For God's sake, Gerry,' she said and tried to push past him. He grabbed her.

'Gerry, let go of me.'

'Darling,' he said. 'Look at me.'

'No,' she said, twisting and turning in his arms. She was determined he would not see her tear-stained face.

'Let's go inside and talk. I've something to say.'

'No,' she cried, almost screaming. 'No, don't. Go away, leave me alone.'

'I want to marry you,' he said.

'Gerry, you're being ridiculous and I have an appointment. Please let me go.'

'No, I am not being ridiculous. I've found out things.'

'And so have I,' said Jeanine, wrenching her arm from his grip and fleeing down the steps.

Jeanine ran to her car, opened the door and got in. Gerry ran after her.

'Jeanine, please, listen to me, I mean what I say. I want to marry you.'

Jeanine's answer was to put the car into gear and drive speedily away from him.

Puzzled, perplexed, angry and frustrated, Gerry decided to follow her. He would speak to her before she got to her appointment. She had to be made to understand he was serious.

Gerry followed her through the streets of Kensington then up to White City and on to the A40. If he started his journey puzzled and perplexed he was even more so as the miles went by and he found himself heading for High Wycombe. Jeanine turned off the freeway and took the direction for Lower Wycombe. Before the village she turned off into a narrow leafy lane. Gerry stopped his car at a notice that said 'Monastery. Trespassers will be Prosecuted.' It was as if he were re-reading the private detective's report. This was the headquarters of Petrov's sex sect.

He was completely bewildered. Why would his darling, his sweet Jeanine, come here, to this place of monstrous iniquity? Then he remembered. She had once said something to him about going to confession. She had mentioned her Confessor. Could this be Petrov? Did she realise what went on in there? He could not believe Jeanine was capable of deceiving him. When she had mentioned her Confessor there had been no hint of sala-ciousness in her voice. No undercurrent of sex. In fact he thought he had caught a hint of fear. Instinctively he knew she had nothing to do with what went on in there. Jeanine was innocent of perversion. Something had forced her to come here. She had been agitated, almost desperate, when he had talked to her on the steps of her hotel. Something awful must have happened.

Gerry felt a disappointed and defeated man. All his energy had dissipated. He let his head fall back against the headrest and fell asleep.

He didn't know what woke him up, the screech of a bird or a car tyre. Whatever it was he was suddenly, instantly alert. He remembered he was outside Petrov's mansion and Jeanine was inside. He had slept for more than an hour. His eye caught sight of the monk's habit on the seat beside him. Gerry was galva-nised into action. He stripped naked and put on the habit. He checked the report in the glove compartment to find the combin-ation number for the gate. He would enter the monastery. He would find Jeanine and save her from Petrov and his sect.

Gerry hoped he wouldn't be too late.

9

'Monsieur Petrov is in a meeting,' Jackson said to Jeanine, thinking how wonderfully sexual she looked as she stood at the monastery door. How ripe. How ready for the taking. He led her to a small ante-room close to the great hall.

Jackson opened a heavily carved Jacobean sideboard.

'Monsieur Petrov said please make yourself comfortable and take a drink. Glasses are here,' he said, indicating the lower shelf, 'and spirits and liqueurs here.' He indicated the upper shelf. 'And over here is the champagne.'

Jackson pushed a button to reveal a refrigerator. 'If you want anything to eat ring the bell and Mrs Klowski will come.'

'Thank you, but I'm not hungry,' said Jeanine, who'd always been more than a little frightened of Mrs Klowski. 'Is Petrov likely to be long?'

'It's possible, but he said it's important you wait. Monsieur has a good selection of books and magazines.' Jackson pointed to the bookcase.

He departed, closing the heavy oak door behind him. Jeanine hadn't been in this room before. There was a full-length mirror on one wall and lithographs on the others. She felt nervous and wondered what Petrov intended for her. She sat idly for a moment then opened the fridge. She saw the pretty, white-flowered bottles of Perrier Jouet Epoque and knew instantly that was the taste she wanted. Jeanine opened the bottle, took down a flute, filled it and began to sip. Then she decided a cocktail would be a good idea. As she opened the spirit cabinet her eyes were drawn to an unusual ivory statuette. It was long and smooth, shaped like a penis. She gently took it down and stroked it. Jeanine liked its feel.

As she caressed the ivory she browsed along the bookshelves. She wanted an easy read, something that didn't demand too much of her attention. The great American, European and Russian classics of fiction were there, but Jeanine had read them all and she was not in the mood to begin reading them again. What was she in the mood for? she asked herself. That familiar tingling between her legs had returned. She hadn't felt it on her journey but now, within the portals of Petrov's manor house, sex seemed to be coming at her through the walls. She continued to scan the shelves. There were some travel books. She glanced half-heartedly at one of them, then put it back. Then her eye caught sight of a leather-bound book with nothing on its spine. No title. A mystery. Jeanine liked that. She took it from the shelf.

She put the ivory down on a small table beside the only chair in the room, opposite the full-length mirror. She sat down, sipped some more champagne and opened the book at random.

'. . . his fingers trailed lovingly over her belly, down to the soft moistness between her legs. He plunged in, taking her, bending her to his will. She had to be made to understand that whatever he wanted she must do. She felt the hard stiffness of his sex plundering her very essence . . .'

It was sex again. Jeanine snapped the book closed and hurriedly put it back on the shelf. She drank some more champagne, then glanced over at the series of lithographs on the panelling. The first one depicted a man in eighteenth-century costume fondling a woman. He had his hands up under her skirt. In the next the same man had his trousers off, his cock in the woman's mouth. In the third the woman had her legs in the air, his penis entering her hidden place. In the fourth one the man's friend had joined them and his cock was now in the woman's mouth. The pictures did nothing to assuage Jeanine's sexuality, but merely increased it. As she stood looking at them she began to rub herself. She undid a couple of the lower buttons on her dress, lifted the silk of her knickers out of the way and felt her own hidden place. She was wet. She let her fingers glide on the wetness, enticing her little bud to emerge. It stiffened beneath her touch. She felt her breasts filling out, her nipples hardening. The tingling between her legs was now desire for something thicker, bigger. She picked up the penis-shaped ivory, undid more of the buttons of her dress, pulled her knickers open, stretched her legs wide and let it drift leisurely along her slowly swelling sex-lips.

From the other side of the mirror Petrov was watching her.

'That, my friend, is a woman waiting to be screwed,' said Petrov to Jackson. Jackson smiled. He and Petrov had been looking forward to this day for some considerable time. The two old friends had plotted and planned over many a boozy evening exactly what they would do to Jeanine when they got the chance.

'What do you say, Vera?' Petrov asked Mrs Klowski, who was standing beside him, watching Jeanine as she played with herself with the ivory dildo.

'I say she needs to be well sucked,' Vera Klowski answered, licking her lips.

Mrs Klowski had a penchant for sucking women's pussies. She had a thick fat tongue that could worm its way into the smallest furl and crevice.

'That was a stroke of genius leaving that Japanese ivory dildo in the drinks cabinet,' said Jackson, pleased with his own idea.

'I want her arse,' said Mr Sawyer, who sat next to Mrs Klowski.

'And you shall have it, Leon,' replied Petrov. That was Leon's agreed reward for planting the photographs of Jeanine in her hotel foyer.

'I'll give her a good buggering,' continued Leon Sawyer, stroking himself in anticipation.

'And what will Auralie and Olga do to her?' said Mrs Klowski.

'As they will,' said Petrov. 'But you can tell them I will see them here in five minutes.'

Mrs Klowski left the room as Petrov closed the panel over the two-way mirror.

Unaware of the existence of the special mirror, Jeanine lay back in the chair in the ante-room, happily enticing herself. She thought of Gerry screwing her and then she thought about her Confessor. She wondered if he would screw her. Would that be her punishment? She had a vision of Petrov tying her down and licking her slowly, his tongue entering her open sex.

Then she heard a raised voice coming from outside the door. Jeanine strained her ears and listened. She suddenly realised it was Auralie. Jeanine froze.

'But you can't do that to me,' Auralie was pleading, almost sobbing. 'You can't. I love you. You know I love you. Please. Kiss me. Say you love me.'

The tone and the tears were most unexpected coming from Auralie, and Jeanine wondered who her cousin was talking to. Could it be Gerry? She was aware that he'd been following her, but she thought she had lost him *en route*. What was he now going to do to Auralie?

The voices on the other side of the door subsided to a whisper. Jeanine pulled down her frock, tiptoed over and tried to hear what was being said. Then she heard Olga's voice.

'*Chérie, chérie,*' said Olga, 'I love you too, but business is business. We have to have that contract. It's absolutely vital. Surely you've realised that Petrov has suffered substantial losses recently. The contract is the one thing that will save us, all of us.'

Jeanine was puzzled.

'You know I love you more than anything,' she heard Auralie say. 'I only married that bloody Gerry because you wanted me to. Kiss me, Olga. Tell me you love me.'

Jeanine suddenly realised who Auralie was talking to. So Auralie loved Olga. She was having an affair with her. The possibility of something that extraordinary had never for one moment crossed Jeanine's mind. She took a deep breath as she considered it. Auralie and Olga were lovers. But why had Olga wanted Auralie to marry Gerry? It was a bizarre twist, thought Jeanine.

'Come, *chérie*, dry your eyes,' said Olga. 'We'll see Petrov in a moment. We'll see what he has to say. Perhaps that bloody bitch Penelope doesn't hate you as much as you think she does.'

'She does,' said Auralie. 'She's never forgiven me. She said she never would, she never has and she never will. And we will never get that contract now.'

'Madame Olga,' Mrs Klowski's voice interrupted Auralie. 'Monsieur Petrov said he is ready to see you now.'

The voices stopped and, curious, Jeanine slowly and carefully opened the door and looked outside. There was no one about but then she heard the same voices, this time coming from within Petrov's office next door. She stood in an alcove close to the door and listened.

'What do you mean "No"!' she heard Auralie screech.

'What I said. No,' said Petrov.

'Olga, say something. Make him change his mind,' pleaded

Auralie, desperately. 'The only way we can get the contract now is if we send the photographs of Gerry and Jeanine to Penelope. When she sees them she'll have to give us the contract to keep the whole thing quiet.'

'No, that's not the way I do business,' said Petrov, flatly.

'After I went to the trouble of getting the photographs taken,' said Auralie.

'And you were out of order,' said Petrov. 'Why did you even consider it?'

'Originally it wasn't for business. It was for my divorce,' said Auralie. 'I knew Jeanine fancied Gerry. I could tell by the look on her face whenever she saw him. Him too, I'd guessed that. That's why I set it up. After we'd got the contract I'd get a good divorce. Jeanine was a half-naked slut, always pretending she's so good, so pure. That fat cow was letting my husband lick between her legs. Dressed like a *putain* she let him screw her, let him stick his prick in her blonde pussy, stick a finger in her tight little arse and let him suck her big tits.'

'You were still out of order,' repeated Petrov, unimpressed.

Standing in the alcove Jeanine held her breath, astounded at what she had overheard. So Auralie knew she had had sex with Gerry. They all knew. She considered making a run for it. She would forget about confession. Forget about her hotel and what had happened there.

Jeanine half turned to go but Auralie's high, agitated voice caught her attention.

'First she marries Laurence . . .'

'Why are you still so bothered about that?' exclaimed Petrov.

'Because Laurence was the only man I ever really loved,' replied Auralie.

My God, thought Jeanine, had Auralie and Laurence been

lovers? She had asked Laurence about it but he'd always denied it. Had he lied to her? Then Auralie, by staying silent, must have lied as well.

'. . . then she screws my husband,' continued Auralie, by now in tears and hysterical. 'And you always feel so sorry for Jeanine. You think she's so pure. Bah. And now that bitch's mother has gone and married Sir Henry. Where does that leave me with the contract? You know Penelope hates me and it was all bloody Stefan's fault. He let me do it. He knew what I was doing and just pretended to be asleep.'

Jeanine's mind was reeling. So Auralie had done something with Stefan. That was the reason her mother so disliked her. But what? Perhaps now she would find out.

'That's why I say send the photographs to Penelope and tell her unless she makes certain we get the contract we'll send them to the tabloid press.'

'No,' said Petrov once more, with a finality in his voice that brooked no opposition.

Jeanine shivered at the thought of her mother seeing pictures of her – the woman taken in adultery – with Auralie's husband, now Penelope's son-in-law. Penelope would never forgive her. It was not the sort of homecoming her mother would appreciate. God, thought Jeanine, what a mess she was in. At least Petrov was endeavouring to protect her from Auralie's spleen.

'We'll think of something else,' said Petrov. 'Jackson tells me Jeanine has arrived. She's finally come to confession. I told her when she came she must tell me everything. I also told her that as her sin was sexual, her penance, her punishment will be too. So, my dear Auralie, I suggest you get yourself dressed. The afternoon will not be wasted. You can give her part of her punishment. Olga, are you returning to London?'

'I will stay,' said Olga. 'Kensit and Nicole are with me and

I think they should be given the opportunity to enjoy themselves.'

Jeanine quickly slipped back into the ante-room, closed the door, picked up a travel book and gulped down some more champagne.

She had no time to mull over the conversation she had just heard. The door opened and Mrs Klowski entered. She signalled to Jeanine sternly.

'He is waiting for you in the confessional,' Mrs Klowski said as she led the way across the Persian carpet and down the long hall with its heavy panelling and gilded pictures. A couple of young novices scuttled past them before disappearing through a side door. The massively built Jackson appeared holding a large silver tray. As a rule he always smiled at Jeanine, now he ignored her. His face was impassive. Jeanine recalled that the young men who tended the gardens, who normally waved at her, today had remained very busy, not seeing her as she passed by. Jeanine had a terrible feeling they all knew of her fall from grace. She had a strong desire to run, run from the shame and mortification. Run, so that none of them, including Mrs Klowski, could see the tears stinging her eyes.

Instead Jeanine followed Mrs Klowski demurely, not attempting any pleasantries. Mrs Klowski's demeanour was not normally one that invited small talk. Jeanine studied the tall thin woman striding in front of her. Mrs Klowski was dressed in the classical housekeeper's uniform, a severe black frock, ringed at her waist by a large leather belt, from which hung a number of keys that jangled with each step. The woman's thick black stockings were without a wrinkle. Her feet were neatly encased in lace-up shoes, with, Jeanine was surprised to notice, quite a high heel. The woman's short cropped brown hair was parted on one side and held in place by a large black grip. Her short and stubby hands were scrupulously clean, her nails short and devoid of any varnish. In contrast, her wide fleshy mouth was painted a deep dark red. It should have made the woman look softer but, instead, the gloss and the darkness of the colour gave those lips a cruel and rapacious look. There was, Jeanine thought, only one word to describe Mrs Klowski and that was 'formidable'.

Mrs Klowski opened a door at the far end of the hall and they entered a carpeted and panelled room filled with rich tapestries and heavy Jacobean furniture. At one end was a minstrel's gallery with chairs arranged as if for watching a spectacle. At the far end of the room, opposite the minstrel's gallery, was a high dais approached by five steep steps. On this dais there was a throne-like chair. The main body of the room was dominated by a long, but not very wide, heavy oak table. Around the sides of the room and in front of the fireplace were high-backed armchairs, each with its own footstool and a couple of chaises-longues covered in cushions. The overall effect was one of wealth, supreme luxury and warmth. Seductive warmth.

'In there,' said Mrs Klowski, ushering Jeanine through a door into a confessional cubicle behind the dais. There Jeanine knelt with her mouth close against the grille. The moment she had dreaded had finally arrived. On the other side of the grille she dimly saw Petrov's face lean towards her.

'You allowed a man to touch you,' said her Confessor, but as a statement not a question.

Jeanine felt herself suddenly grow cold. Her knees trembled on the hard stool.

'You allowed a man to touch you,' he said again.

'Yes,' she whispered.

'How did that come about?' Petrov's deep-brown voice was soft and friendly. Some of her fear subsided. 'You'd better tell me. How did you get into a situation where you could be seduced?'

Jeanine was afraid again. She would have to tell him how she had been playing with herself and what she had been imagining. How she had bought herself some exotic, blatantly sexual clothes. How she had gone to a sex shop and invested in a dildo and a vibrator to help her act out her lurid fantasies. Jeanine lowered her head and her eyes but said nothing.

'Jeanine,' the voice spoke again. 'If you want to join our order then you must tell me. Every thought, every deed, must be brought out into the open. We have no secrets here. If you want to keep secrets then of course you are free to go. You may leave now.'

'No,' she said.

'Very well, then you must tell me what you have been doing.'

Jeanine drew a sharp breath and began her liturgy of sins. 'I ... I ...' Her voice faltered. 'I have been playing with myself.'

'Speak up I can't hear you,' Petrov said sharply. 'What did you say?'

'I have been playing with myself,' Jeanine said, louder and bolder. Repeating it the second time left her freer. Was this the beginning of her contrition?

'You have been playing with yourself?' his voice boomed into the darkness. 'Is that what I heard you say?'

'Yes,' she said, knowing her face was hot and flushed with shame.

'How did you do that?' he said. 'Tell me. How did you do that?'

'I undressed. Then I sat in front of my mirror and spread my legs and stroked myself. And then I put on some clothes I had bought ...'

'What sort of clothes?'

'Do I have to tell you?'

'Yes.'

'Sexy clothes. A basque made of leather and lace, and black silk stockings and satin crotchless knickers. Then I played with myself again until I was wet.'

'And then?' he asked.

Jeanine hung her head in shame.

'Jeanine,' his voice was stern. 'What did you do then?'

'I took out the dildo I had bought . . .'

'A dildo!' he exclaimed, his voice ringing round the cubicle. 'What sort of a dildo? Describe it.'

'It's in a soft, pink leather and it's about six inches long.'

'I see. And you began to play with it. Did you insert it?'

'Yes. I was wet and very open because I'd had my fingers right up inside me. Watching myself in the mirror I shoved it into me, and listened to the little soft noises it made as it glided backwards and forwards on my juices.'

'You sound as if you enjoyed it,' said Petrov.

'I did. I did,' she replied, enthusiastically. 'And as it went to and fro I pretended.'

'What did you pretend, Jeanine?' her Confessor asked.

'I pretended it was a man making love to me.'

'What man, Jeanine?' Petrov tried to keep the real interest out of his voice. He was hoping she would say it was him.

'Oh, I am so ashamed,' she said, aware that she would have to tell him the awful truth. Perhaps if she asked for his forgiveness now she need not admit to the rest. 'Forgive me.'

'I cannot forgive you until I know the full extent of your sin. Which man, Jeanine?'

'Gerry,' she whispered.

'Who?' Petrov shouted. This was not what he wanted to hear. Petrov was jealous. He would make her pay. 'I can't hear you if you whisper.'

'Gerry,' she said.

'Auralie's husband?'

'Yes.'

'You fantasised about Auralie's husband? That is wicked,' he said. 'Wickedness must not go unpunished. But you also allowed him to seduce you? To enter your sacred portals.'

Jeanine didn't answer.

'Jeanine,' Petrov's voice had a menacing quality. 'Why did you allow Gerry to fuck you?'

She felt a strange thrill between her legs, a dampening, as her Confessor used that particular word. Still she didn't reply.

'And how many times did he fuck you?' Petrov persisted.

'Once,' she whispered breathlessly. 'Only once.'

'Only once? Why was that? Did you not enjoy it? The truth now. Didn't you enjoy it?'

'I did enjoy it.'

'You enjoyed it. You enjoyed fucking your best friend's husband?'

Jeanine felt that thrill again, that tightening then closing of the muscles between her legs. She realised she was moving, swaying slightly. A part of her was beginning to feel a vicarious pleasure in the recounting of her sins. Her knickers were beginning to cling to her. Her own soft sweet smell was drifting up to her. She was aroused. She was sexually excited.

'And how do you think Auralie feels about that?' her Confessor inquired.

'I don't know,' Jeanine lied.

'Your wickedness will have to be punished. Will you accept whatever I desire to be your punishment?'

Jeanine was silent.

'Jeanine, I asked you a question. Will you accept whatever I desire to be your punishment?'

'Yes,' she said softly.

'Very well. You will have to be punished twice. The first by me, my choice, and the second by Auralie.'

'Auralie!' Jeanine exclaimed. 'Why Auralie?'

'Because, as it is Auralie you have wronged, it will be Auralie who will punish you,' Petrov said.

'No!' cried Jeanine.

'Yes. Whatever Auralie wants to do with you, will be done. Do you agree?'

'What would she want to do with me?' Jeanine asked.

'Whatever she wants. Do you agree? You have committed a sin of the flesh, a sexual sin, so your punishment must be a sexual punishment. Now tell me, do you agree?'

'Yes,' Jeanine said finally, once more experiencing a kindling of lust, a wantonness, a wetness between her legs. How could Auralie punish her sexually? Jeanine had sudden visions of her own fantasies. Of Gerry tying her down and licking her. But that would not be a punishment. Jeanine had loved his touch and had dreamt of him doing it again. Would Auralie touch her? No, that wasn't possible. Jeanine shivered.

'You will stay and think about your wickedness until some-body comes for you,' said her Confessor, closing the grille and leaving Jeanine in the semi-darkness of the cubicle.

She was surprised to find that all her fear had gone. Neither was she as penitent as when she had first arrived. Was it, she wondered, her Confessor's use of the word 'fuck' that had removed her shame? It was almost as if he had delighted in it, delighted in her mortification. If so, then her response was rebellion. Or had he wanted to fire her sexuality? Whatever the reason she now had a deep longing between her legs. She stood up, lifted her skirt, and wound her hand under her Directoire knickers. She had no idea how long she would be left in the cubicle but she decided she would play with herself to while away the time.

It was Mrs Klowski who opened the cubicle door before she had time to remove her hands from between her legs. Jackson followed her inside and stood behind Jeanine. Mrs Klowski, thin, stern, hatchet-faced and unsmiling, unbuttoned and removed Jeanine's blue crêpe-de-chine frock, revealing her leather-and-lace basque and her black silk Directoire drawers. Mrs Klowski hauled down the drawers and scooped Jeanine's breasts out from the shelter of their lace covering, displaying their full lusciousness. Then she dipped her hands in a bowl and coated Jeanine's breasts with sweet-smelling oils.

It was while Mrs Klowski was flicking Jeanine's nipples with her short stubby fingers that Jackson's freshly oiled, large black hands began stroking Jeanine's thighs between her stocking tops and her vagina. Very slowly these hands caressed her, the pressure becoming heavier as they inched towards her blonde mound. It was only his hands that touched her, the rest of his body seemed to be deliberately standing back. Jeanine remained perfectly still and upright, her arms hanging limply by her side. The muscles in her buttocks responded – contracting and easing, easing and contracting – in time with the slithering motion of the black hands. Jeanine was excited, but felt unsteady in her extremely high-heeled shoes. She was afraid that if she moved any other part of her body she might topple over. A transient sense of irritability washed over her as for the first time she was aware of the pain of the shoes she was wearing.

Suddenly Jackson seized Jeanine's hands, pinioned them behind her back and clapped handcuffs around her wrists. This unexpected action caused Jeanine to jolt her buttocks backwards and her breasts forwards. Jackson grabbed both her rounded cheeks and propelled her arse back again so that she was standing straight once more. As her hips jerked towards Mrs Klowski Jeanine's mound landed on the stern woman's waiting hand. Instantly Mrs Klowski imprisoned Jeanine's outer labia between her thumb and ring finger, trailed her middle finger along the soft unfurling inner flesh, and began teasing it.

The tingling thrill of the woman's finger touching her left Jeanine gasping. It was pure delight and Jeanine wanted more, much more. Her entire body was suffused in the sensation of a gentle electric current. It was as if her sex was the centre of a generator and Mrs Klowski's finger had turned the switch. The whole of her, every fibre, every nerve ending, was lit up. Jeanine moved her muscles invitingly but Mrs Klowski ignored the invitation. She failed to penetrate Jeanine's willing wetness. Mrs Klowski let her finger come to rest on Jeanine's small soft and hidden point. Jeanine let out an instant gasp. She was shaking and her imprisoned hands wanted to hold something, grasp something thick and warm and pulsating. Mrs Klowski rubbed Jeanine's clitoris gently, soothingly, enticingly. Exciting it until that concealed tip emerged victorious and hard, enlarged and engorged.

Jackson knelt down behind Jeanine and caressed her legs. Instinctively Jeanine edged her legs apart but Jackson forced them back together again. Jeanine was endeavouring to take more of Mrs Klowski's moving hand. Instead she was aware of the pressure of the man's body behind her. She felt Jackson's thick, warm and well-greased cock rubbing between the calves of her legs whilst his hands kneaded her buttocks; his lips kissing their roundness and sometimes allowing his tongue to find its way onto her arse.

This was somehow exactly what Jeanine wanted, though she had no idea she possessed an erogenous zone so far down her legs. She responded by rolling her hips. Jeanine had been hoping to ease Mrs Klowski's finger further round, inwards and upwards. But Mrs Klowski knew exactly what she was doing and had anticipated Jeanine's movement. She made her touch lighter, more feathery, even more tantalisingly. Jeanine gasped once more. Her mouth had gone completely dry but her sex-juices were oozing out. The whole of her being was heightened. It wasn't just the nerve endings in her lustful pussy that were on edge. Waiting, excited, every part of her body was screaming the same message. Caress me. Caress me more.

Then Jeanine felt the sweet sharpness of fingernails scraping slowly across her fully rounded pale-skinned bare bottom. This sudden sharpness flipped her over into undulating sexual rhapsody and total abandonment. Jeanine had arrived in unknown territory, the land of ecstatic trance. Mrs Klowski brought up one hand and caressed Jeanine's stiff nipples and breasts, then stepped to one side as Jackson stood up.

Each of them took hold of one of Jeanine's arms. They piloted her out of the cubicle into the darkened hall, where hypnotically sexual music was playing.

As she emerged, an unknown hand turned on a spotlight. Jeanine was unaware of anything or anybody except her own semi-nakedness and the two silent figures guiding her up the five steep steps onto the dais. There they positioned her on the carved wooden throne. The seat was moulded, comfortable, like a lavatory seat. Slowly, with care and precision, as if taking part in a religious ceremony, Mrs Klowski and Jackson each took one of Jeanine's feet and placed them onto tiny foot rests built into the front legs of the throne. Then they shackled Jeanine's ankles.

Jeanine sat acquiescent and motionless, her breasts jutting forward and her shoulders square. Her hands were still manacled behind her back and, with her legs apart, her swollen blonde mound was on display. Her secret inner lips, unfolded like red rose petals, were protruding and aching to be touched.

Jackson stood up. He too was in the full glare of the spotlight and Jeanine suddenly realised that his cock was level with her mouth. Jackson put his hand on her head, wound her hair around his fist, pulled her head towards his belly, then traced the tip of his penis along her lips.

Jeanine was concentrating on the size of the thing in front of her, wondering if she was expected to take it in her mouth. She did not notice that Mrs Klowski had moved behind her throne and was releasing part of the seat so that Jeanine's buttocks and sex suddenly dropped, hung loose and exposed. Jeanine gripped the arms of the chair and her mouth dropped open with surprise. Jackson stuffed his prick between her lips.

'Suck,' he commanded.

Holding onto her hair he thrust deep into her throat.

Jeanine heard a rustling beneath her throne and then felt the tongue licking her secret lips, her vulva. It was a thick tongue, and it was entering every tiny fold and crevice within her. It was opening her, sucking and slurping at her juices.

The unknown tongue caused a reaction in her brain. Vivid and explicit sexual thoughts swamped her. Total wantonness overwhelmed her as she frantically moved her crotch muscles in an attempt to draw the tongue further upwards. But the tongue withdrew and nibbled on her clit.

In the harsh glare of the spotlight Jeanine felt a movement in the darkness beyond. There was an all-pervading smell of leather in the room. Jackson removed his prick from Jeanine's mouth and turned her head so that she saw shapes moving towards her. Some of the shapes wore hooded habits, others had parts of their body covered in black leather. Everyone was masked. As the shapes, in assorted heights and widths, came closer, Jeanine was able to see that there seemed to be an equal number of men and women.

The men wore silver-studded black leather collars and strips of leather down the front of their bodies. This left their chests bare but their stomach, hips and legs encased. Their costumes were cut in such a way that their naked balls were pushed forward, their buttocks bare and their upright pricks clearly on show.

The women also wore studded collars and some wore tight leather costumes that fitted over their shoulders and down their arms, over their bellies and down their legs. Their breasts projected through cut-outs and their bare buttocks swelled out from under the tight leather. Most of the women had shaven pubises and these were emphasised by the lack of any covering. Others wore leather shorts cut high over the thigh and held up with braces which grazed their naked breasts. These braces, attached to a leather necklet, were hoisted hard at the waist-band, tensioning the leather shorts upwards and causing them to pucker and seam into the women's crotches, allowing a substantial showing of their naked fleshy bare bottoms. Some women wore thigh-high boots, others very high-heeled shoes. The men and the women wore long black lace-up leather gloves.

Six men and six women in leather turned away from her and bowed in the direction of the minstrels' gallery. Then one by one the twelve went up on the dais and stood in line before Jeanine and bowed again. The men took their balls and their stiff cocks into their gloved hands and began playing with themselves. It was as if each was offering her a present. And the choice was hers. Then the women entered the spot-light. They spread their legs apart, put their gloved hands over their naked mounds and each began fingering her own clitoris. Jeanine wondered if this was her punishment, to be stared at naked by unknown people playing with themselves. She, who was being brought to a point of exquisite sexual sensation by an unknown, unseen tongue, was to be denied their touch. She sat up straight and perfectly still, her pale voluptuous breasts jutting out. She wondered who was there behind the masks, and if her Confessor was amongst them. Or was he sitting up in the minstrels' gallery watching her, open and squirming? She thought of him, his large body, his broad chest and slim hips cloaked in the robes of a priest. She wondered whether he would take her. Whether his penis would elicit from her the same sensuous response as Gerry's had done.

The tongue inside her pussy moved. Jeanine bent her head to take a better look and thought she caught sight of Mrs Klowski's brown hair and hair grip slithering in and out under her throne. In that instant a blindfold was fastened around Jeanine's eyes and a gag put over her mouth. The deprivation of sight heightened her sense of feel and touch. She felt the tongue keep changing direction, one moment deep inside her, the next licking and nibbling at her clit. While this was happening she sensed people taking up their positions behind her throne.

Jeanine felt gloved hands over her shoulders, clasping her breasts, kneading and slipping on the oil, playing with her nipples. Other gloved hands were stroking her legs. As the tongue moved round to her anus, fingers stroked the space left vacant. The ridged seams of the gloves provoked her wet opening to further abandonment. The hands playing with her breasts pulled her backwards. Suddenly the tongue was replaced by an exploring and gloved finger which was penetrating her arse. Hands were sliding, gliding their way along her thighs; fingers were running along her sex-lips and on her clitoris. Jeanine knew she was in ecstasy. The feeling was superb. Her ever-tingling, further opening, further wanton, further taking sex was opening wider and wider, and so was her other orifice.

Jeanine enjoyed the freedom of not knowing who was sucking her or fingering her. She was relishing the pleasure of stiff cocks being rolled against the skin of her arms, her breasts, her nipples, and being stroked along her thighs. Then Jeanine felt someone kneel between her parted legs. Hands pulled her so that she leant against the back of the throne. From beneath, other hands encased her rounded bare buttocks, dug fingernails into her flesh, pushed her upwards and held her there. Jeanine was wide open.

She was being venerated. She was the woman, the eternal goddess. One by one they knelt before her prostrate figure and soft juicy lips and a variety of different-sized tongues buried themselves into her excited, tingling, wet and juicy sex. Her labia, her hole, her womb, her life centre was being adored and honoured.

This went on for some time until she felt a penis hovering at her carnal entrance. Hands beneath her throne still held her upwards; other hands pulled her thighs outwards. The penis was taken along her outer sex-lips and then slowly began to penetrate. Her breathing was coming faster and faster. It was the only fast movement around her. Everything else was done with a studied slowness. Nothing was hurried. And the effect of this measured rite was to leave Jeanine almost out of her mind with uncontrollable desire.

'Fuck me, fuck me,' she was silently begging.

The man kneeling in front of her took her without ceremony. He pushed his penis in suddenly so that she jerked towards him as he thrust. He kept thrusting and penetrating. Jeanine thought she had never known so much pleasure, had never felt so completely taken or so enjoyed being enjoyed. She was no longer shy and retiring but was moving, shaking and squirming and loving every minute. Never wanting it to stop.

The man came. The hands beneath her moved away and her buttocks and crotch dropped again into the void beneath the commode-like throne. Then, without warning, she felt an ice-cold object against her anus. Her forbidden hole was being plundered by a small, hard shape. She wondered if it was the ivory penis she had discovered earlier. It was being moved backwards and forwards inside her so that her arse was opening, spreading wider to its insistent demands.

Jeanine leant against the back of the throne, willingly taking that hard instrument. Hands encircled her breasts and fingers rolled her stiff nipples, stiffening them further.

Then she felt the object withdraw and a tongue lick her buttocks. Something stick-thin and hard then began to poke into her anus. Her sex was untouched. Concentration was levelled at her other opening. Jeanine was gasping once more.

'Release her,' came her Confessor's voice.

Jeanine felt a sharp pang of disappointment. She had been taken to heights of enjoyment but had not come. She desperately wanted to climax but this had been denied her. Each time she had almost climaxed the touch on her breasts, her sex, her arse, had been relaxed and her orgasm had faded. Then the hands, lips and pricks brought her back again to the same point and took her beyond, but still she had not come.

Unseen hands unshackled her feet and unlocked the handcuffs. Jeanine was helped to her feet. Still blindfolded, gagged and handcuffed, she was led away from the throne and lifted up and bent over what seemed to her to be a vaulting horse. It was in fact a trestle. Her belly was lying on upholstered leather. Her head hung down, her arms, held out in front of her, were chained to the front of the horse. Her legs were splayed and her ankles chained to the back of the trestle. Her hindquarters were domed by added horsehair cushions eased under her belly. She was doubled over, her bottom raised high and utterly inviting.

The tip of the cane-like instrument teased the outer edges of her anus and was then withdrawn, to be replaced by a thick leather dildo that penetrated her, pushing backwards and forwards, harder and harder. Jeanine wallowed in the sentient pleasure and let her unseen accomplices see her pleasure by rolling her hips slightly. Leather thongs attached to the dildo were then tied around her waist and legs. She felt the leather cut into her pussy. Fingers adjusted it so that the leather was pressing on her clit. Jeanine smelled the oils, then felt hands rubbing it into her bare buttocks.

The next moment, and utterly without warning, she experienced the lash. A fine stripe whipped through the air and landed across her naked bottom. Pain seared through her. She clenched her teeth. The gag stopped her from crying out. Hands quickly stroked the mark then the whip came down again. She contracted her muscles. Someone moved the instrument up and down within her arse. The leather thongs were cutting deeper and deeper between her legs. She was imprisoned. The lash came down a third time. In between, the instrument was shoved up harder, stretching her wider. The lash came down another three times. Jeanine knew pleasure and pain. She tried to grasp the moment of pain and transform it into heightened joy. It was exquisite torture.

A tongue licked the marks. The instrument was untied and removed. Then a large prick penetrated her anus. It went straight up inside and thrust furiously at her newly-widened, forbidden hole. Her hips were gripped tightly. The weals across her buttocks were stroked. Jeanine was buggered quite thoroughly, until the man, letting out a great roar, came. Jeanine was still wet and open.

The slowness that had typified everything until the

moment the man rammed at her arse was now gone. Dispelled. Evaporated. Even the music increased its pace and sound. Quickly her hands were unchained from her legs and she was marched across the room. Her hands were brought up above her head and chained. Her legs were spread apart and shackled. Her waist was enclosed in a vice and keyed. She was upright, she could move and she could squirm. Her bare breasts, her naked buttocks and open pussy were available to anybody who wanted access, but she could not escape. She was a captive. One of the monks removed her blindfold but the gag stayed on. Jeanine was able to see that the room was now lit by myriad candles. She also saw that her hands were attached to a leather-covered ring hanging from a cross-bar, and her legs and the iron vice that encircled her waist were attached to the upright wooden posts.

Masked men and the women surged around her. Those in habits lifted them so that Jeanine could see their genitals. Those in leather had themselves already on display. The wood panelling in front of her slid away to reveal a huge mirror. Jeanine was able to turn within the iron ring that encircled her waist and see the bright red weals criss-crossing her buttocks. Men and women moved forward and began to touch her. Jeanine had to watch as they took it in turns, sometimes in ones, sometimes in twos and threes, to possess her chained and imprisoned body. Jeanine was no longer the venerated queen. She was the slave. She was there for their use. Women pressed their breasts to her breasts, to her back and sucked her. Some women held her shoulders whilst a cock was shoved into her sex. A man would play with her breasts while another penetrated her behind. A woman played with her mound whilst she was having her arse screwed. Jeanine found she could take it, accepted it, enjoyed it, wanted more.

She was able to glance about the room and she saw Olga

whipping the large dimpled bottom of a girl in a maid's uniform. She saw a young beautiful black guy sodomising a young woman in a novitiate's habit who was bent over and chained to the wall. She saw Auralie, who was not wearing a mask but had a large dildo strapped around her skin-tight, red PVC suit, take hold of Olga, bend her over and penetrate her.

She saw Petrov screw Jackson whilst he was giving head to a young ginger-haired guy, who in turn was sucking the sex of a slim young girl with a mass of pre-Raphaelite curls tumbling down over her naked breasts.

Everywhere she looked Jeanine saw couplings, people entering each other, enjoying their bodies and their orifices. She became wetter and wetter the more she was sucked and penetrated and handled. She did not know it was possible to have so much juiciness inside her. Her body squirmed sensuously. She rolled her shoulders, her hips, any part of her that could be touched. Every inch of her seemed to be an erogenous zone.

Then Jeanine saw Auralie coming towards her wearing bright-red PVC. She carried a whip. It was a tawse split over the last six inches into finger-like thongs to search out the more intimate areas for a severe leathering. She also held a riding crop. Jeanine instantly knew fear. Real fear. She had been tied and gagged and used. She had already felt the lash. Had felt that pleasure and pain. The pain that had seared across her buttocks. She had learned quickly how to handle it and enjoy it, but an instinct told her that Auralie would show her no mercy. Jeanine remembered Auralie's conversation with Petrov. She had discovered that her cousin, far from liking her, was acutely jealous of her. Jealous of her marriage to Laurence and because she was Penelope's daughter. Jeanine was terrified as she also recalled Petrov's words.

'You will take your punishment first from me and then from Auralie,' he had said to Jeanine in the confessional.

Auralie brought the tawse down hard on Jeanine's bare flesh. The stinging and the pain were so severe she thought she would faint. Auralie hit her again. The pain was almost unbearable. Then Auralie moved slowly away on her incredibly high-heels through the mass of people who were copulating. She jabbed the crop at two naked men who were lying on the floor, busy caressing one another's pricks. Auralie ordered them to kneel. They did so, their buttocks in the air. She stood behind them and brought the crop down hard on their bare arses. They said 'thank you'.

'Now remove her basque,' Auralie's voice pierced the air.

Immediately the two men walked over to Jeanine and carefully, and in harmony, unhooked Jeanine's basque, undid the suspenders from the stockings – letting them fall to her ankles – and removed her shoes and stockings. Then they put her shoes back on. Except for the handcuffs and anklets Jeanine was naked. Vulnerably naked. No part of her body could now escape the crop. Her breasts, her belly, her bottom, her thighs, were utterly unprotected.

The men turned Jeanine so that her bare bottom faced the minstrels' gallery. She was tipped slightly forward. Mrs Klowski grabbed her bottom cheeks and pulled them apart, displaying her inner being to every seen and unseen person in the room. She lowered her head and licked Jeanine's sex, which fear had tightened and dried. Fear had reduced her sexuality. Fear had closed the holes that previously had been so open, used, wanting and wanton.

Mrs Klowski licked at the edges of her vulva, quickening Jeanine's almost dormant desire. The thick tongue knew its route. It found each crevice and fold easily. Jeanine began to unfurl. As she opened she began to sway. Her hips rolled slightly to the incessant rhythm of both the tongue and the music and the juices began to flow again. Jeanine realised it was a familiar tongue wriggling so expertly, flicking her hard, protruding point and licking her arse. It was Mrs Klowski's thick, fat tongue that she had so thoroughly enjoyed before. Jeanine lowered her eyes, not wanting Mrs Klowski to see how much she was enjoying her punishment.

Auralie had watched all the proceedings with a tremendous sense of satisfaction. She had enjoyed seeing Leon Sawyer screw Jeanine's arse; the sight of Petrov first penetrating her, then whipping her, then the whip changing hands; seeing Jackson, then Kensit, rubbing their cocks between the blindfolded girl's legs; Olga bringing those strips of leather up through Jeanine's sensitive sex and flash down over her rounded buttocks. Now she watched with glee as she saw the housekeeper's tongue invading Jeanine's vulva, preparing her simpering blonde cousin for the crop. Mrs Klowski was making Jeanine wetter and juicier.

Auralie watched the tied girl begin to squirm. Whorishly she trailed the tawse through the open crotch of her PVC suit. She liked the feel of its rock-hard stiffness on her sex. She held it to her clitoris and rubbed, exciting her own hidden point into action. She too was preparing herself for the next moment. The moment when she was going to have her revenge.

Auralie struck the tawse against her leather-gloved palm and ordered Mrs Klowski to stop. She raised the tawse high and brought it whistling down on Jeanine's bare bottom. The burning sensation ignited Jeanine's limbs. She twisted and turned as the thin strips of leather flayed her naked flesh. The heat of the impact seared through, marking her skin. Bright red and violet-blue stripes appeared on her belly, her thighs and her buttocks. Nobody came to her rescue. This time no caressing hands stroked the terrible marks. No hands wandered into her softness. Jeanine knew only the tawse and felt she would faint from the pain. Catch the pain, she told herself.

Catch it and hold it. Push it out through the top of your head. For the fragment of the moment that she could do this Jeanine knew exquisite joy, but afterwards only fire. She closed her eyes. She couldn't bear to watch. There was no mercy from Auralie's hand. She felt herself drying, all sexuality used up, evaporated. Auralie raised her hand again. Jeanine saw it and slumped.

Meanwhile, Petrov and Brother Geoffrey had returned to the minstrels' gallery. They had been drinking champagne and watching the novices and acolytes enjoying themselves below. Sister Pierre was being screwed by Brother Leslie, Leon was sodomising Sister Chloe and Kensit was thrusting into Olga's maid, Nicole. Petrov noticed Jill and Mary had Olga on the table. He gave a wry smile. He knew his ex-wife would be enjoying that. He saw Terry screwing the fat-arsed novice, Margaret.

Petrov put his hands under Brother Geoffrey's habit, grabbed the young man's penis and dipped it in his champagne flute. Then he noticed a new young girl beside him whose name he could not remember.

'Your name?' said Petrov a little indistinctly. He had consumed a large amount of champagne.

'Natasha,' replied the girl.

'Suck his cock for me,' ordered Petrov. 'Lay across my lap and take his balls in your mouth.'

Obligingly the girl did as she was asked. Petrov lifted her habit and idly played with her neat bottom as she sucked.

He looked down over the gallery rail and saw Jeanine hooked up to the whipping ring. He was suddenly aware that the punishment that Auralie was handing out was not sexual. It was real. Through his alcoholic haze Petrov realised that Auralie was beating Jeanine beyond the boundaries he allowed. Petrov was immediately sobered. Furious, he shouted. He pushed the girl off his lap and stood up.

'Enough!' he shouted and ran down the gallery stairs. He

rushed up to where Auralie was standing and grabbed her arm.

'You bitch,' he said. 'You absolute bitch.'

He ordered Mrs Klowski to cut Jeanine down and called to Jackson.

'Hold her!' Petrov shoved Auralie into Jackson's vice-like grip.

Petrov organised a group of masked figures to carry Jeanine upstairs where they laid her on a bed covered with soft silk sheets. Her bruises and bitter marks were tended with anti-septics and cool water, then gently rubbed with oils. Her gag was removed and the handcuffs and anklets taken off. Then the masked figures left Jeanine alone to sleep.

Downstairs in the great hall Petrov ordered Jackson to hoist a violently protesting Auralie into Jeanine's vacated place. Then he brought the tawse sizzling down on Auralie's PVC-clad hind-quarters.

'And you will thank me,' he said. 'Is that understood, Auralie? You will thank me in the appropriate style.'

'Yes, master,' squeaked Auralie as the whip came down again, searing her taut buttocks.

'Now strip her,' said Petrov. A number of men gathered round Auralie and stripped her of her suit.

'Give me the crop,' he said. Mrs Klowski handed it to him.

'And the gag?' she asked.

'No gag,' Petrov replied.

He brought the crop swinging down on Auralie's bottom, on her thighs and on her belly. Auralie twisted and turned, struggling to stay silent but the pain was too much. She let out an unearthly howl.

'No mercy,' Petrov said, beating her again. 'Disobedience must be punished. You violated a basic law of my order, and for that there is no mercy.'

In all, Auralie received twenty-four strokes. Twenty-four clearly defined crop marks on her buttocks, her belly and her thighs.

'Now explain those to your husband,' Petrov said with some satisfaction as he threw the crop down and walked away.

Auralie wouldn't need to explain it to her husband. Gerry had witnessed her beating. He had found the entrance to the hall and, wearing the monk's habit, he had edged in amongst the writhing and masked people. In the half-light of the now dimly glowing candles somebody had grabbed his cock. Afraid he would be found out as an impostor he had allowed his prick to be fiddled with. He had stiffened to someone's expert touch and then screwed the girl responsible for his erection before moving on. He had suddenly noticed a female figure tied to a ring and being sodomised, screwed and sucked. He paid little attention to her until, with amazement, he noticed his wife standing near the girl holding a riding crop and a whip in either hand. He watched with growing horror as she brought the instruments down on the swaying, chained girl.

Then he realised the girl receiving the beating was Jeanine. He had been about to rush forward and blow his cover when Petrov had shouted and stopped Auralie. Gerry had been one of the figures who had carried the exhausted Jeanine upstairs. He had made sure he had been the last to leave and that the door of the room where she lay was not locked.

He had arrived back downstairs at the moment Petrov was punishing Auralie. Gerry witnessed this spectacle with a certain satisfaction. It was no more than the bitch deserved, he thought.

It was then that Gerry decided that he would delay his impending confrontation with Auralie. He wouldn't let her know he knew about Petrov's sect until he had enjoyed watching her squirm when he tried to make love to her. He wondered just how she would explain away the marks that Petrov had left on her body. Then he would get rid of her for good. Throw her out of his house, divorce her and marry Jeanine.

With these thoughts Gerry left the hall and made his way upstairs to where Jeanine lay. He had been too late to save her from the excesses of Petrov's sect but he would take her back to London while the rest of the household was otherwise occupied.

Gerry thought Jeanine was asleep but nothing could have been further from the truth. Jeanine's mind was whirring. Her body was in pain but her mind was extra active. She had lain with her eyes closed, trying to work out what she was going to do next.

Jeanine had made some discoveries about herself. Some things inside her she recognised; other things she had refused to acknowledge; some things she hadn't even realised. Now these had been brought to the surface and she had been forced to examine all her motives. She decided she must take charge of her own life. She must recognise that she liked sex. If she wanted multiple sex then she should admit that. She must not pretend to do things unwillingly that she really *wanted* to do. She must make her objectives clear, at least to herself. She must see, recognise and know the person she really was. She must also know who her enemies were, and know whom she could trust. She knew she could trust her mother. She could not trust Auralie, except to be jealous and deceitful. Jeanine lay between the cool silken sheets, her body aching and sore. She had had an experience beyond her wildest dreams, most of which she had enjoyed. That was a revelation. She had a cousin who loathed her. That, too, was a revelation. She had been naïve and foolish and she had been punished. She was not going to allow such a thing to happen to her again. However, Jeanine had to think of a way of overcoming her present predicament. The hotel had to make money. She had to make it a success. It was also imperative that she got her own back on Auralie. But how? That was the question.

Her reverie was interrupted by Gerry gently kissing her cheek. She opened her eyes as his arms enveloped her body and tried to lift her out of the bed.

'What the hell do you think you're doing, Gerry?' said Jeanine angrily.

'My car's outside,' he said.

'I can drive myself home,' she said sharply. 'But I'm not walking out of here like a thief. I'm collecting my clothes, saying goodbye to Petrov and I'm getting myself home.'

Gerry knew from her tone that it was stupid to gainsay Jeanine.

'I really do want to marry you,' Gerry said.

'Do you?'

'Very much,' he replied.

Jeanine said nothing but stood up and wound the bedsheet around her naked, marked body. Gerry thought she looked magnificent, like Dido or Boadicea.

Her only intention was to get away from Petrov's and be on her own to think quietly. And she had a lot of things to think about. How she was going to live the rest of her life was one of them, and she must make the right decision.

'I'll follow you back to London, make sure you're all right,' said Gerry.

'That'll be nice,' said Jeanine. 'Thank you.'

Jeanine walked out of the room and down the stairs. Suddenly she knew what she was going to do. She knew how she was going to survive. It had come to her in a flash. Jeanine knew how she could achieve her goals.

10

It had been with an intense feeling of relief that Jeanine had unlocked the front doors of her hotel. Finally she was home. She could lie in a good hot bath and soak away her aches and pains. Her bottom hurt. It stung. She had difficulty driving. At times she had wondered whether she wouldn't be wiser to flag Gerry down, leave the car in a side road and let him take her home. The longer she had wrestled with the idea the closer she had got to London until, finally, she was so close there was no point in stopping him.

'Hiya,' said Mrs Maclean. Jeanine had completely forgotten about Mrs Maclean. 'Your mother telephoned. Twice. Said she's in London. Wanted to know where you were.'

'What did you say?'

'At a special business meeting,' said Mrs Maclean. Jeanine gave a wry smile. Well, she thought, you could call it that.

'You look exhausted,' said Mrs Maclean.

'I am,' said Jeanine.

'Let me make you something. What would you like, tea or coffee?'

'Tea,' said Jeanine. 'Some nice camomile.'

'That's not the ordinary English tea now, is it?' asked Mrs Maclean.

'No. I want to be soothed. And there's nothing more soothing than camomile,' said Jeanine.

Jeanine made her way down the stairs.

'I'm going to take a bath,' Jeanine called up to Mrs Maclean. 'I'll bring the tea to you,' she said.

Jeanine thought how kind Mrs Maclean was, how lucky she was that she had chosen to remain at the hotel.

In her own apartment Jeanine threw off her clothes and stared momentarily at her body. The marks from Auralie's stripes with the tawse were livid. Jeanine felt an intense rush of anger and an acute desire for revenge. She wasn't that happy with either emotion and tried to expiate them by standing under the shower and washing her hair. Afterwards, with none of her anger assuaged and her desire for revenge increased, she filled the bath with water and bath salts. Jeanine lay luxuriating in the expensive foaming fragrance as various thoughts jockeyed for her mental winning post. It was then that the full impact of Auralie's conversation with Petrov and Olga hit her. Auralie had said she and Laurence were lovers. That meant they had both lied to her.

Jeanine hated lies and liars. She was very open and honest. Perhaps, she thought, that was a defect in this world. She must learn from recent events. She must learn to be devious. A shiver went through Jeanine's body. She leaned forwards, turned on the gold taps and added more hot water to her mahogany-surrounded Victorian bath tub. She took stock of her own position. Her hotel's reputation was in tatters; her plans for earning money and making a good living had disappeared; the cousin she loved really hated her and had plotted her downfall; her cousin's husband was in love with her and wanted to marry her. If he could have sex with her when married to Auralie, when Jeanine was his wife he could easily screw somebody else. To Jeanine's mind that was a negation of commitment. And marriage was a commitment. Perhaps, she thought, fidelity was impossible. Now if she looked at the whole question from that point of view then she might arrive at completely different answers.

Thinking in the bath was most invigorating. Jeanine let out some water and added some more hot. Jeanine explored her other relationships. Her mother, remarried and on a high with her new adoring husband. She would talk to her later but she had seen the photographs in the newspapers and now she knew what her mother looked like when she was really happy. Penelope was in love and a woman in love is totally occupied with her lover. Jeanine could not rely on her mother. Not in the long term. She would have to grow up. She must not depend on anyone. She must make her own decisions. But what should she do? There was a lot of money invested in her hotel. Some of Petrov's too. What else could she use the hotel for?

A variety of ideas began to push their way into her mind. As she thought, she idly stroked her breasts with the foamy water. It was only then that a thought struck her. What had Gerry been doing at Petrov's – at Petrov's and wearing a monk's habit? Surely he wasn't part of the order. If he was had he screwed her there? She thought she would have remembered the feel of his cock above all the others. A part of her could hardly believe she had submitted to unknown hands fondling her breasts, feeling her sex, screwing her, sodomising her. Erotic memories enticed her wayward hands and all too soon her nipples had hardened. She washed between her legs and realised she was wet inside as well as outside. She was excited again. She wanted sex again. She lay back, closed her eyes and softly smiled to herself.

'You look pretty as a picture,' said Mrs Maclean. Jeanine opened her eyes with surprise. 'I knocked and knocked but you didn't answer.'

'Oh, I was miles away thinking, Mrs Maclean,' said Jeanine.

'Call me Henrietta.' Mrs Maclean handed her a steaming cup of camomile tea, then picked up her own cup and sipped. 'I thought I'd have mine with you. I must say from the look on your face they sure was happy thoughts.'

'They were, Henrietta, they were. I was being fucked.' Jeanine was surprised by her forthright admission but there was something about the American that inspired a confidence.

'Lucky you! Is that why you're so exhausted?'

'To be quite frank, Henrietta, yes. I have been attending a sex orgy.'

'Oh my!' exclaimed the other woman. 'Do people really have those? I thought that was only fantasy land. Can you tell me what you did? I mean, did you like it?'

'I liked most of it,' replied Jeanine. 'I liked it until my cousin arrived and beat me. Look what she did.'

Jeanine stood up in the bath and to Mrs Maclean's complete surprise showed off her voluptuous creamy bottom covered with magenta red and Persian-blue stripes.

'Oh my heavens! You need witch hazel on those, fast,' said Mrs Maclean, disappearing out the door.

By the time Mrs Maclean returned Jeanine was out of the bath and covered in her thick, ankle-length, corn-yellow towelling robe.

'Can you rub it in for me,' asked Jeanine, letting the robe fall to the floor and standing in front of Mrs Maclean, stark naked.

'I sure can,' she said. 'And when I'm doing it you can tell me what was done to you.'

Jeanine leant over the bath and, while Mrs Maclean's soft hands rubbed her sore buttocks with witch hazel, Jeanine told her how she'd had to confess her sins. And how she'd had to tell Petrov she had had sex with her cousin's husband. And how he had told her that her punishment would be sexual. Then Jeanine told Mrs Maclean how Mrs Klowski had rubbed her breasts and Jackson had put his cock between her legs whilst Mrs Klowski had played with her pussy.

'Like this?' asked Mrs Maclean. Trance-like, she had been

encircling the young woman's buttocks, noticing Jeanine's swollen pink bud easing outwards invitingly, and had longed to touch its soft, full wetness. Now, slowly, gently, she let her finger edge round into Jeanine's open wet pussy.

'Yes,' said Jeanine, rolling her hips, enjoying the touch. She had wanted someone to feel her. Jeanine was past caring who it was, just someone gentle. Someone who would stroke her lovingly.

'Just like that,' she said, then continued her story. 'Then Jackson chained my wrists together.'

'Who's Jackson?' asked Mrs Maclean.

'He's a huge, very black man,' explained Jeanine. 'He's also my uncle Petrov's best friend and business partner who enjoys playing at being his butler. I think they could also be lovers. Petrov swings both ways and the two have been together a long time.'

'Tell me, Jeanine,' said Mrs Maclean intrigued, 'is it true what they say, that black guys have big pricks?'

'I don't know generally, but Jackson had. A very big one.'

'You saw it?'

'I saw it, and he shoved it in my mouth and made me suck it.'

'Oh!' Jeanine's bald statement gave Mrs Maclean a vicarious thrill. 'And then what happened?' she asked, enjoying the feel of Jeanine's wet opening expanding beneath her probing fingers. 'They removed my dress. Left me only in my basque and stockings and high-heeled shoes, and took me out of a cubicle into a hall filled with people. Then they walked me up onto a dais, sat me on a throne and tied my legs to either side of it so my pussy was wide open and on display.' The memory of it was exciting Jeanine, and she wriggled and squirmed under Mrs Maclean's sure touch. 'Then men and women dressed exotically in leather came up onto the dais, and while Jackson's prick was in my mouth someone blindfolded me.'

'What happened after that?'

'Unknown hands felt me, unknown tongues licked me and unknown pricks screwed me.'

'And you enjoyed that.'

'Oh yes. Wouldn't you?'

'I think I would, yes,' Mrs Maclean gulped excitedly. 'Given the chance I think I would. What else?'

'The throne I was sitting on had a seat that opened up and somebody lay under the chair sucking my pussy.'

'Sucking your pussy?'

'Yes. Have you ever done that to anyone, Henrietta?'

'No.'

'Would you like to?'

'Yes.'

'Would you like to suck mine?'

'Yes,' said Mrs Maclean, thrusting a couple of fingers hard up into Jeanine's juicy pussy.

'Then I'll turn round and open my legs and you can put your tongue just here . . .' Jeanine said. She stood up, turned round, leaned her hindquarters against the side of the bath and splayed herself open with her fingers. Mrs Maclean knelt in front of her and put her tongue to Jeanine's soft, succulent opening.

Today, thought Mrs Maclean, is a remarkable day. She had been screwed doggie fashion by the waiter early in the morning and, for the first time in her life, had had an orgasm. This had led to her discovery that, far from disliking sex, she enjoyed it. With the purest intentions in the world she had rubbed witch hazel into Jeanine's well-rounded but badly marked bottom. As she had done so, she had listened to Jeanine's extraordinary account of her sexual activity and it had aroused her and her hands and fingers had started to play with and mould Jeanine's beautiful fleshy bum. Henrietta Maclean had become wetter and wetter between her legs and her nipples had stiffened and her throat had contracted. She too had been having sexual visions. She too had been thinking about penises and pussies.

'Hold my thighs apart and let your tongue go right in,' said Jeanine.

As she knelt exploring Jeanine's yielding fleshy folds, feeling the slightest contraction of the woman's muscles and her opening enlarging and throbbing under her tongue, Henrietta Maclean made her next major discovery. She enjoyed sucking another woman.

'Let your tongue wander up and down,' said Jeanine. 'Yes, yes just there.' Mrs Maclean had found Jeanine's clitoris. 'Oh, that's wonderful.'

Mrs Maclean had a full, fat, liquid tongue that worked amazingly well. Jeanine was enjoying this unexpected pleasure. She straightened her legs slightly, gripped the side of the bath harder, and continued with her story.

'Then they stopped screwing and licking and sucking me and tied me over a trestle, stuck my arse up in the air with a load of cushions and somebody pushed a dildo up into my arse.'

'Into your arse?'

'Yes, into my arse.'

'Like this?' said Mrs Maclean, excited, and did the most natural thing in the world. She brought a hand round from inside Jeanine's thighs and pushed a finger into her newly stretched rear opening.

'Just like that,' said Jeanine, squirming and shaking from the finger and the tongue. 'And then I felt the whip.'

'Was that your cousin?' said Henrietta, raising her head briefly then returning to her welcome task and flicking her fat tongue over Jeanine's clit.

'No, she did it later. This was done properly.'

As she rememberd the lash searing down over her domed

buttocks Jeanine went completely rigid with desire. She trembled. A lump came into her throat, her stomach tightened. From somewhere deep within her belly a spark ignited and, gathering momentum, flew down through her loins. Suddenly and very quickly Jeanine came.

'Henrietta, would you like to be screwed?' Jeanine asked moments later as the two of them sat happily sipping camomile tea. There was no sour atmosphere between the two women. One had needed, the other had given, joyously. They might do it again. They might not. It was of no concern. Both had gained from the experience. Both were content.

'I would. I'd very much like to have sex,' replied Mrs Maclean.

'Then I'd like you to go out this minute, get your hair cut and dyed. Grey doesn't suit you. It's too ageing.'

'My hair dyed!' she exclaimed, thinking that Jeanine was confirming everything she thought about herself.

'Yes. Get it dyed brown and buy yourself some new clothes. Throw away everything you brought with you. You've got money, haven't you?'

'Yes.'

'Good. Go to this shop,' Jeanine wrote a name and address down on a piece of paper and handed it to Mrs Maclean. 'You'll have to go to Soho. Any taxi driver will know the way. I want you to buy the following items to fit you. And I mean really fit you. A good snug fit.'

Mrs Maclean looked with some alarm at the list that Jeanine had written down for her.

'You'll look wonderful,' said Jeanine, reassuringly, sensing Mrs Maclean's trepidation. 'When you've got that lot, go to this shop –' Jeanine wrote down another name and address, '– and buy these items. It's not far away so you won't have any problem.'

'And then what?' asked Mrs Maclean.

'I'd like you to stay with me and help me run my hotel,' said Jeanine. 'Would you do that?'

'I'll get myself screwed if I do?' asked Henrietta.

'Definitely,' said Jeanine, smiling mischievously. She had suddenly decided what she was going to do; how she was going to run her hotel and make money. But she could only do it with loyal help. Henrietta Maclean's loyal help.

'Then I don't see that I have any option,' said Henrietta, returning her smile then departing.

Jeanine picked up the telephone and called her mother. When she had finished talking to her she called the carpenter who had worked for her when she was renovating the hotel. She made an appointment with him for that evening. Then she called Petrov and Olga and informed them she was calling an extraordinary family meeting for three days' time and wanted various members of his sect to attend, including Auralie. When Petrov endeavoured to quiz her, Jeanine cut him short. She was brooking no inquisition.

Then Jeanine dialled Gerry's number at work. His secretary told her he had gone to a meeting. Jeanine tried him at home but he wasn't there. She left a message on the answering machine telling him she would be very busy for the next few days and would not be able to see him.

Jeanine was not yet dressed when she heard them arrive for the meeting. She picked out Petrov's deep hypnotic voice; Jackson's, even deeper, with its slight American intonation, and Olga's French accent. She heard Auralie laugh, and Terry call to Nicole and Kensit. Jeanine presumed they were Olga's maid and chauffeur; she never seemed to go anywhere without her entourage. They were all punctual but Jeanine had every intention of keeping them waiting. She had told Mrs Maclean to show them into her dining-room and to their allotted place at the table.

Jeanine had called an extraordinary meeting; how extra-ordinary they would soon discover. In the past few days, since her return from Petrov's monastery, Jeanine had decided upon a plan and had set that plan into action. It was about to come to fruition. Jeanine had all to play for and nothing to lose. She knew she was in the top position. But they did not.

Naked, Jeanine stood in front of her walnut inlay wardrobe and opened its doors. Her eyes lighted on a French-navy, heavy, silk jersey ankle-length frock. It had long sleeves, a bias-cut skirt that hugged her hips, and a cross-over bodice. That, she decided, was perfect for what she had in mind. Jeanine glanced at her buttocks. She noticed how the vicious red and blue marks had almost faded. She pulled the dress over her head and eased it down and along her full figure. It was a superb fit. She would wear nothing under it, allowing the form, folds and fluidity of the jersey to highlight the curves of her body. But she would wear stockings. She picked out some very dark-grey, pure silk hold-ups with a fine lacy top and rolled them gently up her legs. She took her shoe horn and eased her feet into black suede high-heels. She brushed her hair and let it tumble sexily over her shoulders. She sat at her dressing-table and made-up her face with a soft luminous foundation. She lightly mascara'd her eyes and brows, dabbed rouge on her cheeks, outlined her full lips with a brown pencil then filled them in with a bright, slightly pinky red that enhanced her skin colouring.

Henrietta Maclean put her head round the bedroom door.

'They're all here and waiting,' she said.

'Is everything ready?' asked Jeanine, putting away her lipstick.

'Everything,' confirmed Mrs Maclean.

The two women smiled conspiratorially at one another.

'I won't be long,' said Jeanine.

Mrs Maclean left, closing the door. Jeanine stood up. With

the aid of the mirror on the wall and the cheval mirror Jeanine was able to see herself from every angle. She was chic but sexy. The soft fabric completely covered her large breasts, but her hard nipples distorted the line and managed to make them look thoroughly immodest. They were an enticement, to anyone even vaguely aroused, to touch. Jeanine smiled. That was exactly the effect she wanted. Jeanine looked at herself from behind. She noted with satisfaction how the falls of the silk jersey draped over her buttocks, fell neatly into the crack of her bottom, emphasising its shape, and proclaiming loud and clear that she was completely naked beneath her frock. Jeanine was ready to do business.

She felt a ripple of lust as she walked slowly into her dining-room, her head held high and her large breasts wobbling. Her erect nipples strained against the silk jersey fabric and her hips swayed invitingly. She stopped at the empty seat between Petrov and Olga.

Olga stared at her, regretting the time she had spent with Nicole at Petrov's when she could have been having Jeanine. She was looking unbelievably desirable. Her breasts were saying 'touch me', her stiff nipples almost shouted out 'squeeze, stroke and tweak me'. Olga was convinced Jeanine was not wearing any undergarments and felt a strong desire to lift her skirt and smack her bare bottom.

'Olga, put your hand palm upwards on my seat,' said Jeanine.

Olga licked her lips and did as she was asked. Jeanine hoisted her skirt. Her bare bottom was momentarily visible to Olga and Petrov. Then she sat down, imprisoning Olga's hand beneath her and the leather of the chair. Jeanine squirmed and wriggled slightly, making sure that Olga's fingers were positioned so as to glide on her wetness, touching her clitoris and slowly entering her wanton sex.

When Jeanine was seated she glanced round the table. Henrietta had placed everyone exactly as she had requested. Beside her, Petrov, wearing his habit, was playing with his prick and balls. Auralie, in tight jeans and a white fine lawn blouse, her lack of brassiere allowing the outline of her pert upright breasts to be clearly visible through the transparent fabric, was deliberately seated opposite her cousin so that she was forced to watch every movement of Jeanine's body responding to Olga's exploring fingers. Auralie sat still, icily feigning indifference whilst jealousy stormed through her body. Jackson, in a suit, was sitting between Petrov and Nicole. He gave a half-smile, realising what Jeanine was up to. His hands disappeared beneath the table and undid his flies. Jeanine knew that he would be watching her with his massive cock and balls spilling out. That gave her a thrill and she wiggled spontaneously on Olga's fingers.

Jeanine looked around the table and was quite sure that everyone there had itchy loins. Terry, summery in T-shirt and shorts, sat between Nicole and Auralie. Nicole was demurely dressed in a maid's black frock. But her appearance belied reality as Jeanine recalled having seen her behaviour at Petrov's. She watched Terry's hands move over and begin to massage Nicole's thighs as the girl's legs opened to receive his fingers. Kensit, dressed in his chauffeur's uniform, sat quite still. He was disinclined to touch Auralie, who remained impassive and stony faced. Olga continued to occupy herself with Jeanine's expanding pussy. Jeanine flexed her crotch muscles around Olga's fingers.

'As you know, I am a good fuck,' she announced to the assembled company.

This was not quite what any of them had expected to hear. They stayed silent as Jeanine continued.

'And one way or another each one of you has endeavoured

to stop my hotel being a success.' She looked at Nicole and Kensit. 'But some less than others.'

Jeanine's pussy was gliding nicely now on Olga's gently moving hand, and it was obvious to everyone in the room she was thoroughly enjoying herself. Jeanine looked at Auralie, whose face was black as thunder. Jeanine's revenge was beginning to take shape.

'However, as you have managed to wreak a certain amount of havoc I have decided not to continue in the hotel business as such. Instead I propose to turn this place into a club. A specialist club. An expensive and exclusive specialist club. It will cost a lot of money to join and a lot of money to stay here, but I shall offer certain services that are not otherwise readily available to people with, shall we say, certain foibles.'

Jeanine stood up, the folds of her frock settled down around her body.

'I have made certain alterations in the last few days and I want you all to come with me to see what I have done.'

Jeanine led the way out of the dining-room, down the stairs and through her bedroom into the carpeted, windowless room beyond. She tapped on the door then stepped slightly to one side as Mrs Maclean opened it. Jeanine enjoyed watching Terry's mouth drop open as he stared in amazement at Mrs Maclean.

She was dressed à la Nell Gwynne and seemed to have shed at least ten years. Her newly dyed mid-brown hair was beautifully cut, with soft waves framing her face. Her face had been made up without a heavy, dark shade of foundation cream. The green-blue eye shadow had been replaced by a soft grey eyeliner and the dark-red, blue-tinged lipstick by a gentle shade of pink. But it was the clothes she was wearing that made her different. Her bare breasts were jacked up by a boned and corseted black and green silk bodice, her nipples barely covered by a fragment of écru lace. Her waist was nipped in hard with the lacing, and the dark-green silk skirt billowed out over her large hips. She wore small high-heeled side-buttoning black boots. Over her left arm she carried a basket of oranges and in her right hand she held a bull's pizzle.

'Welcome to the dungeon,' said Jeanine.

A frisson of licentiousness wafted through the group as they walked into the room and Henrietta locked the heavy door behind them.

Petrov and Olga wandered round the room inspecting and noticing everything. Rafters had been put in across the ceiling and a couple of large steel rings with leather straps attached hung from them. Petrov tested the rings for strength.

Nicole checked out some of the harnesses hanging beside the rings. Olga took down some of the canes displayed along one wall beside an array of paddles, whips and leather straps. She swished the air with them and pronounced them excellent. Auralie did nothing except stare at the extensive range of dildoes Jeanine had exhibited on a shelf. Large and small, fat and thin, short and long, including a magnificent black leather double dildo complete with harness and belt.

Jeanine reached out and began to stroke Jackson's massive and excited prick. He instantly responded by leisurely leaning against the wall and putting his hands through the gap in the cross-over of Jeanine's bodice. Jeanine lifted her skirt so that Jackson could poke his prick through her thighs whilst she rested her back against his chest and let him play with her breasts. Jeanine knew this was exciting every male and female in the room.

Auralie let her eyes graze over Jeanine's punishment equipment including a whipping post with ropes and chains hanging from it, as if in readiness for an occupant. An instinct told her it could very well be her. She was grateful that she was wearing tight-fitting jeans.

Surreptitiously she edged back towards the door and tried the handle. Mrs Maclean noticed.

'It's locked,' she said. This increased Auralie's sense of fear. She gave Mrs Maclean a wan smile and moved to the far side of the room.

The floor area had three raised dais. On each there was a most particular piece of furniture. A padded punishment stool, a whipping bench with a stocks-like fitting for the head with steel anklets and bracelets let into the side, and a trestle with leather bindings hanging ready to enclose spreadeagled legs and arms.

'You've done well,' said Petrov, turning to Jeanine.

'Haven't I,' she purred, bringing her hand down and catching hold of Jackson's moving cock as it shoved backwards and forwards between the tops of her thighs. Jeanine looked across at Henrietta. 'But I couldn't have done it without Henrietta's help.'

Mrs Maclean came over and stood beside Jeanine.

'Everyone, I want you to meet Henrietta, my new partner in this venture.'

Jeanine took her hand. Mrs Maclean thought she was going to hold it up as some sort of introduction. Instead she lowered it and placed it over the visible part of Jackson's enormous penis protruding between her thighs.

'Rub it,' said Jeanine. 'Better still, bend over and lick it.'

Holding Jackson's shaft in her hand but keeping her legs straight, Mrs Maclean bent from the waist and licked Jackson's gliding member. At which point Terry, who had been excited and intrigued by the transformation in Mrs Maclean, undid his flies and, standing behind her, lifted the hem of her green silk skirt, gripped her waist and slid his cock between her thighs.

Henrietta Maclean continued attending to Jackson as she

felt the pleasure of another cock gradually pushing its way upwards into her wet and wanton vulva. She didn't know whose it was but hoped it was Terry's. It felt like Terry's. No wonder Jeanine had enjoyed her sex orgy – the feel of two cocks was extremely pleasurable. Henrietta edged backwards onto Terry's penis which plunged into her as far as it could go, taking her and riding her as Jackson's cock rode her mouth. Jeanine smiled licentiously. She had promised Henrietta a screw if she stayed with her and her promise had been fulfilled.

'Now listen, everybody,' said Jeanine. 'I propose to continue our meeting in here, so would you all like to find a comfortable spot while I outline my plan. And, of course, if anybody is overcome by a sudden desire to fuck or suck, be my guest. And, if anybody wants to take advantage of any of my toys they are more than welcome. Today is free of charge. Oh yes, and I have to tell you, the room is completely sound-proofed.'

Kensit, cane in hand, had lifted Nicole's maid's frock, pulled her long frilly drawers down to her knees, and was gently flicking her bare bottom with it.

Auralie immediately rushed over to Olga.

'Why did you do that?' said Auralie. 'Why did you play with that bitch's pussy?'

Jeanine heard Auralie's comment but suppressed her anger. Her moment would come; she was not going to rush anything. She had planned her revenge and it would not be run off-course by a sudden stupid flash of emotion.

'Because I wanted to,' replied Olga.

'But you're mine, not hers!'

'I'm not anybody's,' said Olga. '*Chérie*, I thought you understood that. That's the whole point of belonging to the Order. We screw, suck, bugger and whip anybody we want.'

'I know that, but you're special to me,' wailed Auralie. 'And I thought I was special to you.'

'*Chérie*, don't be ridiculous. I love feeling your sweet juicy pussy, but I like touching up Nicole, too.' Olga beckoned to Nicole who had been busy sucking Kensit's cock. She came tripping over to Olga.

Olga kissed Nicole's lips, fuelling Auralie's despair.

'Which of Jeanine's little toys do you fancy?' Olga asked Nicole.

'Whichever is your choice, madam,' said Nicole.

'You see, Auralie. Instant obedience,' said Olga. 'What makes you think you're any more special to me than Nicole?'

Auralie didn't answer.

'Have you been sucking Kensit's cock again, Nicole?' asked Olga.

'Yes, madam.'

'Did I give you permission?'

'No, madam.'

'Then get that thin cane and bend over the trestle.'

'Yes, madam.'

Nicole walked over, took down Olga's choice, raised her maid's dress, stepped onto the dais and, showing her full rounded bottom to everyone in the room, bent over the trestle.

'Twelve strokes,' said Olga.

'Twelve!' exclaimed Nicole.

'Yes, twelve. Six from me and six from someone of my choice.'

'Yes, madam. Thank you, madam,' said Nicole.

Olga brought down the cane on Nicole's fat rump. Petrov looked at Mrs Maclean and rubbed his thick, stiff prick even harder.

'Would you like to screw my new partner, Petrov,' said Jeanine, as the huge man held her under her arms and positioned her over the tip of his massive penis. Jeanine spread her legs wide open and let out a great sigh as Jackson thrust his cock into her. She had been longing for it, wanting it, and now he was filling up every space inside her. She wiggled as he raised her up and down, up and down. She loved every second and enjoyed the covetous looks on the faces of the others as she held her silk frock high so that they could see his big black cock entering her soft, creamy white and swollen pussy. Henrietta, no longer occupied with Jackson's cock, put the tips of her fingers on the floor, steadying herself as Terry continued to screw her.

'Oh, I would,' answered Petrov. 'I would love to screw your new partner.'

The sight of Henrietta Maclean in her seventeenth-century outfit had sent the blood rushing to his prick the moment he had seen her. He had wanted to fondle her breasts and her full fat bottom, feel her opening under him, feel his cock sliding into her sex.

'Then take Terry's place,' said Jeanine. 'Henrietta said she wanted to be screwed. I see no reason to restrict her to one man, do you? In fact, she might be bored having it like that. Why don't you lie down and let her sit on you.'

Petrov lay down between Mrs Maclean's fingertips so that his erect dick was pointing up to her mouth. He pulled her down and away from Terry's probing cock.

'Put your pussy on my cock and sit on me,' said Petrov, feeling Mrs Maclean's rounded breasts.

Swishing the skirt out behind her and putting her feet either side of his flanks, Mrs Maclean squatted over Petrov. She held her pussy to the tip of his prick for a moment then, in one quick movement, sat on him taking him right inside her. Petrov grasped her ample buttocks with both hands and guided her up and down onto his stalwart member. Terry came over and knelt beside Henrietta. He began to stroke her tits before turning her head, forcing her mouth open to take his prick between her lips. This was better than her wildest expectations. When Terry put his hand round and began to play with her bottom-hole Mrs Maclean knew that with every orifice being attended to she was in heaven.

'Jackson,' Jeanine whispered in the man's ear. 'I'd like you to do something for me.'

Jackson was still pushing and probing inside Jeanine's soaking wet pussy.

'Anything,' he said.

'See poor little Auralie. She looks so forlorn,' said Jeanine. 'I think she needs some attention.'

Jackson looked towards Jeanine's cousin who was leaning disconsolately against the wall watching Olga give Nicole her punishment for sucking Kensit's prick without permission.

'What do you suggest?' Jackson asked.

'Take her blouse off and suck her breasts.'

'Is that all?'

'For the moment.'

'You mean I've to stop screwing you just to suck that bitch's breasts?'

'Yes,' said Jeanine.

'You don't want her jeans off?'

'No. I think she feels safer with them on.'

'Safer. What do you mean?'

'Wait and see,' said Jeanine, licking his neck and wiggling one last time before gently easing her pussy off his cock. 'Do it now, Jackson.'

'What about you?'

'Oh I'll manage,' she said, picking out the black leather double-ended V-shaped dildo. She stepped onto a dais so that she was in full view of the whole room and raised her dress. She put one end of the monstrous instrument inside her, strapped it on, and left the other end poking forth, the folds of her frock draped either side of it.

Olga's fingers explored Nicole's sex and arse between stripes. She looked licentiously at Jeanine. 'My God,' she thought, 'that girl's learnt fast.'

Jeanine stepped down from the dais, enjoying the feel of the leather phallus inside her as she moved. She began to look around, searching for something. Henrietta was still being screwed by Petrov and sucked by Terry, so she left her alone. Rubbing his stiff penis Jackson made his way over to Auralie who was feeling humiliated by Olga's rejection and intensely jealous as she watched her licking Nicole's arse. She did not want her jeans taken down, or Jackson's prick inside her. She moved slowly along the wall, further and further away from him. But he caught up with her and grabbed her wrists. She wriggled and twisted as he pushed her up against the wall. She tried pushing him away. She didn't want anybody touching her. She preferred to torment herself, watching her lover suck, stroke and stripe Nicole. Jackson pinned her to the wall and put his hands over her pert breasts. She pulled away and he grabbed the collar of her blouse. The fine lawn ripped, leaving her breasts exposed and her arms held awkwardly to her side by the torn fabric. He stuck his bare prick between her jeans-clad thighs and rubbed, enjoying the sensation of cloth and ridged seams against his naked flesh. He held her shoulders back with one large hand as he brought the other over her breasts and stroked them, then bent his head and licked her nipples.

'She doesn't seem to know a good man when she feels one,' said Jeanine. 'Take her to Olga.'

But Olga was still fully occupied with Nicole and didn't want to know.

'Sit her there,' said Jeanine, pointing to a dais above which a steel ring was hanging. 'I've something else to say. Olga, stop that for a moment, this is my dungeon and what I say here goes.'

Olga laid down the cane. Nicole stood up and Kensit helped her down from the trestle. Petrov and Jackson sat on the floor. Terry put away his cock and Henrietta pulled down her dress with a look of satisfaction on her face.

'I want a seat on the board of Petolg Holdings,' Jeanine announced, without any preamble, to the astonished assembly.

'Impossible,' said Olga.

'Outrageous,' said Petrov.

'You're a joke,' scoffed Auralie.

'Why?' asked Jeanine.

'Because you've nothing to offer,' said Auralie.

'I see,' said Jeanine, knowing she was in command and savouring the situation. 'I am a very good screw.'

'So are a lot of people,' snapped Auralie, 'but that doesn't get them a seat on the board.'

'Why not? Didn't it get you yours?' replied Jeanine. 'And I enjoy sex. Except for your little escapade with my body, Auralie, I had a fantastic time at Petrov's. I loved being felt and licked, sucked and screwed by so many unknown people. In fact it makes me wet just thinking about it.'

Jeanine went over and stood behind Olga. Watching Auralie's face, Jeanine put a hand over Olga's breasts and stroked them. Olga liked her touch. She put out a hand and ran it up Jeanine's legs. Jeanine allowed her to do it. She knew she was driving Auralie insane with jealousy. Jeanine lifted Olga's chiffon skirt and stuck the leather dildo between her legs and began rubbing Olga's naked sex. Auralie watched Jeanine's fingers moving underneath the chiffon and gritted her teeth. Jeanine saw Petrov lick his lips and rub his penis harder. She knew he wanted to put it into her. She wiggled her tongue at him invitingly.

'Open your legs wider,' Jeanine stage-whispered to Olga. She looked at Auralie knowing full well that her cousin wanted to throttle her. Jeanine bent Olga slightly then jerked the hard black leather dildo into Olga's wet pussy as she let her hands tweak Olga's tits.

'I also propose to join your order. Not as a novitiate but as the High Priestess,' said Jeanine. 'I want to take Auralie's place.'

'I've no objection,' Olga gasped, rolling back and forth on the dildo.

'I've seen and heard enough,' said Auralie, starting towards the door.

'Stay where you are, bitch!' Jeanine called to Auralie, at the same time giving Olga's pussy another hard jab and squeezing her nipples. Olga sighed contentedly, enjoying dancing to Jeanine's tune. 'I haven't finished with you yet. Your husband is going to divorce you.'

'Never,' said Auralie.

'Oh yes, and I am going to take your place in his bed.'

'You want to marry Gerry?' exclaimed Auralie.

'I didn't say that,' replied Jeanine, calmly. 'All I said was I'm going to take your place in his bed. And I will have a controlling seat on the board of Petolg Holdings. You will no longer be a member of the board, but I do propose that you stay on as designer.'

'Go screw yourself,' spat Auralie.

'I prefer to screw Olga,' said Jeanine. 'And I would say she's enjoying it, wouldn't you? So listen. You will receive no settlement from Gerry but as my designer and with the de Bouys contract you will earn enough.'

Everyone in the room was speechless. They could not believe what they were hearing.

Jeanine was wet and horny, and wanting to be screwed herself. But she held her desires in check and moved away from Olga.

'What makes you think we'd agree to any of your demands?' asked Petrov.

'You will give me what I want because without me you will not get that contract, and I know how much you need it,' said Jeanine.

'And how do you work that out?' hissed Auralie.

'Because my mother hates your guts,' said Jeanine, triumphantly. 'Because you climbed into bed with her husband and sucked his cock and she has never forgiven you. She never will. You know that, and now I know that.' Jeanine whisked round to Petrov and Olga. 'Do you two agree to my proposal? If you do I will make sure you get the airline contract. I will talk to my mother. She will talk to Sir Henry. And Sir Henry dotes on her, absolutely dotes on her. Whatever she wants, she'll get. If she wants the contract to go to Petolg Holdings, the contract will go there. But if she doesn't, it won't. It's simple isn't it? You, all of you, agree to my suggestion and everything's fine. If you don't, well, everybody suffers. So, Olga, Petrov, do you agree?'

Petrov and Olga recognised that Jeanine held the trump card. If they refused her they could see their multi-million dollar contract disappearing down the drain and with it their entire lifestyle.

'Yes,' they said.

But Auralie chose to be stubborn.

'You stupid bitch, you think you can win,' said Auralie. 'Without me there is no company. Without me there are no designs, and I'll never work for you, ever.'

'We can always find another designer,' countered Jeanine. 'But I wouldn't bother because without your agreement, Auralie, there's no deal.'

'*Putain*,' said Auralie, venomously. 'I'm going home. Unlock that door and let me out. Do you hear me? I said unlock that door and let me out.'

'I hear you,' said Jeanine. 'But perhaps you ought to know you don't have a home to go to.'

'And why not?'

'I told you. Your husband is going to divorce you. He doesn't want you back, ever.'

'And how do you know that?'

'He told me.'

'When?'

'He came by this afternoon,' said Jeanine, serenely.

Henrietta looked quite shocked. She had been with Jeanine the entire afternoon and Gerry had not put in an appearance. In fact, since her return from the monastery she had blocked all his calls. Henrietta wondered what Jeanine was up to. Why was she being devious? Telling lies?

Jeanine picked up the bull's pizzle and, stroking it, walked towards Auralie. Auralie shivered involuntarily.

'I thought you loved me, cousin,' said Jeanine. 'I thought you helped me because you loved me. As I loved you. Now I find out you hate me. I also discover that you and Laurence were lovers. You knew I loved him. I wasted four years of my life mourning for him. Both of you lied to me. And you, Auralie, are going to be punished for it.'

Flicking the bullwhip Jeanine turned to Jackson.

'Tie her to that ring,' she commanded.

Auralie tried to leap from the dais but Jackson was too quick for her. He caught her and pinioned her arms. Auralie struggled violently.

'Petrov, help Jackson,' said Jeanine.

Petrov took hold of Auralie's legs. Auralie twisted and turned as they fastened the leather straps to her wrists and pulled her arms up to the steel ring.

'Olga, your protégée needs to be calmed down,' said Jeanine. 'Do it in the way you know best. But do not remove her jeans.'

Olga went up to the writhing woman on the dais and began slowly kissing her mouth while stroking her pert, naked tits. 'There, there,' said Olga, feeling Auralie's pussy through her jeans. 'Don't worry, *chérie*, Jeanine's only play acting.'

Olga kissed Auralie's lips again.

Jeanine joined them on the dais. The others in the room began to feel a sense of vicarious excitement as they realised that Jeanine had every intention of punishing Auralie. Jeanine began to stroke Auralie's thighs with the bull whip. Auralie kicked out.

'Don't do that, cousin,' said Jeanine, menacingly. 'You might hurt me and I don't want to be hurt by you again. However, I do want your agreement. I think the time has come for you to realise I mean business. Real business.'

Jeanine ordered Olga to leave the dais and then raised the whip high. Everyone in the room took a sharp intake of breath. Auralie felt the atmosphere and twisted on her bindings.

'No!' Auralie yelled, seeing the angle of Jeanine's hand.

'Yes!' said Jeanine, bringing the pizzle with vigour down hard on Auralie's jeans-clad bottom.

Auralie jumped violently. It seared her more than if she had taken it on her bare bottom. Her encased flesh was held so firm it could not retreat from the savagery of the stripe. She let out a shriek of pain and clenched her fingers together, screwing up her eyes in an effort to stop her tears.

Jeanine felt a rush of pleasure as she watched Auralie squirm and wriggle. She was going to whip her again. She would enjoy it even more the second time knowing that her cousin's back-side was feeling the intensity of her stripe.

'You cannot be trusted,' hissed Jeanine, lashing her once again. 'But you are a good designer. A very good designer, so I plan to keep you. Keep you where I can watch over you. I'm offering you a home here with me.'

Auralie was dumbfounded. 'Never!' she screamed furiously through her tears.

'Auralie, I think it's better if you agree to Jeanine's terms,' advised Petrov.

'Never, never!' cried Auralie.

'*Chérie,*' whispered Olga to the helpless girl. 'I will never make love to you again unless you agree. Agree. Then all will be just as it used to be.'

'No,' said Jeanine. 'No, it won't. Nothing will be the same again. Auralie, you deliberately ruined my business. Not for something I'd done, not consciously done anyway. In fact, had you been honest with me I would have kept away from Laurence and never got involved with him. I would have regarded him as yours.'

'Like you regard my husband now?' said Auralie, sarcastically.

'No, not like that,' Jeanine replied. 'You forfeited your right to Gerry.'

But Jeanine didn't want to talk about Gerry. She changed tack. 'Auralie, I want your agreement on a number of counts,' she said. 'And unless I get it I shall punish you again. You see, Henrietta and I need help. Willing help. Very willing. In fact I need a slave. You will be my slave, Auralie.'

'No!' yelled Auralie.

Jeanine raised her whip hand again. 'You are going to be my slave, Auralie. You are going to live here and do exactly what I want when I want it. Isn't she, Olga?'

Olga's eyes glinted. The idea appealed to her no end. And she liked this new commanding Jeanine with a mind of her own. She also liked the feel of Jeanine's wet pussy and wanted to touch it again. Jeanine instinctively realised what Olga was after and turned slightly to face her, rubbing the dildo between her thighs as she did so. She was silently telling the other woman, 'OK, I'll screw you, just back me with this bitch.'

Olga was excited. There was no way she could refuse Jeanine's unspoken invitation. She was already imagining the two of them making love. She smiled salaciously at Jeanine.

'Auralie,' said Olga, slyly. 'As Jeanine's slave I will be able to feel you, touch you when I want. That is right, isn't it, Jeanine?'

'That is correct.' replied Jeanine, unctuously.

'No!' exclaimed Auralie.

'I've lost patience,' said Jeanine. She advanced towards Auralie, who, seeing her coming, turned this way and that in a vain effort to avoid those long leather thongs. Jeanine brought the pizzle down again on Auralie's rump, this time considerably harder than before. Auralie danced and swung and jumped to the tune of the lash. Her hindquarters stung. 'You've had your last chance. No deal.'

Auralie could not believe what she was hearing. This was not the same Jeanine. She had always suspected the woman was neither as mousy nor as saintly as everybody had thought. The ease with which Jeanine had slipped into the role of dominatrix shocked the dark-haired girl swinging from the steel ring. Through her tears she caught a glance of Olga's face.

Olga was looking pleased, almost deliriously happy. She was enjoying the girl's extreme discomfort.

Jeanine raised her whip hand once more.

'OK. OK, I agree,' said Auralie, turning on her bindings, her bottom stinging and unwelcome tears pouring down her face.

'To everything?' said Jeanine, harshly.

'Yes,' Auralie replied, resignedly. Her arms were aching. She wanted to be taken down.

'You agree to my seat on the board?'

'Yes.'

'To your staying on as designer?'

'Yes.'

'To my becoming High Priestess of the order instead of you?'

'Yes.'

'To your being my slave?'

'Yes.'

'Yes what?' said Jeanine, raising the bull whip again.

'Yes, *madam*,' said Auralie.

'Don't forget. Never forget,' commanded Jeanine.

She threw the whip to one side.

'OK, someone cut her down, and do what you want with her.' Jeanine unstrapped the dildo and handed it to Terry, who placed it back on the wall. 'Come with me, Henrietta.'

The two women left the room as Jackson and Petrov untied Auralie's bindings.

'It's a pity that Terry didn't have his camera with him,' said Henrietta Maclean when they were both outside the door. 'We could have taken some photos of Auralie being screwed and whipped.'

'Maybe we still can,' said Jeanine. 'Where did he leave his camera?'

'In the dining-room, I think,' said Mrs Maclean.

'Did Auralie bring her portfolio with her? I'll need it for the presentation.'

'I didn't see it.'

'In that case I'll phone Gerry to bring it over,' said Jeanine. 'As soon as he arrives I'll go with Olga for the presentation, and you can keep Auralie here. If there's time, I might screw Gerry before we go.'

Jeanine left Mrs Maclean and made her way to her upstairs office. *En route* she noticed Terry, Kensit and Nicole sidling out through the hotel entrance, but they didn't see her. She allowed herself a smile as she imagined what Jackson and Petrov and Olga were doing with Auralie.

At her desk she telephoned Gerry, who agreed to come over with the presentation kit within the hour. Then she went in search of Terry's digital camera and found it in the dining-room.

'Now I can take those photographs of Auralie,' thought Jeanine, smugly.

She made her way back to her bedroom. Through the inter-connecting doorway to the dungeon beyond Jeanine saw the remaining four enjoying an orgy of sex. Auralie, now naked, flat on the floor being screwed by Jackson. Olga was astride her face, queening Auralie whilst fondling her neat breasts. Auralie was in ecstasy, her hips rising up and down with every thrust of Jackson's prick, whilst her tongue slurped and sucked at Olga's open sex. Auralie's arms were thrown out from her side in total abandonment, one of her hands working furiously on Petrov's cock. He was kneeling beside her, one of his hands ringing Jackson's shaft as it charged in and out of Auralie's pussy.

From her vantage point Jeanine took a number of shots and put them in her handbag which was beside her bed. Then she went into the dungeon.

Demonstrating her new-found power Jeanine clapped her hands loudly.

'That's it, everybody. You've had your fun,' she announced.

Everybody stopped what they were doing and got to their feet. Jeanine instructed Petrov and Jackson to tie Auralie to a sturdy Georgian chair positioned close to a large two-way mirror on the wall near her bedroom door.

'Now gag her,' said Jeanine.

She took Olga to one side.

'I've made the necessary phone calls,' said Jeanine. 'We are to meet Sir Henry in two hours at his office. Gerry's bringing the presentation kit over any moment now, so you'll need to get ready.'

Jeanine dismissed them all and then pressed a button in the wall. Heavy red silk curtains descended across the breadth of the dungeon, hiding all the paraphernalia. This left a small area between the curtains and the bedroom where Auralie sat bound and gagged.

Jeanine closed the connecting doors and waited for Gerry. He arrived an hour later, entering Jeanine's sitting-room as she was talking to her mother on the telephone.

When she saw him Jeanine's heart gave a leap. She let out a squeal of pleasure and ran to Gerry. He caught her up in his arms and kissed her passionately, as his hand pressed the small of her back. Gerry's prick made a sudden surge into thrusting life. Jeanine felt it through the fabric of his suit. Kindled with fresh desire Jeanine began to sway and undulate under Gerry's insistent pressure.

Jeanine's response was more than Gerry had hoped for. He lifted the heavy silk jersey of her frock and let his hands roam over her soft skin. His fingers found her voluptuous breasts and he began playing with her nipples. His tongue searched out every crevice of her mouth. He turned her slightly so that his hands could easily travel down from her breasts, and down over her belly to the opening between her legs. He was surprised to find her so wet and wanton. Jeanine sighed as his fingers played softly with her swollen and fully aroused sex-lips. She held her breath as he played a game with those lips, moulding them backwards and forwards between his fore and ring fingers, increasing her wantonness. She took a sharp intake of breath as his middle finger alighted on her hard, stiff clit.

Gerry was astonished to find Jeanine so excited. But he was pleased because he desperately wanted to have sex with her. His cock was itching to be inside her, feeling her muscles gripping him, taking him ever further inwards and upwards to the peak of desire and satisfaction.

Jeanine was squirming beneath his touch. Her big breasts were pushed forward, her hard nipples responding to each gentle caress. She was standing on tiptoe, her hips jutting out, allowing him full access to her wayward pussy as his fingers played gently with her highly sensitive clitoris. The more he did that, the greater her desire became, the more she was inflamed, and the more her mind conjured up visions. Erotic visions. She sighed and tenderly played with Gerry's erect penis through the restricting fabric of his trousers.

Impatiently she undid his flies and wound her fingers under his underpants until she was finally able to touch the naked throbbing hardness of his cock.

'I think I would like to suck your dick,' said Jeanine teasingly, removing her frock and slithering down his body. She took it between both hands and placed it to her lips. Her tongue flicked across the dangerous pink dome, feeling along its crimson ridge. Her mouth formed into a perfect 'O' shape as her lips enveloped his vibrant tool. She moved one of her hands to cup his balls, gently rolling their soft malleability between her fingers.

Excited almost beyond endurance, Gerry bent slightly so that his hands could encircle Jeanine's breasts. He played with her hard nipples, exciting them, hardening them more. He watched her bare bottom sway and move as her mouth slid up and down, up and down, on his cock. Leaving his member entrusted to her mouth, her fingers undid the waistband on his trousers.

'Take them off,' she murmured, sexily.

She wanted him. Wanted him more than she could think; more than she realised. She desperately needed to feel his cock inside her, filling her up, taking her, taking her higher. Feeling his body on hers, feeling his skin, smelling his sweet scent never clouded by aftershave.

Gerry took off his clothes as Jeanine wandered through into

her bedroom. She lay on her queen-sized double bed, her hips arched, her legs splayed, her fingers down between her legs playing with herself. She was the embodiment of the seductive enchantress. She turned and saw her reflection in the two-way mirror. Cat-like, Jeanine smiled. She knew that on the other side of the mirror, Auralie, powerless to move or speak, would be watching.

Gerry came towards Jeanine, his shaft proudly extended. His athletic, beautifully formed body bent down over her. He licked her wanton sex.

'Sit on me,' he whispered.

They changed places. Jeanine sat astride Gerry and gradually lowered herself on to his upright cock. She took it slowly, teasing him. She edged her pussy down onto his shaft, at first only taking in the head. Up and then down again. Each time she went down she took in a little more. Gerry found he was in a state of exquisite agony. He wanted to thrust hard up inside her but knew he would lose the thrill of anticipation. He held his breath and waited. The total wetness, the full juiciness of Jeanine's opening was taking him out of himself, making him high. Working her crotch muscles round his cock she made her slow progress down his provoked and highly stimulated prick.

Gerry lay back savouring every moment. Jeanine made one more slow movement upwards. Suddenly with a great force, she came down on him. Then she rode him like a rider on a stallion. Up and down she went, faster and faster. His head was rolling this way and that, his hands busy massaging her breasts. His legs were shaking and he didn't know whether he was on this earth or in paradise.

Jeanine spread her body along his. He relished the pleasure of her full breasts against his chest. She wound her arms around his neck, gripped his flanks with her knees and, locked together, managed to turn the two of them over. She wanted to be ravished.

'Now screw me, hard,' she ordered, biting his ear.

Gerry needed no further invitation. Keeping her feet and shoulders on the bed she raised her hips. He brought his mouth down to hers, and at the moment his tongue slipped through her lips, his cock thrust into her pussy. The sweet agony was over. He could ride her, give full vent to his raging desire.

Her swollen sex was aching, longing and tingling as she took him. His thick, thrusting shaft plunged into her, his willing captive. Blissfully locked together in one long kiss, their heads turned from side to side as if they could never get enough of the feel and taste of each other. Rapturously, their inflamed bodies were totally united. Their movements were in unison as they rode backwards and forwards, wallowing in the pleasure and the delight of the other's body. They came in an explosion so violent, so all-pervading, that for a brief moment neither realised the other had come. They stayed entwined in each other's arms. Their ecstasy was complete and fulfilled.

'You must go now,' said Jeanine, easing her way off the bed. 'But first I have a present for you.'

She reached over to her handbag and took out the prints of Auralie being screwed in the dungeon.

'Now you have the evidence to divorce Auralie,' said Jeanine.

'How did you get these?' said an astonished Gerry as he stared at the photographs.

'I took them myself,' said Jeanine.

'Where?' he asked.

'Right here,' she replied, taking Gerry's hand and leading him towards the connecting doors which she opened wide. Initially Gerry saw only the heavy red curtain of silk which hid the trappings of the dungeon. Then, with horror, he saw Auralie, gagged and bound to the chair.

He couldn't believe his eyes. He walked over to her to touch her hair. Glancing sideways he saw that the whole wall was a window onto Jeanine's bedroom. But how could it be, he puzzled. Then it dawned on him that it was part of a two-way mirror.

'Did she see us?' he whispered anxiously to Jeanine.

'I hope so,' said Jeanine, triumphantly.

'You hope so!'

'Yes,' said Jeanine. 'You see, she's my slave. If I want her to watch me making love, she has to watch. That's part of the deal.'

Auralie squirmed silently.

'What deal?' Gerry asked Jeanine. 'And for what?'

'Oh, for everything,' said Jeanine airily. 'You don't have to worry about anything. Just divorce her, that's all. She won't be making any claims upon you. She's capable of earning her own living. And as my slave she'll live here with me. I'll keep her in food and clothing. You can rest assured she'll behave herself from now on. If she doesn't she'll be punished. I'll have her whipped.'

'Whipped!' exclaimed Gerry, a passing flush of pleasure surging through his loins at the very idea.

'Yes,' said Jeanine. 'Whipped. Perhaps *you* might like to do it.'

'Yes,' said Gerry enthusiastically, falling more in love with Jeanine than ever. What she was suggesting was his greatest fantasy come true.

'I thought you might,' said Jeanine. 'But that's for another day. Right now I've got a very important meeting and must ask you to go.'

'Jeanine,' said Gerry, earnestly. 'After I've divorced Auralie, will you marry me?'

'I don't think so, Gerry,' she replied. 'I don't think it would work. You see, I'm planning on running my own highly specialised business and I'll be too occupied with other people's needs to consider a full-time relationship with only one person. But we could come to an arrangement. One that won't interfere with any of your ambitions. Why don't we set a regular date for you to come and screw me and hear my report on my slave's progress. If she's been a naughty girl, you can give her her punishment. And this is where you can do it.'

Jeanine glanced towards Auralie, seeing the frustration in the captive girl's eyes. She smiled victoriously as she operated the control that lifted the silk curtains revealing her working dungeon. The full impact of the room with its impedimenta hit Gerry with a great force. He stepped back, both terrified and curious.

'You see what I mean, Gerry,' said Jeanine, putting a hand over his prick. 'I intend to run a very specialist establishment. Perhaps you'd like to become my special customer?'

'Oh, yes,' he said, swallowing hard.

'Now if you'll excuse me, I really must get ready,' Jeanine smiled. 'Henrietta is already taking bookings. Just let her know when you want to come.'

Gerry followed Jeanine out of the dungeon, kissed her softly on the mouth, then left. Jeanine went to the wardrobe and selected a soft apricot suit for the presentation. So very suitable. So subtle. So virginal. And so completely acceptable.

She hoped Olga was ready. Not that there was really any need for either of them to attend, but it would look better. The presentation was a mere formality. Her mother had already had a word with Sir Henry and the contract was theirs.

After she had finished dressing, Jeanine went back into the dungeon.

She removed Auralie's gag but not the bindings.

'Olga and I'll have some good news for you, when we get back,' said Jeanine. 'And, slave, I have to tell you my next pleasure is that you watch me being sucked by your lover.'

'No,' shouted Auralie, at last able to voice her feelings.

'You will be whipped for that,' said Jeanine maliciously. 'The reply is "Yes, madam. Thank you madam." Remember that, Auralie.'

Jeanine picked up the glass of champagne she had put beside the chair. She held it to Auralie's lips.

'Drink.'

Auralie bent her head and sipped.

'What do you say?'

'Thank you, madam,' said Auralie.

'You see, cousin,' said Jeanine, 'I'm quite certain we're going to be very successful.'

Jeanine held the glass until Auralie had finished drinking, then she picked up her handbag and walked towards the door.

'I shall tell Henrietta to release you after we've gone.'

Jeanine walked triumphantly out of the room leaving Auralie still tied to the chair.

Auralie watched her leave. The triumph's not all yours, she thought. 'I might enjoy this. Might enjoy not having to think and scheme all the time. At least for a while. But when I no longer enjoy it, then watch out Jeanine, just watch out.'

Visit the Black Lace website at
www.black-lace-books.com

FIND OUT THE LATEST INFORMATION AND TAKE ADVANTAGE OF OUR FANTASTIC FREE BOOK OFFER! ALSO VISIT THE SITE FOR . . .

- All Black Lace titles currently available and how to order online
- Great new offers
- Writers' guidelines
- Author interviews
- An erotica newsletter
- Features
- Cool links

BLACK LACE — THE LEADING IMPRINT OF WOMEN'S SEXY FICTION

TAKING YOUR EROTIC READING PLEASURE TO NEW HORIZONS

LOOK OUT FOR THE BLACK LACE 15TH ANNIVERSARY SPECIAL EDITIONS. COLLECT ALL 10 TITLES IN THE SERIES!

All books priced £7.99 in the UK. Please note publication dates apply to the UK only. For other territories, please contact your retailer.

Published in March 2008

CASSANDRA'S CONFLICT
Fredrica Alleyn
ISBN 978 0 352 34186 0

A house in Hampstead. Present-day. Behind a façade of cultured respectability lies a world of decadent indulgence and dark eroticism. Cassandra's sheltered life is transformed when she gets employed as governess to the Baron's children. He draws her into games where lust can feed on the erotic charge of submission. Games where only he knows the rules and where unusual pleasures can flourish.

Published in April 2008

GEMINI HEAT
Portia Da Costa
ISBN 978 0 352 34187 7

As the metropolis sizzles in the freak early summer temperatures, identical
twin sisters Deana and Delia Ferraro are cooking up a heat wave of their own.
Surrounded by an atmosphere of relentless humidity, Deana and Delia find
themselves rivals for the attentions of Jackson de Guile – an exotic, wealthy
entrepreneur and master of power dynamics – who draws them both into a web of
luxurious debauchery.

Their erotic encounters become increasingly bizarre as the twins vie for the rewards
that pleasuring him brings them - tainted rewards which only serve to confuse
their perceptions of the limits of sexual experience.

Published in May 2008

BLACK ORCHID
Roxanne Carr
ISBN 978 0 352 34188 4

At the Black Orchid Club, adventurous women who yearn for the pleasures of exotic,
even kinky sex can quench their desires in discreet and luxurious surroundings.
Having tasted the fulfilment of unique and powerful lusts, one such adventurous
woman learns what happens when the need for limitless indulgence becomes an
addiction.

Published in June 2008

FORBIDDEN FRUIT
Susie Raymond
ISBN 978 0 352 34189 1

The last thing sexy thirty-something Beth expected was to get involved with a much younger man. But when she finds him spying on her in the dressing room at work she embarks on an erotic journey with the straining youth, teaching him and teasing him as she leads him through myriad sensuous exercises at her stylish modern home. As their lascivious games become more and more intense, Beth soon begins to realise that she is the one being awakened to a new world of desire – and that hers is the mind quickly becoming consumed with lust.

Published in July 2008

JULIET RISING
Cleo Cordell
ISBN 978 0 352 34192 1

Nothing is more important to Reynard than winning the favours of the bright and wilful Juliet, a pupil at Madame Nicol's exclusive but strict 18th century ladies' academy. Her captivating beauty tinged with a hint of cruelty soon has Reynard willing to do anything to win her approval. But Juliet's methods have little effect on Andreas, the real object of her lustful obsessions. Unable to bend him to her will, she is forced to watch him lavish his manly talents on her fellow pupils. That is, until she agrees to change her stuck-up, stubborn ways and become an eager erotic participant.

To be published in September 2008

THE STALLION
Georgina Brown
ISBN 978 0 352 34199 0

The world of showjumping is as steamy as it is competitive. Ambitious young rider Penny Bennett enters into a wager with her oldest rival and friend, Ariadne, to win her thoroughbred stallion, guaranteed to bring Penny money and success. But first she must attain the sponsorship and very personal attention of showjumping's biggest impresario, Alister Beaumont. Beaumont's riding school, however, is not all it seems. There's the weird relationship between Alister and his cigar-smoking sister. And the bizarre clothes they want Penny to wear. But in this atmosphere of unbridled kinkiness, Penny is determined not only to win the wager but to discover the truth about Beaumont's strange hobbies.

To be published in October 2008

THE DEVIL AND THE DEEP BLUE SEA
Cheryl Mildenhall
ISBN 978 0 352 34200 3

When Hillary and her girlfriends rent a country house for their summer vacation, it is a pleasant surprise to find that its secretive and kinky owner – Darius Harwood – seems to be the most desirable man in the locale. That is, before Hillary meets Haldane, the blonde and beautifully proportioned Norwegian sailor who works nearby. Intrigued by the sexual allure of two very different men, Hillary can't resist exploring the possibilities on offer. But these opportunities for misbehaviour quickly lead her into a tricky situation for which a difficult decision has to be made.

To be published in November 2008

THE NINETY DAYS OF GENEVIEVE
Lucinda Carrington
ISBN 978 0 352 34201 0

A ninety-day sex contract wasn't exactly what Genevieve Loften had in mind when she began business negotiations with the arrogant and attractive James Sinclair. As a career move she wanted to go along with it; the pay-off was potentially huge. However, she didn't imagine that he would make her the star performer in a series of increasingly kinky and exotic fantasies. Thrown into a world of sexual misadventure, Genevieve learns how to balance her high-pressure career with the twilight world of fetishism and debauchery.

To be published in December 2008

THE GIFT OF SHAME
Sarah Hope-Walker
ISBN 978 0 352 34202 7

Sad, sultry Helen flies between London, Paris and the Caribbean chasing whatever physical pleasures she can get to tear her mind from a deep, deep loss. Her glamorous life-style and charged sensual escapades belie a widow's grief. When she meets handsome, rich Jeffrey she is shocked and yet intrigued by his masterful, domineering behaviour. Soon, Helen is forced to confront the forbidden desires hiding within herself – and forced to undergo a startling metamorphosis from a meek and modest lady into a bristling, voracious wanton.

ALSO LOOK OUT FOR

THE NEW BLACK LACE BOOK OF WOMEN'S SEXUAL FANTASIES
Edited and compiled by Mitzi Szereto
ISBN 978 0 352 34172 3

The second anthology of detailed sexual fantasies contributed by women from all over the world. The book is a result of a year's research by an expert on erotic writing and gives a fascinating insight into the rich diversity of the female sexual imagination.

Black Lace Booklist

Information is correct at time of printing. To avoid disappointment, check availability before ordering. Go to www.black-lace-books.com.
All books are priced £7.99 unless another price is given.

BLACK LACE BOOKS WITH AN HISTORICAL SETTING

BLACK LACE BOOKS WITH A PARANORMAL THEME

❑ THE PRIDE Edie Bingham ISBN 978 0 352 33997 3
❑ THE SILVER COLLAR Mathilde Madden ISBN 978 0 352 34141 9
❑ THE TEN VISIONS Olivia Knight ISBN 978 0 352 34119 8

BLACK LACE ANTHOLOGIES
❑ BLACK LACE QUICKIES 1 Various ISBN 978 0 352 34126 6 £2.99
❑ BLACK LACE QUICKIES 2 Various ISBN 978 0 352 34127 3 £2.99
❑ BLACK LACE QUICKIES 3 Various ISBN 978 0 352 34128 0 £2.99
❑ BLACK LACE QUICKIES 4 Various ISBN 978 0 352 34129 7 £2.99
❑ BLACK LACE QUICKIES 5 Various ISBN 978 0 352 34130 3 £2.99
❑ BLACK LACE QUICKIES 6 Various ISBN 978 0 352 34133 4 £2.99
❑ BLACK LACE QUICKIES 7 Various ISBN 978 0 352 34146 4 £2.99
❑ BLACK LACE QUICKIES 8 Various ISBN 978 0 352 34147 1 £2.99
❑ BLACK LACE QUICKIES 9 Various ISBN 978 0 352 34155 6 £2.99
❑ MORE WICKED WORDS Various ISBN 978 0 352 33487 9 £6.99
❑ WICKED WORDS 3 Various ISBN 978 0 352 33522 7 £6.99
❑ WICKED WORDS 4 Various ISBN 978 0 352 33603 3 £6.99
❑ WICKED WORDS 5 Various ISBN 978 0 352 33642 2 £6.99
❑ WICKED WORDS 6 Various ISBN 978 0 352 33690 3 £6.99
❑ WICKED WORDS 7 Various ISBN 978 0 352 33743 6 £6.99
❑ WICKED WORDS 8 Various ISBN 978 0 352 33787 0 £6.99
❑ WICKED WORDS 9 Various ISBN 978 0 352 33860 0
❑ WICKED WORDS 10 Various ISBN 978 0 352 33893 8
❑ THE BEST OF BLACK LACE 2 Various ISBN 978 0 352 33718 4
❑ WICKED WORDS: SEX IN THE OFFICE Various ISBN 978 0 352 33944 7
❑ WICKED WORDS: SEX AT THE SPORTS CLUB Various ISBN 978 0 352 33991 1
❑ WICKED WORDS: SEX ON HOLIDAY Various ISBN 978 0 352 33961 4
❑ WICKED WORDS: SEX IN UNIFORM Various ISBN 978 0 352 34002 3
❑ WICKED WORDS: SEX IN THE KITCHEN Various ISBN 978 0 352 34018 4
❑ WICKED WORDS: SEX ON THE MOVE Various ISBN 978 0 352 34034 4
❑ WICKED WORDS: SEX AND MUSIC Various ISBN 978 0 352 34061 0
❑ WICKED WORDS: SEX AND SHOPPING Various ISBN 978 0 352 34076 4
❑ SEX IN PUBLIC Various ISBN 978 0 352 34089 4
❑ SEX WITH STRANGERS Various ISBN 978 0 352 34105 1
❑ LOVE ON THE DARK SIDE Various ISBN 978 0 352 34132 7
❑ LUST BITES Various ISBN 978 0 352 34153 2

BLACK LACE NON-FICTION

To find out the latest information about Black Lace titles, check out the website: www.black-lace-books.com or send for a booklist with complete synopses by writing to:

Black Lace Booklist, Virgin Books Ltd
Thames Wharf Studios
Rainville Road
London W6 9HA

Please include an SAE of decent size. Please note only British stamps are valid.

Our privacy policy
We will not disclose information you supply us to any other parties. We will not disclose any information which identifies you personally to any person without your express consent.

From time to time we may send out information about Black Lace books and special offers. Please tick here if you do not wish to receive Black Lace information. ❑

Please send me the books I have ticked above.

Name ....

Address ....

....

....

....

Post Code ....

Send to: Virgin Books Cash Sales, Thames Wharf Studios, Rainville Road, London W6 9HA.

US customers: for prices and details of how to order books for delivery by mail, call 888-330-8477.

Please enclose a cheque or postal order, made payable to Virgin Books Ltd, to the value of the books you have ordered plus postage and packing costs as follows:

UK and BFPO – £1.00 for the first book, 50p for each subsequent book.

Overseas (including Republic of Ireland) – £2.00 for the first book, £1.00 for each subsequent book.

If you would prefer to pay by VISA, ACCESS/MASTERCARD, DINERS CLUB, AMEX or SWITCH, please write your card number and expiry date here:

....

Signature ....

Please allow up to 28 days for delivery.